# 2194

## REBELLION

A NOVEL BY

# G. J. PAGE

*Gwyneth*

**PAGE PUBLISHING**

Note for Librarians: A cataloguing record for this book is available from Library and Archives Canada at www.collectionscanada.ca/amicus/index-e.html

Cover & Layout Design:
Jenny Engwer, www.jennyengwer.com

Book Images:
*Grass Sunset* by TintaNegra, Shutterstock ID: 180218315
*Futuristic City Scene* by Tithi Luadthong, Shutterstock ID: 1924252175
*Couple* by Tithi Luadthong, Shutterstock ID: 1099575602
*Meteorites* by Tithi Luadthong, Shutterstock ID: 1063277267

ISBN:978-1-989302-13-2 (paperback)

**PAGE PUBLISHING**
*www.gwynethjanepage.com*

10 9 8 7 6 5 4 3 2 1

# CHAPTER ONE
## YEAR 2194

**C**harlotte was at a loss for words. Emi had become her best friend over the last few years and she had no idea how to break the news to her.

The flight back to New York had been torture as her mind went around in circles. She'd thought of multiple scenarios of how she was going to say what she had to say but all of them she'd rejected. She didn't want to be the one to have to tell Emi but she knew she had no choice. *What a difference a week makes!*

After disembarking from the Hovercraft she'd gone to the hospital to see Dez, needing to know what state he was in before seeing Emi. He'd been worse than expected and given that she'd imagined some pretty horrific scenarios — she shook her head. The doctor had allowed her into the intensive care unit but what confronted her had made matters even more impossible. Dez's arms and torso were badly burned. The skin regeneration machines hovered over him, sending out impulses that would slowly heal his skin over the coming weeks. His head was wrapped in a bandage and he was as white as the thin cotton sheet that covered the lower part of his body. But it wasn't his physical condition that shocked her, it was his mental state.

As she approached his eyes flickered open.

'Hi, Dez.'

'Hey.' His mouth moved but the simple response was barely audible.

'You look a bit rough.'

'Yeah, feel as good as I look,' he rasped. Charlotte could only just make out the words above the hum of the machines in the room that were keeping Dez alive.

'Can I get you anything?'

'Water.'

She filled the glass from the jug by his bed, placed a straw in it and brought it to his lips.

He leaned back, exhausted by the small effort. 'Thanks.'

'I was just going to see Emi, let her know you're alive. We all thought you had been killed by the Blues in the raid.'

'Emi,' he whispered.

'She'll be so relieved to know you're okay. Well, maybe not okay but at least you're not dead.'

'Emi!'

Charlotte stared at Dez, concern etched into the weariness on her face. She didn't want to ask her next question. Dread settled like a rock in the pit of her stomach. 'Do...do you not remember Emi?' She held her breath and waited.

Dez moved his head slightly on the pillow. 'I don't want...don't want her to see me like this.'

'But...' Charlotte exhaled and closed her eyes momentarily. 'Oh God!' she muttered under her breath. 'But...she'll be so happy to see you. She thought you'd been killed.'

'I'd be better off dead than like this,' he replied bitterly as he waved his hand to indicate his burned, mutilated body.

'You can't mean that. We need you.'

'For what?' He gave Charlotte a withering glance. 'Since I've been leader, the Blues have started attacking again *and* they've destroyed

The Cloud, the thing that is supposed to save us all, and it was while *I* was on guard duty.'

Charlotte tried to hide her dismay. 'But none of that is your fault.'

'Yeah, well, I still don't want Emi to see me like this.'

She didn't want to overwhelm Dez, but maybe if she highlighted the positives for him he would change his mind. 'But, you're the leader of the Network and everyone loves you. You managed to get all of the Network to help the Fringe build The Cloud. The Fringe respect you. If one of The Cloud sites was destroyed by the Blues, you're hardly to blame.'

Dez looked at Charlotte and shrugged his shoulders but he obviously did not want to hear any more.

'Well, I'm sure Emi will want to see you and I don't think she'll take 'no' for an answer,' said Charlotte bluntly as her sympathy turned to anger at his defeatist attitude.

Dez turned his head away. His eyelids closed.

'Excuse me, you need to go now,' said the doctor as he popped his head in at the door.

Charlotte turned to go. When she looked back from the doorway to say goodbye, Dez was already asleep, or at least he was pretending to be. She slid quietly from the room. Reporting to Edward and breaking the news to Emi before either of them heard about Dez through the grapevine were of priority but the short encounter with Dez had made her life infinitely worse. To tell Emi that Dez was alive was going to be hard enough; to tell her that he was alive but didn't want to see her was unimaginable.

Charlotte dawdled as she headed over to Emi's apartment, head down, she stared unseeingly at the pavement. Even though many of the streets of New York had been dug up and planted with trees and grass to try and help keep the city cool, some days the sun's scorching rays felt impossible to bear. Today was one of those days. Though it was late in the day the blistering heat radiating from the sidewalk beneath her feet seemed worse than usual. But maybe it was just a reflection of her depressed spirits. Try as she might she could not conjure the words necessary that would further crumble the world of her friend.

She pushed the buzzer and waited.

'Hello?'

'Emi, it's Charlotte. Can I come up?'

'Of course.' The doorbell buzzed. She let herself in and headed up to the penthouse suite.

The door to the apartment was open. Emi was there waiting for her. The evening light streaming through the windows behind her brought out the highlights in her raven hair and silhouetted her still slender figure. Charlotte thought she seemed out of place — the opulence of the apartment at odds with Emi's character just as the grandeur within these four walls was in stark contrast to the world beyond.

'Charlotte, you look a bit done in. What can I get you?'

'A glass of wine wouldn't go amiss.' She needed something to steady her nerves. 'I don't suppose Edward is still here, is he?'

'No, he just left to head back to the office. Another meeting with The Cloud engineers,' Emi answered. 'Please, Charlotte, tell me, what did you find out? Were *any* of the guards found alive? And The Cloud…is it *totally* destroyed?'

Charlotte sipped from the wine that Emi handed to her before forming her reply. 'Yes, The Cloud is ruined. At least, the panels are all smashed. The superstructure is still intact, although blackened in parts,' she said. She much preferred focusing on the massive problem of The Cloud being destroyed rather than the personal one of Dez being alive but inconsolable. 'I don't know if they'll be able to salvage anything. I guess we'll have to wait and see if Edward and the committee can figure something out. I can't imagine what we'll do otherwise.'

'And the guards? Jax?' Emi hesitated. 'Dez?' she whispered.

'They found Jax and a couple other guards alive,' said Charlotte. She paused before she drew a big breath and added, 'and they found Dez.'

'Dez. He's alive?' gasped Emi as she brought her hands to her mouth. The misery reflected in her eyes fled as hope lit her countenance.

Charlotte nodded and then watched as realization dawned in Emi's mind and her face crumpled in horror.

'Oh God, what have I done?' Emi cried as she slid down the cupboard to the hard tiles of the kitchen floor, shock caused her legs to buckle beneath her.

Charlotte sat next to her and reached out her hand. 'You weren't to know. The chances of him surviving were miniscule. You did what you had to do.'

'But I shouldn't have given in so easily. I should have waited. What will Dez think of me?'

'Emi!'

Emi looked at Charlotte, her eyes haunted, her expression forlorn. Charlotte hated having to utter the next few words.

'Emi, he doesn't…want to see you.' Charlotte cringed at her own words. She hated the pain she was inflicting on her friend.

'He doesn't want to see me?' said Emi slowly as she tried to make sense of the information being thrown at her. 'Why ever not?'

'I don't know. I think he feels like a failure. He was a guard and didn't protect his people or The Cloud.'

'But that's ridiculous,' Emi sputtered. 'It was a surprise attack by the Blues. The guards didn't stand a chance.'

'I know. But I think he feels responsible,' said Charlotte. 'And he's in rough shape. Badly burned, bed ridden, dependent on others for every little thing…'

'That's just plain stupid. I don't care about any of that. How shallow does he think I am?' Emi spat the words out and then clamped her mouth shut as she realized how shallow she would appear when Dez learned she had taken up with Edward immediately.

Charlotte shook her head and watched the emotional turmoil flit across Emi's face as she slowly came to grips with what she was being told.

'Oh God, whatever am I to do?' Emi asked with a strangled cry.

'We'll figure something out. I'll do whatever I can to help. We can only hope that he'll be okay in time.' Charlotte said as she tried to bolster Emi's spirits and offer comfort that she was far from feeling.

'I don't know. Maybe it's better if he *doesn't* want to see me. I don't know how I'm going to face him, I really don't.'

'I know you don't mean that. It's just the shock. Give it time.' Emi was usually so resilient, it was hard to see her like this. 'Unfortunately, I need to go and report to Edward.' She paused. 'Are you going to be okay?'

'No. Yes. I guess. No. I don't know. What choice do I have? I have Dez's unborn child to think of and people need me,' Emi replied. 'Edward needs me.' Her words trailed off as her head sank into her hands, resting on her bent knees. 'I think I'll go for a walk. I don't want to be here right now.' She brought her head up to gaze at the stark opulence of the apartment that she could not bring herself to call home.

'Good idea. You can walk me as far as the park,' agreed Charlotte. She hated to leave but Edward and the committee would be expecting her.

Getting up off the floor, Charlotte gave Emi a hug. She felt her friend's ribcage expand as Emi drew in a long, shuddering breath. They headed down to street level in the elevator and as they emerged from the apartment building they were greeted by a blast of hot air. Even with the previously black streets of New York being replaced with light grey concrete footpaths and the additional boulevards of grass and trees, the stifling heat retained by the city could feel like a physical impact. The sunlight glinting off thousands of solar-windows was blinding, intensifying the feeling of warmth that permeated the atmosphere.

'Crap it's hot today. Not even a breath of air,' said Charlotte as she donned her sunglasses to block the low slant of the summer evening's rays. She pulled her white mesh sunhat from her bag and gave it a snap, releasing the cooling mechanism contained in the brim. 'I don't know how you survived in The Network all those years without these. They're a lifesaver on days like today.'

'I can't *imagine* going back to how we used to live but with even *worse* conditions,' said Emi miserably.

Charlotte looked sideways at Emi. 'You at least had food and water…and shelters and a community. It's hard to imagine life could become even more…primal.'

'I was still hungry most of the time. Growing or hunting for food was a constant challenge. Then there was always the worry that one of the villages might get raided by The Blues. That was what I hated the most — always worrying that maybe The Blues had moved further north and would find our valleys. The fear never went away.'

'Given the circumstances, your fear was a rational one.'

'I rather wish it had turned out to be irrational.'

'Don't we all.'

'I still don't understand why The Blues would bother smashing The Cloud. They only ever raided for food. It just doesn't make sense.'

'Does violence need a logical reason?'

'No, I guess not, but still.'

'Looks like we're all going to have to start living with your rational fear.'

'I hope not,' Emi responded. She cast a glance at Charlotte, alarm etched on her face. 'I can't figure out how they got as far north as where The Cloud was. It seems impossible. It was so far from their last known whereabouts and…how *could* they find it? It was so well hidden.' Emi shook her head.

'I have to report to Edward. Will you be okay on your own? It's been a lot to take in.'

Emi shrugged. 'I'll try to focus on a solution rather than the problem, or problems, since there seems to be more than one,' she said as she tried to make light of their situation but failed miserably.

'Well, when you want to see Dez let me know. If we go in under my security clearance then Ed…no one ever need know that you visited.'

'Thanks, Charlotte. You're a gem. Don't know what I'd do without you.'

'Can't believe you consider me a gem when all I ever seem to do is deliver bad news.'

'Well, I don't believe in shooting the messenger,' Emi replied with the slightest hint of a smile, before giving her friend a hug and parting ways.

———

Emi wandered down to the sea wall and climbed the grey, stone steps to the walkway along the top. As bleak as life was, the engineering that had gone into building a sea wall big enough to save New York from the rising tides never ceased to amaze her. It gave her some small hope that they could still salvage their world from the mistakes made by past generations. How was she to salvage her own life from the mess she had made of it — her own mistakes? They were so easily made and so hard to undo. She was engaged to Edward, the most powerful man in what was left of the world. But she was in love with Dez and carrying his baby but he didn't want to see her. That he didn't want to see her hurt more than she wanted to admit, even to herself. Really it would probably be best if he never wanted to see her again, then she need not rock the rickety raft she had made for herself.

Wearily she rested her elbows on the rail of the sea wall and let her pent up tears slip down her face to mingle with the vast ocean below. She would allow herself this moment of weakness and let go of all her own hopes and dreams. Lifting her head, she took a deep breath, dashed the tears from her cheeks and turned to go back to her four walls.

The beauty of the setting sun was lost on her.

# CHAPTER TWO

**C**harlotte left Emi and made her way through Central Park towards Edward's office. Normally, Central Park would soothe her soul. She loved the vast array of colourful vegetable plots, the immense variety of trees bearing fruit and nuts — everything from almonds, olives and avocados to apples, peaches, bananas and oranges — and the ever changing aroma that came from the herbs planted as borders along the walkways. But this evening it went unnoticed. She'd broken the news to Emi and now she must lay an equal but vastly different burden at the feet of Edward.

She found Edward, with ten engineers and environmentalists, some of the best minds in The Fringe, seated around the conference table in the boardroom. The last of the sun's rays barely penetrated the tinted windows. There were screens, papers and coffee cups in front of each of them. At the centre of the massive conference table was displayed a 3-D map of the world with the current temperatures of different areas colour coded onto the map. Many…most…were red, some were orange/yellow and a few, a very few, had a blue/green tone. The same map was shown in 2-D at the end of the table on an otherwise blank, white wall. Charlotte felt her body grow warmer simply by looking at the map. So much of the earth was red, orange or yellow. How were the people in this room going to save them all now? She didn't think they had an answer. Everyone gathered around the table looked very serious.

'Charlotte, come on in. Have a seat.'

She sat in one of the spare chairs. All eyes turned in her direction as they waited for her to speak. Where to start? There could be no sugar-coating her report to these people — they couldn't be fooled into a false sense of security.

'I've just returned from the site of Cloud III. I've spent the last week, at Edward's request, surveying the site, talking to those employed there and waiting to see if any of the guards were found alive. The damage is extensive. Most of the panels have been destroyed. The superstructure is still intact but there are no functioning components. In order to make it operational every panel would need to be re-made, the smashed ones removed and new ones installed. The people who work at the site figure it would take the better part of a year to restore Cloud III to working order, possibly longer. As you all are *more* than aware, a year is a long time given our current circumstances. And then there is the added fear that The Blues will attack and destroy everything again. For all their stupidity, the attack was well executed. The guards didn't stand a chance,' Charlotte paused for breath as she looked at the expressions on the faces of what was left of the world's elite. What thoughts were churning in the minds of those gathered around the table? Did they still have hope of saving the planet and the human race or were they ready to give up, put it in the 'too hard' pile, and live out the rest of their days unconcerned for the future?

It was almost as if Edward had read her mind.

'The general feeling around the table is that trying to live at peace with The Blues has been our downfall. We were talking of planning our retaliation before they eradicate all of humanity,' stated Edward calmly, the thought of wiping out The Blues obviously not giving him a moment's hesitation. 'We may be able to make enough panels for Cloud III to be operational again in the time we have left or we may be better off making other Cloud sites bigger, ones where The Blues are not a threat. But if we choose to enlarge other facilities it would most likely mean that the area around Cloud III, so all The Network valleys, would eventually become part of the red zone. No one in the area would be able to survive.'

Charlotte looked at Edward. 'And have you come to a decision?'

'Not yet. There's a lot to consider regarding logistics. And if the area around Cloud III becomes a hot spot, rather than the planned cool spot, then it effects weather patterns,' explained Edward as he pointed to the map. 'If the weather patterns here are different then we need to know how they might affect the rest of the planet. Winds may be stronger, it may generate more storms, rainfall could be affected. There's a lot to consider and the calculations are far from simple. But if we choose to maintain the cool spot at Cloud III then the very real continued threat from The Blues needs to be...discussed.'

Charlotte nodded her head in understanding but had little to offer regarding a solution to their problems.

'And what of the guards?' asked Elizabeth, one of the key people within the ruling class of The Fringe. She was a classic beauty by Fringe standards. Perfect skin, glossy hair, a figure to envy in that it was toned but shapely. Her impecable genetics were obvious for everyone to see. It had been Elizabeth who had first made contact with The Network and enlisted their aid as a workforce to get them to where they were, to the point where they had some small hope of saving the planet — until The Blues had ruined all their plans.

'They found four left alive but just barely alive. Many were badly burned so it was difficult to identify the bodies. It seemed a couple of guards were missing, but with the chaos, and the bodies being burned, we couldn't be sure. And then Jax and Dez were discovered.

They had managed to crawl into the forest and….' Charlotte left her sentence hanging in mid-air as Edward coughed and sputtered — choking on the sip of coffee he'd taken.

'Sorry,' Edward gasped as he reached for his glass of water. 'Dez! Dez is…he's still alive?'

'He is, yes. I've….'

'Oh, thank God,' muttered Elizabeth. She closed her eyes and pinched the bridge of her nose. 'I don't know what we'd do without him, especially given the current situation.'

'I'm afraid the news I have is not good. I've just come from Dez's bedside at the hospital. He's very badly burned and also weak from exposure to the elements and dehydration. And he is also in a fragile emotional state. Blames himself for not protecting his people or The Cloud.'

'He can hardly hold himself accountable for that. None of us expected an attack at Cloud III,' exclaimed Elizabeth, her brow drew down in a frown.

'Is he expected to live?' asked Edward.

'I believe so. But even if he makes a full recovery physically, I'm not sure if he'll be willing to resume leadership of The Network, or help in any way with restoration of The Cloud, given his current state of mind.'

Edward glanced around the room. 'Well, Emi is perfectly capable of leading The Network. Everyone likes and respects her and we must have an immediate and smooth transition.'

All those around the table nodded their agreement. Charlotte sensed undercurrents in the room. She was sure that if anyone had thought to defend Dez and suggest he be given time to recover and resume his leadership role that the words would not be uttered out loud — or if they were, it would be to that individual's detriment.

Undermining Edward's authority, and that of his new fiancee, would not be politically correct in the present company.

'The restoration of Cloud III, and whether or not it will be feasible *in time*, as we were discussing prior to your arrival, is of utmost importance. We cannot be distracted by a leadership debate,' Edward continued. He grimly fixed his gaze on Charlotte.

'I wish I could be the bearer of better news.'

'But we need to encourage Dez. We can't allow him to wallow in self-recrimination. He's such a good leader and familiar with every aspect of The Cloud. His perspective would be invaluable right about now,' Elizabeth volunteered. It was almost as if she were talking to herself as her head rested on her hands and she massaged her temples. She stared at the tabletop, her exhaustion palpable. She didn't look up in time to catch the look of thunder on Edward's face.

But Charlotte did. She shivered though the room was far from cold.

# CHAPTER THREE

The early morning light filtered through the thin curtains covering the floor-to-ceiling windows. Matthew stirred and turned his head on the pillow to gaze at Zoe, only to find her staring back at him, a smile hovering around the corners of her mouth.

'Good morning, doctor.'

Matthew raised himself up on one elbow and planted a kiss on her mouth by way of reply.

'This 'end of the world catastrophe' we now find ourselves in certainly has stirred your passion for making the most of every moment,' she teased.

His second kiss was more lingering; his lips slowly made their way to her ear and then down to her neck, extracting a groan from Zoe in response.

The Satcomm beside the bed buzzed loudly in the quiet room.

'Damn,' Matthew swore before rolling over to answer the call. 'Hello. Yes. Yes. Good God. Yes, I'll head there immediately. Yes. Thanks for letting me know. Bye.'

'Who was that?'

'Charlotte. They found Dez and Jax.'

'Alive?'

'Yes but not in good shape. Dez is badly burned and Jax is still unconscious. I have to go. They've been flown to the hospital here.'

Matthew quickly got dressed into his hospital garb — a light cotton shirt and dress pants — and headed to the hospital. Although it was only 5am, the day already felt sultry and oppressive. There wasn't a breath of air. He could see puffy, white clouds billowing high into the sky to the southwest where the New York Cloud was in operation, but other than that the sky was its usual clear blue. It promised to be another stiflingly hot day. By the time he'd walked the six short blocks from his apartment to the hospital, his shirt was glued to him and he could feel the sweat trickling down his back. He grimaced. When the weather was this hot and still it was sometimes a pre-cursor to a Hyperstorm. He took the elevator to the hospital roof but all seemed serene on the distant horizon; there were no black-green storm clouds gathering. He shuddered involuntarily as he took the elevator back down to the intensive care unit. At least he could dismiss the thoughts of having to give warning for a hospital lockdown from his mind.

He took big breaths as he walked down the corridor, trying to ease the tension building within him before reaching the unit for burn victims. It would not help Dez if he arrived wound up like a spring. He wasn't sure if his mounting tension was from trying to keep his relationship with Zoe a secret and having to suddenly leave her alone in his apartment or if it was from the eerie feeling of the stifling weather or if it was to do with the news that Dez and Jax had been found alive.

He took one more steadying breath and pushed open the door to Dez's room.

'Well, you're a sight for sore eyes.'

Dez turned his head on the pillow and fixed Matthew with a bleak gaze. 'Yeah, I'm sure I must make sore eyes even more sore, given my current state.'

'You aren't looking your best, I must admit,' said Matthew as he gave Dez a hint of a smile. 'But we'll see what we can do to fix you up.'

'You'll either need a lot of luck or a lot of help or both,' said Dez bitterly.

'Well, I tend to be fairly lucky much of the time and help is not hard to come by.' Matthew attempted to instill a lighthearted tone to his voice to disguise his growing concern which was increasing the tension he didn't seem able to shake. 'I would like to do some tests and scans if that's okay? See if there's any internal damage.'

Dez nodded his agreement and lay back as Matthew connected his scanner to the screen and hovered it over parts of his torso and then inch by inch around his head. Matthew kept his eyes fixed to the screen as the scanner beeped loudly in the quiet room.

'I don't see any lasting damage. There's no reason you shouldn't make a full recovery, both physically and mentally.'

'What do you mean…mentally?'

'I was informed that you're blaming yourself for the traumatic events you've just been through, which is preposterous.'

'Is it!' Dez rasped, his response obviously not meant as a question but as a challenge.

'Nobody blames you. We were all caught off guard. How The Blues managed to find and plan an attack on Cloud III is beyond me but it's certainly *not* your fault. In my opinion, when you're back on your feet, you should shake off these thoughts and resume your role as leader,' said Matthew, trying to encourage Dez with his best bedside manner. 'You're an excellent leader and we're going to need you now more than ever.'

'Yeah, well, I didn't ask for your opinion and I wasn't a good enough leader to save my people was I? And they're not going to get the chance to 'make a full recovery' are they?' Dez turned his head away to stare at the far wall. 'Leave me be would you? I'm tired,' he added as he closed his eyes to feign sleep.

'Very well. But I'll be back to check on you again soon,' said Matthew, before turning to exit the room.

There was no response from Dez.

---

Matthew checked on Jax, but he was still unconscious and hooked to a multitude of machines so there was little more he could do for him until he woke up. With shoulders slumped, and not able to shake his sense of impending doom, he slowly made his way back to his apartment, in no hurry given the uncommonly hot weather. He gazed up at the oppressively blue sky, his mouth pulled down in a grimace.

'Damn Blues,' he muttered to himself. His thoughts turned to Dez and the fragile state he was in. They were all in a precarious state now, life teetering on the edge of a knife. If anything else went in the slightest bit wrong the entire planet would be doomed to a stay on its current trajectory of a slow and painful death. He shifted his gaze to the clouds on the distant horizon emitted by The Cloud. 'I wish those were heading this way, a bit of shade would be a welcome relief,' he said to the sultry air. But he knew for The Cloud to do its job that the cloud cover was not best optimized by having it over New York. Its dual purpose of reducing the heat from the sun and providing shade and some rain for the new crops planted in the purified soil was fulfilled by directing the clouds to the surrounding countryside and not having them over the city. He sighed and carried on. It was nearing noon so there was little shade on either side of the street. The sweat trickeling down his back was captured by his belted pants at his waist. As his head started to throb, he scowled at the heat shimmering off the pavement. 'Damn, I hope this eases up soon and isn't the new norm.' He wiped the perspiration from his forehead before it stung his eyes. His gaze was again drawn to the precious clouds on the distant horizon. He shook his head. They really should have built the New York Cloud elsewhere. If a Hyperstorm hit it would be in danger of being damaged and they couldn't afford to lose another Cloud. They should have considered more places, even if they were further away. His stomach cramped with his looming sense of dread. There were no green-black clouds on the horizon and not a breath of air — he needed to stop worrying.

Purposely redirecting his mind, his thoughts turned to Zoe. Surely with Edward now being openly engaged to Emi it meant that it was no longer illegal to be in a relationship with someone from The Network. Since the vaccine — the vaccine he had created and the highlight of his medical career — they were now as pure as The Fringe. There was no reason to not change the laws. He was tired of keeping his relationship with Zoe a secret and life was so fragile he no longer wanted to wait passively for the changes to be instigated. He would talk to Edward and push to have the laws re-written. Who knew if any of them would survive. They needed to make the most of what time they had. He increased his pace as his longing to be with Zoe and talk to her about a future together, however short, infused his mind with renewed hope.

But first he might take a cold shower, he thought as he tried to pull his shirt away from his torso.

# CHAPTER FOUR

'What a disaster. What on earth are we going to do now?' Tom stared at the wreckage of what had been the Cloud III site. Panel fragments were everywhere, blanketing the ground. The frame was still intact but it resembled a blackened maze of metal fingers. The grass surrounding the structure continued to emit smoke into the hazy atmosphere.

'I don't know. Cleaning all this up and putting in new panels will take forever,' replied Abe. 'Or, at least it will probably take longer than we have,' he added. He wiped his arm across his smarting eyes, the smoky air causing them to sting and water. He was beginning to wish he hadn't suggested coming out here on the Hoverboards to see if there was anything they could do. He realized now that it had been a stupid idea, one without any hope and it was depressing to see the devastation.

'We can't give up so easily. If we do then The Blues have won the battle but we all have lost the war because no one will survive,' said Chi vehemently.

The group from The Network turned to stare at her.

'We have to fix this,' she declared. She stared back at each one in turn, her eyes burned with determination. 'We have to. Don't you understand…this is our future! We have to fix this,' she waved her arm to encompass the desolation before them.

'How?' asked Tom.

'We'll start by getting every person we can to help clean up. The superstructure is charred but surely that doesn't really matter. And then…'

'But where are we going to get more panels? When this was built The Fringe had been making panels for years and they were ready to go….' Tom trailed off, not wanting to make matters worse by being negative.

'There are some spare panels in the storehouses,' said Abe.

'There are?' asked Chi. Why should she be surprised? Of course there would have to be extra panels in case something went wrong. But nobody had thought of it going this wrong.

'Sure. But not enough to re-build this.' Abe said, echoing her thoughts.

'I don't suppose The Fringe will care if we use the spares.' stated Chi.

'I don't know. I doubt it. And I don't know if they even keep track.' Abe looked at Chi and shrugged his shoulders. 'Dez was in charge. After his close call at the New York Cloud he liked to order extra panels just in case of an emergency. He had Jax or I put them in the storehouses for safekeeping.'

'So how many do you have?' Chi's face lit up at the thought of there still being some small hope for survival.

Abe stared out across the massive structure. 'Maybe enough for one or two rows.'

'One or two rows! That's not enough,' said Tom before relapsing into silence and wishing he had bitten his tongue.

'No, it's not.'

'Can each row be programmed to work independently?' asked Chi.

'Don't know but I don't see why not. Be a bit of extra work but I would think it can be reconfigured.'

'Then what are we waiting for? Surely *something* is better than *nothing*,' said Chi, her enthusiasm was starting to bubble over.

'And The Fringe…they must have some more panels,' said Tom as he caught on to a ray of Chi's optimism.

Abe looked around at the group and grinned. 'I think we should gather as many people as we can from the villages in Sectors A and B and get stuck into it. What have we got to lose?' he said as hope took hold. He glanced over at Chi, who had a stupidly happy grin on her face. He was amazed they could be so happy given what they were faced with but he was thankful for Chi's practical mind.

'Shouldn't we check in with The Fringe and see what they have planned?' suggested Tom. 'Besides, we'll need their help for making sure the relays that we fix are connected to the solar-power grids.'

Abe wasn't sure what made him hesitate. A part of him didn't want the help of The Fringe. He wanted to get on with cleaning up and fixing things without being told what to do or how to go about it. 'I have Dez's SatComm. I guess I'll call Peter and ask him if he could fly us out any spare panels they have…and a couple engineers to reconfigure the grid,' he said as he attempted to disguise his reluctance.

They headed back to Sector A on their Hoverboards, skirting around the dry brittle trees, the long-dead leaves now turned to lifeless dust. The chemical sprays that had once been used in the area had destroyed the circle of life. There had been a tipping point, when the trees leaves could no longer replenish the soil as they fell to the ground in the autumn, the toxic levels within the trees too high. As the ground became more toxic, it also was able to absorb less moisture, the tree roots took up the chemicals, but without enough water the trees became stunted, then they started to dry out, the leaves dwindled in number each year, those left took on the toxins and the circle continued until all life in the forest ceased. What rainfall there was no longer permeated the ground but ran off into the rivers, carrying the toxins to the oceans to further multiply the damage done there. Animals and birds could not survive in such a hostile environment so they either died or found a new place to live — except there were few places anymore where animals or people could exist.

The brittle forest barely registered in the minds of Abe and his friends — they had never known the world to be any other way. They snaked their way through the tall dry grass that seemed to cover most of the surrounding area. The abundant grass waved above their heads. They had learned to harvest it and weave it together to make mats, beds, seats, children's swings, and covers for shade. It grew new every year in a never-ending, heartbreaking cycle. It was the one crop that had been genetically modified and thrived on the toxic soil, eventually wiping out most other crops which could not compete with its tenacious hold. But other than its usefulness in making physical items it had no nutritional value and every year added its toxicity back into the already barren soil.

Finally they descended into the valley that Abe called home. Security had been doubled since the raid on The Cloud and Abe gave a wave to the guards before they headed down the path that led to the valley floor. The lushness of the valley was astounding given the desolate landscape around them — although he was beginning to wonder if the valley was not as fertile as it used to be or if it was just his imagination playing tricks on him. Abe looked around him as he headed home, trying to notice the small details of his surroundings. He could only surmise that the river that fed the valley came from mountains untouched by humans and that since past generations had never bothered to commercially farm the valley its soil could still sustain life. He smiled his appreciation as he neared home, where he was sure his little red-headed charges, Fie and Lea, would be cooking up a storm.

'I'll go put that call through to Peter and then I'll gather as many Hoverboards as I can. I'll also see about getting some carts for us to haul the debris in. Can you guys gather as many helpers as possible? Then we'll meet back here, say a few days from now, and get started,' Abe instructed. As Abe watched everyone depart he realized that he felt much better for having a plan. But he wished Dez were back as he would gladly relinquish the role of leadership he'd taken up to keep Sector A running smoothly. He also felt like he had a rock in the pit of his stomach. He didn't want to re-build a portion of The Cloud only to have The Blues destroy everything again.

Surely something could be done about The Blues.

———

By the following week they had two hundred helpers clearing The Cloud III site. They worked from dawn until dusk picking up tiny shards of the shattered panels, placing them in the carts and hauling it away. It would take weeks to clear the area but nobody was willing to sacrifice the hard work of the last couple years that had gone into creating The Cloud.

Abe, Tom, Liz and Chi worked alongside everyone else.

Abe ripped up one of his oldest shirts and tied a bandana around his head to prevent the sweat from trickling into his eyes. His t-shirt soon stuck to his back but the sun was too scorching for him to think of removing his shirt for most of the day. As one of the bigger, stronger men around he figured the best thing he could do to aid with the clean up was to haul the carts of debris off site. It was exhausting, grueling work. He clenched and unclenched his sore and callused hands and then stretched to ease the pain in his back and shoulders. He was accustomed to hard physical work and being exposed to the elements but this was more taxing that anything he had done before. Every muscle hurt — he felt like he had been trampled.

Abe looked over to where Liz and Chi were placing panel shards into a cart. They were both soaked with sweat, their clothes darker where the material was saturated and glued to their glistening skin. Chi had a long scratch down one arm where she had obviously lost an argument with a piece of debris. Liz had a strip of cloth wrapped around one hand, blood had soaked through the temporary bandage but Liz seemed oblivious as she kept on picking up piece after piece of the sharp panels.

'You guys want to take a break? I brought quite a lot of extra food with me today, figuring we were going to need it,' offered Tom as he rummaged in his pack.

'Thanks, Tom.' Liz took the proffered apple. She looked around and sighed as she shook her head. 'I still don't get why The Blues did this.' She waved her arm at the destruction surrounding them. 'What was the point? There's no food here. And how did they travel this far? How did they find The Cloud when it is so far from where they were last known to be?'

'Maybe it was another set-up,' suggested Tom.

All eyes turned to stare at Tom.

'What?' asked Chi and Abe in unison.

Tom glanced from one to the other. 'Yeah, you know, like the one on Sectors C and D.'

'*What* are you talking about?' asked Chi, her apple halfway to her mouth, her hand frozen in mid-air.

Abe's eyebrows were drawn down, his expression perplexed as he fixed his gaze on Tom. He glanced at Chi, who wore a similar expression.

'Obviously Dez has not shared his thoughts with everyone,' commented Tom.

'Care to enlighten us?' asked Chi.

'Dez thinks that when Sam was dying he was trying to warn him that the raid was a set-up. He thought I was behind it.'

'You! Why on earth would he think something like that?' asked Chi as she passed around the water canister after spraying some on her head.

'He thought I was trying to plan the death of my uncle…because of what he did to my mom. He thought that I had arranged to exchange food with The Blues and in return they would kill my uncle…but that the plans had gone wrong and they ended up raiding the villages.'

'How on earth do you know what Dez thinks…or that he would think something like that, at least?' asked Abe, his forehead puckered in disbelief.

'Because he asked me…he asked me if I had set-up the raid.'

'Good God. What a thing to have to ask one of your own people,' said Chi, her eyes large with surprise, her voice incredulous. 'And what a thing to be asked.'

'Yeah. It wasn't a good moment. But I could see why he thought what he did.'

'But it obviously wasn't you,' Liz piped up. 'So, if the raid was a set-up, then who planned it and *why*?'

Tom shrugged.

Abe looked from Tom to Liz and back again. 'And does Dez *still* think it was a set-up…the attack on Sectors C and D?' he asked. He took the bread roll that Tom handed to him.

'I think so,' said Tom.

'But what makes you think this was a set-up as well?' asked Abe as he waved his arm to encompass what had once been the structure that was supposed to save humanity and the world.

'I don't see how The Blues would have got this far without help,' stated Tom bluntly. He paused to take a swig from the water canister as it came round. 'I mean…a handful of Blues have been seen to the far south of Sector A, near the water holes…but that is still a days walk. And this…this is what…at least a weeks walk north if we didn't have Hoverboards? I just don't see how they got this far. It's hot and dry with little shelter and no food and the grasslands are almost impossible to navigate…'

Abe looked around at the years of hard work now reduced to fragments littered across the ground. 'But why?'

Tom shrugged his shoulders and shook his head. He didn't have an answer.

'I think I need to go to New York and have a chat with Dez,' stated Abe.

———

Edward and Emi were alone in their apartment. The late evening light streamed in through the floor to ceiling windows. There was no warmth in the last of the sunlight — it was filtered out by a protective coating on each window pane. They had just finished a succulent dinner of salmon, sweet potatoes and vegetables, all raised and harvested within the confines of New York City and prepared by Edward, which Emi had barely been able to choke down. They now sat on the sofa, watching the firey display of the fading sunset. Emi wondered how there could still be so much beauty in the world when there was so little hope of survival.

'You do realize, I hope, that I need you to assume Dez's role as leader,' stated Edward as the sun disappeared in a final glow of red and orange. He got up and turned on a light. The bright light seemed harsh after the radiance of the sunset. Edward pushed the button that controlled the dimmer. The glare abated — he did not want this to seem like an interogation. He had picked his moment carefully.

Emi shook her head, misery eminating from her eyes. 'Please, Edward, can't we wait and see how long it takes him to recover? Surely him being in hospital for a couple of months will not matter to the leadership too much. Everyone understands.'

Edward shook his head. 'It's not his physical recovery I'm concerned about. It's his mental one. Charlotte informed me that he is in a very fragile state of mind and does not want to resume his leadership role. I can't have someone in charge of The Network who is not one hundred per cent committed. You must understand.'

'But I'm sure as he recovers physically he'll also recover mentally. He's never backed away from a challenge in his life. He's a born leader. I'm positive that once he's recovered from the burns and has had time to distance himself from the trauma that he'll be back to normal. Can't we give him a few months?' Emi knew she was pleading and that it wouldn't sit well with Edward but the thought of taking Dez's position as leader after abandoning him for Edward was not something she wanted to contemplate.

Once again, Edward shook his head. This time there was a hint of annoyance in the movement and his eyes held a steely, almost angry, glint.

Emi swallowed and stared back at Edward, her mouth a hard line of defiance. The quietness of the room stretched between them.

Edward broke the silence.

'I'm sorry. I can't wait for Dez to recover…if he recovers. We are at a very crucial time. If we can't fix the Cloud or come up with an alternate solution…and fast…people will get disillusioned, restless. We could end up with a rebellion on our hands. I can't lose control after coming so far. I have to have a leader who will work with me and who the Network trust. You're the only person who can fill the role. The only person I can rely on. I'm sorry it is so soon after our engagement. I had hoped we could have had some time just for us… as a couple…but it can't be helped.' He paused. 'I'll be here for you. We'll rule together.' Edward offered up a tentative smile, trying to alleviate the tention. He must use his charm to win Emi over.

Edward had convinced himself with his monologue but Emi felt frightened and trapped. She shook her head. The smallest movement of denial. Her eyes darted to the door. She wanted to run, to escape. She felt the walls of the opulent apartment, her home, closing in on her. The dinner and the sunset were nothing more than agents of manipulation.

Edward reached for her hand. She flinched. His grip tightened and his eyes became hard.

'You have to do this, Emi. I need you. Now more than ever. The world, all of mankind, needs you. You can't turn your back on your people when they will look to you for guidance. They trust you. This is your destiny now, You must embrace it.'

She returned Edward's gaze. 'I…' She trailed off. There was no escape. There was never any escape. From the moment Elizabeth had found them in the forest, or even long before that, their paths had been set by those in the Fringe…by Edward. She shut her eyes, head bent and heaved a sigh.

Edward tightened his grip on her hands. She winced in pain.

Raising her head she looked Edward in the eye and nodded.

'That's my girl. I knew you would see reason.' Edward grinned. He had won his point and had no doubt that Emi would realize he was right once she was over the emotinal trauma of the raid on the Cloud. 'Maybe when Dez is fully recovered he can become a board member,' he offered by way of consolation.

'Yes. Perhaps.' Emi agreed. *Heaven forbid* she thought. But she had a role to play…a role that required her to put on the biggest act of her life if she wanted to protect the man she loved, her baby and her people. She nodded more emphatically and gave Edward a smile.

'You're right of course. The people will miss Dez but they must have a leader, especially now. We have no time to lose or we shall all perish.' She heaved a sigh. 'Sorry, I'm just still upset by the raid. Becoming leader of the Network was not something I was contemplating. You took me by surprise. I'll be alright now.' She put her hand protectively over her tummy, hoping Edward would not attribute any significance to the gesture. She could not tell him yet. It was not time.

Edward's face lit up with her capitulation. He leaned forward and kissed her on the lips, savouring his triumph.

# CHAPTER FIVE

'So, what now fat-ass?' Shade glared at Spike.

They were back in their decrepid concrete box of a room in the partially ruined building on the outskirts of the city. They had not received any extra food for 'services rendered' and the little they had was almost gone. Beyond the cracked, grimey windows nothing moved — the ancient sidewalks were a sea of broken slabs, hauled upward by the weeds that engulfed them. Not even a rat stirred as there was no food to be found in the area.

'I don't know.' Spike shrugged his shoulders and scowled at Shade. He was tired and didn't want to be badgered by anyone. His plans hadn't worked and he felt defensive and angry at being duped. He'd killed the guards like he was supposed to. He was pretty sure it had been on the right day but it was hard to know seeing as he had no way of judging what day it was. But he'd made marks on the wall and then on his arm on the long treck north to count off the days so had been fairly certain. But no food had arrived. He slammed his fist into the straw mattress they were lying on but it didn't aleviate any of his pent up rage. He got up and kicked over a chair, taking pleasure in watching it smash into the wall and fall to pieces. The hike north had been a long hard walk for nothing. And of course, on the way back, there hadn't even been the food drops. Obviously the fellow who had given him the tip-offs had needed them to arrive at the site in good shape but hadn't cared if they all died on the way back. A bunch of their gang *had* died on the hike back and others had snuck off, trying to return to their old stomping grounds in the city where they could at least get food from the Exchange. Now it was just him, Shade and a few others. 'Why should I have to do all the thinking and planning?' he asked as he returned Shade's glare.

'You call that thinking and planning,' mocked Shade, her eyebrows raised in feigned surprise, causing the zipper tattoo across her forehead to stretch. 'Fat lot of good that did us. We walked for forever and for what…to kill a few people and smash up whatever that was. No food, no crops, no better shelter or clothes. Nothing. Yeah, bloody brilliant plan.'

'Not my fault. I was promised a lifetime supply of food.'

Shade craned her neck around as her gaze flitted from one part of the room to the other. 'Yeah, and where might that be? I don't see any food, dumbass.'

'No,' grumbled Spike. 'I don't think we should have smashed up the panels,' he muttered.

'You don't say. Bloody brilliant thinking that now!' her face creased in such a way that it made the zipper imprints look like they were being pulled apart.

'Yeah, well, I was mad. There was supposed to be food left for us. I was promised food and there wasn't any.'

'Oh, you don't say. I hadn't noticed.'

'Piss off. Who asked you? Don't see you thinkin' of any way to get us some food.'

'We could have just stayed where we were. At least we had something to live on. Now we've got nothin'.'

'So, leave if you want. I don't give a crap.'

'Nah. It's your brat and when it arrives I'll need someone to get me food. Won't be in no shape to try huntin' squirrels on me own.'

'I can't feed myself, never mind feedin' you and some brat,' said Spike. 'Never have managed to catch a squirrel,' he added under his breath.

'Should have thought of that before you came up with all these brilliant plans and got me pregnant. I didn't get pregnant all by myself you know.'

Spike growled and stomped off down the stairs.

'Where you goin' asshole?' yelled Shade.

'Find some food so you'll shut up for a bit,' shouted Spike over his shoulder as he emerged from the building into the blinding sunlight. He shuffled down the street, trying not to trip over the broken bits of concrete jutting out of the ground, and headed further out of town. A few weeks back he'd found a spot where some trees still grew that looked like they might produce some kind of fruit. At the time the things he'd tried had been bitter and hard, causing his stomach to cramp painfully, but maybe it had been too early to pick. He didn't like fruit, at least not the half-rotten stuff the Exchange gave them, but it was better than nothing. He needed to find the place again and see if anything tasted better.

He trudged on, his feet burned on the hot pavement while the sweat trickled into his eyes, causing them to sting. He stopped to stand on a clump of dry grass and weeds to give his feet a chance to cool. He took his shirt off, wiped his face and then tied it onto his head. He rubbed at his empty belly and admired the massive spike imprint that looked like it was impaling both him and the snake tattoo on his stomach. It was the reason for his name. He liked the spike imprint — it made him look menacing.

It was nice to be on his own for a while, away from every one glaring at him and blaming him for all that had gone wrong. He shouldn't have smashed the panels. He knew that now. It hadn't been part of the plan and he was sure his punishment would be not getting the promised food. Now they were going to have to fend for themselves and have even less than they had before. Death seemed more appealing than having an even harder life with Shade nagging at him all the time. But he hadn't yet given up all hope of having some of the promised food delivered to them. He'd wait a while longer, see what happened.

He stopped to take a piss up against a wall and purposefully aimed the yellow stream at a weed growing from the crevice in the sidewalk. 'Ha,' he said out loud to the weed that was drooping under his steady stream. 'That's one thing that still feels good,' he added, thinking of when he was forcing himself on Shade. 'I'll get her some bloody food and then make her pay for it and for her nagging.' He grinned and put himself back together before carrying on.

He turned the last corner where the crumbling buildings spewed out over the pavement and came to the field where the fruit trees grew. The trees had grown together into a single massive canopy, their branches a snarled, intertwined mess, but the filtered light they offered was pleasant. Spike headed for the small stream that flowed on the far side of the field. From the fall of the land it seemed that the stream had once been a bigger river, but the fact that there was still water flowing explained how the trees had survived since someone, long ago, had dug a couple trenches to redirect the water and use it for irrigation. He waded into the stream, and cupping his hands drank as much as he could before submersing his entire body into the coolness.

He emerged from the water and rang out his shirt before laying it on the ground to dry. It was the only thing he had to carry food in since he hadn't thought to bring a sachel in his hurry to leave. As he walked slowly between the trees, his neck craned up, he scanned the branches for whatever he could find. The trees were different from one another and evenly spaced — an orchard from a different era. He wasn't sure what it was that he was picking — fruit, nuts, maybe some kind of vegetable? Did vegetables grow on trees? He didn't know and didn't care. He would take what he could get. There were a variety of colours — red, orange, green and brown. Some still hung from the trees while others were lying on the ground.

Spike reached down to pick up an apple and bit into the soft skin. The sweet tanginess wakened his taste buds. He had never tasted anything so good. With a few more bites he devoured the apple. Moving further along the row he found something small and yellow growing on a tree. He plucked the fruit from the branch and bit into it, anticipating the sweet goodness of this new type of fruit. His lips puckered and his throat closed as the sour taste assaulted his mouth. He spat out the offending fruit and looked at it. The skin was thick, his teeth barely penetrating to the juicy insides. He peeled the skin off and took a tentative nibble of the flesh…nope, still sour. Why would anyone plant such a thing? He threw it down. Even though he was starving he was obviously still going to have to pick and choose what to haul back with him. Shade would never let him live it down if he turned up with a bunch of food that made your stomach clench in revolt. And he wanted his reward.

A rabbit hopped from behind a bush and sat in front of him, unafraid, eyeing him up. He raised his arm above his head and hurled the hard nut in his hand directly at the rabbit's head. The rabbit fell sideways, knocked unconscious, if not dead. Spike grinned. Meat as well as all this. He looked at his haul with a smirk and rubbed at his crotch. How happy Shade was going to be. He picked up the rabbit by its hind legs and then gathered up his shirt of colourful fruit, nuts and berries. Time to head home and claim what was rightfully his. She was too immense to climb on top of anymore but there were other ways. His grin split his face from ear to ear, making the snakes appear as if they were slithering upwards on his cheeks.

Spike retraced his steps, whistling tunelessly as he went. The pavement still burned his feet and the heat radiating upwards from the city streets caused the sweat to trickle in a steady stream down his back but the snakes continued to dance on his face as he neared their desolate home.

He hauled himself up the stairs. Nobody else was about, just Shade resting on the thin straw mat on the hard concrete floor furthest away from where the sunlight streamed through the grimey, broken glass.

'Look what I found,' Spike said in triumph. He layed his shirt down in front of her.

'Where'd you get all this?' she asked as she reached for the red piece of fruit and bit down into its juicy sweetness.

'Found some trees on the edge of town. There's lots. At least enough for us if we don't tell the others,' said Spike. 'And I got this,' he added. He pulled the rabbit out from behind his back.

'Rabbit.' Shade's eyes glowed with happiness. 'I can't remember the last time I had meat.'

'Yeah, well, I need a reward before I give you any more of this,' Spike demanded as he reached out to squeeze her breast.

'Piss off,' said Shade and hit his hand away. 'Why should I? I don't owe you anything. You're the one who got us into this mess in the first place.'

'Yeah, well, I'm also the only one who knows where the food is and can help you now, aren't I,' said Spike. His hand ripped aside her shirt.

Shade remained silent as he continued to maul her. Her eyes strayed to the food that was just out of reach.

Spiked looked up at Shade's face and noted her expression of longing — not for him but for the food. His irritation deepened. He'd done all he could, walked on the blistering pavement, under the scorching sun to get her what she wanted and yet she still scorned him. He squeezed her breast hard.

'Ouch,' she yelped and glared at him.

'Look, I'll take you there. We'll figure out how to ditch this lot and go. Just you and me. There'll be enough if it's just us and there's a building close by for shelter. We'll survive…and if the asshole who promised me food doesn't come through…then we'll plan our revenge. We're rebels, right! We'll get what we want and we'll make him pay.'

Shade continued to stare at him. Then she shrugged her shoulders and nodded.

He freed himself from his shorts.

Shade stare was icy, the zipper imprints on her face looking as if they were drawing together. 'Creep.'

'It's not like I can get you pregnant,' he grinned menacingly, the snakes slithered upwards in excitement as he gave her a shove so she knew that he meant it.

# CHAPTER SIX

Peter knocked and quietly slipped into the conference room. Filtered sunlight streamed in through the tinted full-length windows, covered by sheer curtains during the hottest part of the day. Leftover remnants of lunch littered the middle of the table. Those gathered around the table looked exhausted, their eyes bloodshot, their clothes rumpled. The maps were unchanged — the hot spots too many, the cool green spots too few for survival. Expressions were grim. Conversation came to a halt as everyone turned toward him.

'Peter, come on in.' Edward waved him to a chair and invited him to state what he had come to say, happy for the interruption.

'I've just had a call from Abe at Sector A. He says they're clearing the Cloud III site and asked me to fly out with whatever spare panels we have,' Peter announced to the stunned group seated around the conference table.

'But we haven't finished calculating if repairing Cloud III is feasible with the time constraints that we have or if it's even advisable since The Blues are obviously close enough to destroy it. We might be better off making the New York Cloud bigger. It's closer by and not at the mercy of The Blues,' Edward responded in frustration. 'They're just wasting resources and manpower.'

'Abe said they felt like doing something was better than nothing and even if Cloud III is only partially functional it would still be helping to cool the earth and provide the rain they so desperately need in the area.' Peter lifted his hands in resignation as he passed along the message.

There was a hum around the room as everyone commented on the unexpected development. Edward raised his voice to be heard. 'That may be but I've suggested enlarging the New York Cloud, which would be a huge benefit to us as it would lower the temperature of the city and increase our local crop production,' he said as he glanced at each member of the board seated around the table, 'and then we could ship extra panels to the UK Cloud site, making it bigger and... sacrifice Cloud III.'

'I thought we required *each* site for optimum efficiency,' said Emi, fear knotted her stomach at the thought of Cloud III being abandoned and the surrounding valleys left desolate. She was suddenly quite sure that if Cloud III were sacrificed then the world temperature would not be lowered fast enough for the valleys of The Network to survive.

Since she'd agreed to take over as the official new leader of The Network she had resigned herself to the fact that she probably was the best candidate for the position. She'd been the leader of Sector B, had the trust of The Network, was — or at least had been — close to Dez and now had access to the plans of The Fringe. She would do her best until Dez recovered — if he recovered. As leader, she tried to attend the board meetings and was very glad she'd decided to come to this one. An inner instinct also warned her that Edward could be quite selective in what he shared with her when they were alone together. She felt a desperate need to keep her finger on the pulse of what was happening.

'That's the ideal. But Cloud III will obviously remain at risk due to its proximity to The Blues,' said Elizabeth. 'We'll need heightened security and a better warning system in place…and more adequate defence,' she added reluctantly.

'Or perhaps we should rid ourselves, once and for all, of The Blues. We all know we have the firepower,' suggested Edward as he cast a steely glance at those gathered and took in the grim set of mouths and worried expressions reflected back at him. 'Until now The Blues have never been a threat to us personally,' he paused, 'but things have changed.'

'But the mandate of The Fringe has always been to live at peace. We've spent the last hundred years trying to devise a way for the human race to survive,' Elizabeth stated. 'Are you now going to annihilate them instead?'

'The Blues are not the type of humans we are trying to save the planet for,' said Edward emphatically.

'Surely there is a better way. Maybe if we explained to them what is going on and…what if Matthew's vaccine worked on them — the new one he made after Sal died,' countered Elizabeth. 'They should at least be given a chance.'

Edward turned a hard stare upon Elizabeth. He did not appreciate being argued with. 'And who would you put forward — be willing to sacrifice — to enter their camp and try to *converse*? Reasoning is *not* their strong point,' he added, his voice reverberated with condescension.

Elizabeth yielded and shook her head.

'Now, shall we carry on?'

'So, do I have your permission to fly the panels out to Cloud III?' asked Peter.

'I'm not convinced that's our best course of action,' said Edward, the coldness of his expression left no one in the room in doubt that he was not accustomed to being argued with or dictated to — by them or by The Network.

'We should let them try.' Emi bestowed her most alluring look of hope and confidence upon Edward. 'The structure is already there, they are willing to do the work, we only need to supply them with spare panels. Surely, it is the easiest thing to do at present?' she paused and then added, 'It doesn't prevent us from making more panels and fulfilling our own plans, does it?' she asked in an attempt to appeal to Edward's need to rule and make the decisions.

Edward looked around the table as everyone exchanged glances. 'I suppose if the work to clear the site is already being done,' conceded Edward reluctantly as he interpreted the silence around the table as agreement with Emi.

They had not really come up with a better solution yet and he was not willing to look petty and foolish by starting an argument in front of everyone in the room. 'But if we are going to re-build Cloud III then we need to eradicate The Blues,' he stated. He locked eyes with each person in the room — challenging anyone to contradict him.

There wasn't a person present brave enough to argue with Edward when his face looked as it did at the moment — his jaw locked, his forehead creased in anger, his eyes daggers of fury. He stared each of them down until they nodded their head in agreement. The hatred he felt toward The Blues and their stupid act of violence was more than he could express. Their one senseless act may yet turn out to be the tipping point — enough to jeopardize his ideas of ruling the new world that The Fringe had been planning for the last hundred years. 'It's unanimous then! Peter, once you've delivered the panels to Cloud III, report back here to me immediately. We'll need a few Hovercrafts with experienced pilots to deliver our own destructive power onto the heads of the unsuspecting Blues,' ordered Edward with an icy blue stare.

The Blues would not be allowed to survive.

———

Emi left the meeting early, claiming a headache, and headed for the hospital. Edward had not given her security clearance to see Dez and she knew not to ask. Edward's jealousy would never allow him to permit her to see Dez but he would be in the meeting for hours yet so she would not need to explain where she'd been. She desperately needed to talk to Dez even if he said he didn't want to see her. Edward's decisions were starting to worry her and she felt the need of Dez's calm reassurance as a leader to carry on in her assumed role until he was better. But more than that, she missed Dez — the ache in her soul was a constant gnawing, reminding her of the mess she had created of her life.

Heading through Central Park she meandered along the paths where the overhanging canopy of the trees offered shade. All of the trees were in full bloom and many of the fruits were ripe for picking. She took her time, enjoying the dappled green light filtering through the leaves overhead, formulating her thoughts into what she was going to say. Reaching up she plucked an orange from a tree, peeled it and popped a segment into her mouth. The refreshing taste of the sweet, tangy fruit brought a smile to her face. If The Fringe could salvage so many types of food she had never encountered before, and modify the soil and the atmosphere to allow them to grow in abundance, then surely they could still save the planet. They couldn't let go of hope so easily just because one Cloud structure had been damaged, especially if The Network could get some of it back to working order. She savoured the flavour of the orange as it restored her faith in the path she had chosen — to support Edward as he found a way forward for their salvation and to be the leader The Network needed until Dez was better. She must use her influence over Edward to make sure The Network were not abandoned, along with The Blues, in the precarious situation they now found themselves in.

As she left Central Park she crossed the street to be able to walk in the shadows cast by the tall buildings. Some streets, which were wide, had shade structures over them but most streets did not need the additional shade structures as the buildings offered enough protection from the sun on one side of the street or the other. She stayed in the shadows, her sunglasses on and her white hat pulled low, not wanting to be noticed walking in the direction of the hospital. Charlotte had told her what room Dez was in, she just needed to figure out how to get in unobserved.

She entered the hospital through the front doors and headed for the burn unit. It was three o'clock — the beginning of visiting hours and also the time when nurses would switch shifts. She removed her hat and sunglasses, feeling too conspicuous indoors with them on, and walked purposefully to Dez's room. If she made her way to his room with a confidence she was far from feeling she hoped no one would stop and challenge her. The burn unit reception nurses were, thankfully, absent. Coming during shift change was working in her favour. She found Dez's room number, and taking a big breath, slipped quietly inside.

'Emi!'

The room was sterile. White walls, light beige floor and a single bed — placed so the patient could look out the window to the tops of the surrounding concrete buildings and patch of blue sky. There was one hard chair she could choose to sit on, or not, and the rest of the room was filled with medical instuments, their lights and graphs quietly beeping in the stillness.

'Hi, remember me?' she asked, trying for lighthearted nonchalance to disguise her overwhelming emotions. She could barely take in the number of tubes sticking out of Dez. The skin regeneration machines hovered over him, slowly restoring his burned skin and the rest of him was wrapped in bandages. The parts of him that were visible were badly burned, or bruised and swollen with the less severe cuts showing as red slashes. The only thing that looked familiar were his eyes — except they were now filled with reproach and not the loving glow she was accustomed to.

'I told Charlotte to tell you not to come. I don't want to be seen like this,' his hostility immediately apparent as his anger bubbled to the surface. The beeping on his heart rate monitor increased.

'I know,' Emi whispered as she blinked back the tears. 'But I needed…wanted to see you.'

'Well, that makes one of us,' Dez took a big breath and glanced at the monitor with a frown. He took another deep breath before turning his gaze back to Emi.

'I don't care what you look like,' her raw emotions causing her to retaliate. 'I love you and…you'll get better,' she whispered as the momentary anger vanished.

'Maybe, but that still won't make me into a good leader. Go away, Emi. I'm not the person you think I am. Not the person you or The Network needs,' he leaned back, rested his head on the pillows and stared at the ceiling as the heart monitor slowly returned to its usual rhythm.

'But I…we do need you. I'm trying to fill your shoes as leader but Edward is so powerful. I don't know if I fully trust his judgment anymore and…'

'He's done a perfectly adequate job of running things and planning how to save the planet up until now. I highly doubt he needs, or wants, me holding his hand during this crisis…a crisis that I should have been able to prevent if I had put a bit more thought into our safety and the protection of the Cloud.' He continued to focus on the ceiling and control his breathing.

'How can you plan for something you're not expecting? You're not being reasonable.'

'That's just it you see…it is perfectly reasonable in this god-forsaken world to expect an attack by the Blues. Or have you forgotten about what they did to Sectors C and D?' he asked. He turned his head once again to look her in the eyes, his expression challenging.

'No. No, of course I haven't forgotten.' She paused and swallowed the lump in her throat. 'How could I?' she whispered, fighting back the tears that were threatening to undo her attempt at staying calm. 'But still…this took us all by surprise…not just you.'

'But I'm the leader. I'm the one who should have given it the extra thought and been prepared.'

'But…but Edward has been a leader for ages…and he didn't think to prepare the Cloud for an attack by the Blues…other than surrounding it with…guards. Nobody dreamed they could get that far north.'

'Yes, but Edward has not had to deal with the Blues like I have. I should have seen it coming, had a plan, made some kind of effort to protect…' He choked off the rest of what he was going to say and clamped his mouth shut.

Emi shook her head. She had run out of arguments. After a while of waiting in silence she muttered, 'You don't understand. Edward… he's different somehow. Not listening to the others on the board and I…I…as Network leader I only have so much sway over him. He…'

'There are lots of people who support you, Emi. You don't need me.'

'Please Dez…'

'Just leave, Emi,' he said as he turned his head away and closed his eyes.

'Dez?'

There was no response.

Emi quietly let herself out. Dashing the tears from her cheeks she fished out her sunglasses, feeling the need to hide behind them as she left the hospital and despair overwhelmed her. Though she had been warned that Dez didn't want to see her, she still had not expected him to be so hostile or so down on himself as a leader. How on earth was she going to change his thought process and get him back to the person she knew him to be? She couldn't do it on her own. She needed help.

# CHAPTER SEVEN

They worked tirelessly clearing the Cloud site. It was backbreaking work in the scorching heat. The dust and the soot coated everything and the panel shards were sharp and menacing. Staying nourished and hydrated was a constant challenge. The mesh hats they wore did little to keep them cool or prevent heat stroke — yet few complained.

Finally, the last of the destruction was cleared away.

The Fringe engineers arrived to re-configure the relays so that each could work independently of the others. They meticulously checked over each row, ensuring that everything was properly connected to the new control board. The control board was now a myriad of buttons — each relay had to have its own emergency shut-off as well as sliding scales for how much cloud output was desired at a time.

'Looks like there will be enough panels to get five of the thirty rows working once I've brought over the last shipment of the ones we have on hand.' Peter watched as the panels were unloaded from the Hovercraft.

'It's not much but it's a start,' replied Abe. 'Put them over there would you,' he instructed the guys who were hauling the heavy panels out of the Hovercraft. He indicated the side of the control room where temporary bracing had been built to house the panels until they could be put in place.

'Each time enough panels are made for an entire relay I'll fly them out…unless Edward changes his mind in favour of some other plan,' said Peter, his mouth turned down at the edges. 'I have to tell you… warn you…Edward would never have agreed to this if it wasn't for Emi's influence. I don't think he listens to anyone else anymore. Thank God she agreed to be his wife,' he added.

Abe glanced at Peter. He wasn't so happy about Emi being with Edward but he could see that her influence was invaluable. With Dez incapacitated they needed someone that The Network respected who also had the ear of The Fringe, especially Edward.

'We'll see how long it takes to get the whole thing operational again *and* if we now have enough time to make a difference to the atmosphere.' Peter squinted up into the clear, blue sky as he brushed his hand across his forehead to wipe away the perspiration forming at his hairline.

'Yeah, it might not be enough but at least it's something and nobody has come up with a better plan in the time that I know of,' said Abe. He followed Peter's gaze at the relentlessly cloud-less sky above, his forehead furrowed into a scowl. 'At least it restores a little bit of hope,' he turned to look back at Peter, his lips twitched up in an effort at a half-hearted smile.

'Hope is pretty hard to come by lately,' said Peter, sounding somewhat morose. 'I was happy to help out with your plan to restore Cloud III — or at least the part of it that we can.'

'It would have been a pretty damn long walk with the panels if you hadn't flown them here,' joked Abe, trying to lighten the mood as he too wiped the sweat from his brow. 'Now we just need to protect this new lot from The Blues. I'm going to double security, provide the guards with weapons and a Satcomm so they can call for help if need be. Why such measures weren't already in place is beyond me. You would almost think that someone didn't want the guards to....' He trailed off, not wanting to voice his doubts out loud and make them into a concrete thought. 'Anyway, we definitely can't have them destroy everything again or none of us will survive.'

'The Blues won't be a concern for much longer. My next task is to take some experienced pilots, with some loaded Hovercrafts, and show them what kind of firepower we have,' stated Peter with a scowl.

Abe's eyes dilated and his eyebrows rose. 'Firepower?'

'Edward's orders. The Blues won't know what hit them.'

'How much firepower *do* you have?'

'Lots,' Peter paused and then added, 'enough to annihilate the city and surrounding area of their last known whereabouts. We also have infra-red heat detectors so if we see anyone moving on the ground below they…well, I'm sure you get the picture.'

Abe was silent. He stared at Peter, trying to absorb what he'd just been told. Although there had been raids, there had never been war, or a complete masacare of one group by another, since the collapse of government control in the aftermath of the catastrophic climate change which had wiped out most of the population. 'I have no love for The Blues but I never thought of torching them to the ground.'

'No. I understand the necessity but I don't relish the assignment,' stated Peter. He frowned. 'It makes us no better than them.'

'Yeah. They wiped out my entire family but I've never been able to bring myself to retaliate…although I have thought about it plenty, especially since the raid on Sectors C and D.'

'Elizabeth wanted to make contact with them. See if we could try and explain what we're doing and get them to leave us alone…but Edward shut her down.' Peter's scowl returned to his face. 'Although reasoning with them may be pointless anyway,' he added with a shrug of his shoulders.

'Yeah, probably,' agreed Abe. 'But still!'

'I know,' said Peter. The look he gave Abe acknowledged all that was not being expressed.

Abe shook his head. The Fringe had spent decades meticulously planning The Cloud and how to save the planet and now it seemed as if everything was haphazard, with plans being executed with little thought. They needed Dez back as leader, someone who understood the nuances of each group and the overall working of The Cloud. 'Can you give me a lift back to New York? I'd like to see Dez.'

'Sure. I was planning on leaving as soon as the panels are unloaded. Can you be ready to go soon?'

'Yeah, I have a change of clothes in my pack. I just need to find Chi to send a message to the girls. I'll meet you back here as soon as I can.'

———

'You look a sight lot better than when we found you,' stated Abe as he let himself into the sterile hospital room. The overhead light was glaring and the smell of disinfectant was unpleasant but Abe kept his expression cheerful as he approached Dez's bedside.

'Well, I must have looked pretty rough because as far as I'm concerned I still look a sight,' replied Dez with a frown at what he could see of himself — burned skin, bandages, scars forming where the gashes had been. The bruising had gone but he could see that his muscles were already starting to atrophy. His tan from always being outside was long gone and he now seemed to be a shade close to that of the sheet that covered the lower half of him. He turned his frown upon Abe.

'But at least you're not dead,' said Abe before realizing it was probably the wrong thing to say since most of the other guards had been killed.

'Hmmm,' was Dez's only response, indicating death might have been his preferred option compared with lying in a hospital bed, incapacitated, with a myriad of tubes sticking out of him.

Abe's eyebrows drew down as he absorbed Dez's attitude. 'Do you want me to come back some other time?'

'Depends. What do you want?' asked Dez, his voice surly.

'We really could use to have our leader back soon. I realize you're not quite well enough yet. But things are getting messy…I don't like it. Emi and I are trying to fill your shoes but…there are undercurrents…'

'I'm sure you'll get along just fine without me,' Dez growled at Abe.

Abe stared at Dez. 'No. We won't!' he bristled, his tone indicating his frustration with Dez's attitude.

Dez turned his startled gaze upon Abe. It dawned on him that Abe was not the type of guy who was going to tip-toe around his feelings just because he was lying injured in a hospital bed.

'I don't like it. Things don't feel right. We've taken things into our own hands and started the process of re-building Cloud III…'

'You're re-building Cloud III? I wouldn't have thought that was possible,' said Dez in astonishment.

'We are. We couldn't sit by and do nothing and lose everything we've spent so long building. The structure is still intact and we have the spare panels you ordered and we've asked Peter to bring whatever else is on hand. The Fringe engineers have made a new control panel so we can operate each row independently of the others. As we get more panels we can bring on each row as it becomes functional. But to protect The Cloud from further attack Edward is planning on using…firepower…to obliterate The Blues…although the primary mandate of The Fringe is to live in peace. I don't like the control he seems to have,' explained Abe, noticing that he had at least captured Dez's attention.

'They have firepower? Enough to wipe out an entire city?' said Dez, his eyebrows momentarily arching to his hairline before the sudden pain the motion caused made him resume a more neutral expression.

'That's what Peter told me. I chatted to Chi before coming here and she thinks we should at least try to talk to them, explain what we're doing, that it's in their best interest to leave us be. It's what Elizabeth thinks as well but apparently Edward shut her down when she expressed her opionion to the council.'

'I thought weapons of mass destruction had been outlawed long ago.'

'It seems as though Edward has taken over…become more of a dictator…and nobody is willing to stand up to him, although Peter did say that Emi is still able to sway him. As his fiancee she still has…'

'Emi! Emi…is…is with Edward!' Dez sputtered, barely able to form the words.

Abe's forehead furrowed and his pupils dilated as he realized that nobody had yet informed Dez about Emi's surprising decision. 'You…you didn't know?'

Dez shook his head and squeezed his eyes shut.

'I thought that was why you wouldn't see her…why you were… refusing to be leader and…feeling sorry for yourself.'

'No, my own personal pity party is because I don't think I'm a good enough leader. The Cloud was destroyed under my watch and all the guards killed,' he said angrily. 'It had nothing to do with Emi…until now…although I did turn her away.'

'Why did you turn her away if you didn't know?'

'Because I'm like this.' He waved his arm to indicate his pathetic condition. 'So…useless.'

'Well, as your friend, and someone who has always had your back, I would suggest giving the…uhh…pity party a rest, become the man you once were, resume your role as leader…we wouldn't have even thought of trying to restore Cloud III if you hadn't had the forethought to order extra panels in case of an emergency…and win Emi back,' said Abe, his anger resurfacing as he became exasperated with Dez's defeatist attitude.

'You make it sound so easy. Just hop out of bed and carry on as before,' said Dez resentfully. 'What do you know?'

'I know lying here with a bad attitude is not going to do you, or anyone else, any favours. So, yes, when you are physically healed, you should hop out of bed and get on with it. You're needed,' said Abe, almost yelling, desperately wanting to snap Dez out of his mental lethargy.

Dez glared at Abe, and then fell back against the pillows. 'I can't believe she turned to Edward,' he whispered.

'She thought you were dead. We all thought you were dead. The likelihood of finding you alive after a week in those conditions was miniscule,' said Abe in defence of Emi. 'Knowing Emi she must have thought it the best decision she could make to ensure the survival of our people. She *must* have had a good reason.'

'I can't imagine what it might be.'

'The survival of our people and you being dead isn't good enough?' questioned Abe, his eyebrows raised.

'After only a week. She could have mourned me for a bit…' Dez trailed off, tired from being at war with Abe and at war with his own conflicting emotions.

'You could win her back. It's not too late. She isn't married yet.'

Dez didn't respond.

'Well, we still need you to be leader. Emi doesn't want the job and either do I,' stated Abe before he abruptly turned and left. He doubted his visit had done any good. If anything he might have just made things infinitely worse.

# CHAPTER EIGHT

aylight was just starting to seep into the room between the floor to ceiling curtains. Emi could hear a couple of early morning birds chattering away on the balcony rail. She wished she felt as happy as they sounded. Rolling over to her side of the king size bed, trying to put as much distance as she could between her and Edward, she sighed. Sleep eluded her. Edward's lovemaking had been passionate yet somehow he did not leave her feeling loved, merely possessed. It was as if he was trying to generate enough love for the two of them and in failing he became more desperate. She wished she could love Edward as he loved her, especially now that she had lost Dez. She cared for him, and he was unfailingly kind to her, but her heart was not ready to relenquish its love for Dez. And Edward's passion for her *had* changed — he was no longer as loving and gentle as he'd been; just to be with her was not enough. Now, it was if he was being denied some part of her that he needed to conquer. She'd noticed the subtle difference in his attitude after she had challenged him in front of everyone at the meeting about fixing Cloud III. But her reason for being with Edward was to use her influence to help her people, she couldn't have sat there and kept silent. She had not yet told him about the baby, although he was sure to notice soon. Maybe if she told him it would restore the balance to their relationship. It would give him what he so obviously craved and, hopefully, the gentle, kind man she knew would be restored to her. But she couldn't yet bring herself to share Dez's baby with Edward and let Edward think it was his. A few tears seeped out of her eyes and soaked into the pillow as she took a shuddering breath. She must play her part unerringly to find a way through the tangled web of lies and misunderstandings.

Tomorrow she would go and visit Dez again and see if he was in any better shape, either mentally or physically. She couldn't give up on him just because he said he didn't want to see her. He had to come around eventually. Didn't he?

———

The hospital building stood before them like a sentinel. A rectangular, concrete block painted white to reflect the sun. Every window was covered with a black solar-film to block the harsh light from entering into the rooms and to give power to the building. No imagination had gone into the construction. It was a place you came to either be healed or die. It was a place for medical procedures, not for emotion or compassion, and it showed in the bleakness of the solid structure.

Emi's heart missed a beat and she swallowed her nervousness as she and Charlotte headed into the hosiptal. The wide hallway was busy with doctors and nurses efficiently going about their business, dressed in their sterile hospital uniforms. There was no acceptance of error. The Fringe did not like any form of sickness — they were genetically pure. If you were a patient here it had better be because you'd had an accident and not because you had a disease. The atmosphere made the fine hairs at the base of her neck prickle. She swallowed the lump in her throat as Charlotte pushed open the door to Dez's room and she followed her in.

'I told you not to bring her. I don't want her to see me like this.' Dez waved an arm at his body, his voice gravelly with instant anger, an anger that was always hovering just below the surface, ready to erupt at a moments notice.

'If I didn't bring her then she would have come on her own and it's better if she comes in under my security clearance,' replied Charlotte, in no mood for an argument but more than willing to stand her ground.

Dez shrugged, grimaced at the pain, and turned away. 'What difference does it make?'

'Dez? I don't care how you look,' said Emi, desperately hoping he would relent and look at her. 'When I thought you were dead it was the worst moment of my life…and there have been some pretty horrible moments. I want…need to see you.'

He didn't turn his head in her direction but resolutely stared at the featureless wall opposite as if mesmerized by the colour white.

'Why's that Emi? To reassure yourself that you picked the right man?' Dez turned his hostile stare upon her. 'Now that you're engaged to the all powerful Edward Black you can have the world — what is left of the world — at your feet. No more scavenging for food. No more grubby clothes or rotten little shelters. Even if we don't save the world you'll still live out your days in luxury. I'm sure seeing me will be a happy reminder of your lucky escape.'

'Dez, please…' gasped Emi.

'What…surprised I happen to know about your little secret? Abe informed me of your decision.'

'You don't understand…'

'You got that right. I don't.'

'I…I had to. I had no choice…' Emi whispered, her voice breaking in misery.

'Yes, I'm sure. You never have a choice do you? I think I've heard you say that before. It's always your excuse, isn't it?'

'I…I…' Emi turned to Charlotte, her eyes pleading for help. She didn't know what to say or how to turn the diatribe around.

'Dez, regardless of how things turn out between you and Emi, and regardless of her decision to…be a support to Edward…we still need you to recover and step back into your role as leader,' interjected Charlotte.

'Dez, please. You'll get better. You have to get better. The Network needs you. The world beyond these walls is a mess.' As is my world she added in her head. But she couldn't lay her own burdens on Dez right now; he was barely coping as it was.

Dez turned an icy stare on her. 'Yes, a mess, a mess of my making. I was the leader and I didn't manage to protect The Cloud or my people,' he replied bitterly. 'I told you…you will be just fine without me,' he said before turning his gaze back to the blank wall.

'It's not your fault. It was a well executed, surprise attack. You didn't stand a chance,' said Emi, hoping to snap him out of his self-pity.

'It wasn't a surprise.'

'What? What are you talking about?'

'It wasn't a surprise. At least it wasn't a surprise to someone.'

Emi glanced at Charlotte, her forehead furrowed. Doubt and confusion whirled in her mind.

'What do you mean, Dez?' asked Charlotte, treading carefully into the maze of Dez's thoughts.

'It was a set-up, just like the raid on Sectors C and D. I knew we had been set-up but I couldn't figure it out in time and more people died. And now The Cloud is destroyed as well,' bitterness dripped from every syllable he uttered.

Charlotte and Emi exchanged glances.

'What on earth makes you think the attack at The Cloud was a set-up? Why would *anyone* want to destroy The Cloud?' asked Emi, her eyebrows drawing down in disbelief.

'I heard him — The Blue leader. He flipped me over thinking I was dead. He thought I was the one who tipped him off. That was right before I passed out and didn't hear anything else.'

'I don't understand. What did he say?' asked Emi. She shook her head in confusion. 'What would you have tipped him off about?'

Dez shrugged. 'He *said* I was the person who tipped him off. I can only assume he meant about how to destroy The Cloud.'

Emi exhaled between pursed lips. How to respond? What to say? She was walking on eggshells, navigating a minefield. What Dez was saying didn't make *any* sense. It didn't add up. But she couldn't say *that* out loud or he would only end up even more angry at her denial. 'Well, it obviously wasn't you. Nobody would *ever* believe that! And with the mess we're in you're the best leader we have. You know The Cloud; everyone in The Network loves you and The Fringe respect you. We need you,' said Emi, trying her best to stir Dez's sense of duty.

Dez turned his angry gaze upon her once more, sending a shiver coursing through her body. 'People will need some one to blame. If it gets out that I set up the attack the love and respect of the people will quickly vanish,' Dez stated coldly.

'Why would anyone think it was you?'

'I *don't know* but the Blue leader thought so. So why not other people? They'll want someone to blame…and as I told you…I'm the best candidate…I failed at everything.'

'We'll just have to prove it wasn't you,' said Charlotte, matter-of-factly. 'Logically it doesn't make any sense. I mean, why would you set up an attack on The Cloud on a day when you are going to be one of the guards, knowing you're likely to be killed? And why would you have The Cloud destroyed when you've put the last couple years of your life into building it? Nobody will think it was you,' added Charlotte, trying to justify her line of thought and convince Dez that he wasn't thinking clearly.

'But who was it?' asked Emi, looking from one to the other. 'I don't even know where to start.'

'Would you both please leave now? I'm tired,' said Dez. He turned his gaze back toward the stark white, featureless wall and shut his eyes.

———————

Dez's eyebrows drew down in a frown as his next guest entered his sterile hospital room.

'I was infromed that you'd survived. Sorry that I haven't been able to escape my duties before now to pay a visit. How are you? You look better than I would have expected, all things considered.'

'I'm better than I was but have a ways to go yet. But, as you say, at least I'm not dead. Although, I've often wished myself otherwise over the last couple of months.'

'I would've thought you were more resilient than that given the life you've led.'

'What do you know about the life I've led?'

'More than you might think.'

'Spying on me?'

'Let's just say I've been kept informed.'

Dez glared at Edward.

'Surely you're not surprised. Be reasonable. I needed to make sure that you were the leader we needed.'

'Sorry to be such a disappointment.'

'Not at all. Everything was going to plan until the Blues took things into thier own hands and destroyed the Cloud. Though you were a guard, I do not hold you accountable.'

'Gee, thanks.'

'Well, I was informed that you were blaming yourself. There's no need. The Blues are stupid and brutal and will be dealt with as they deserve.'

'Meaning what exactly?'

'That is yet to be decided.'

'For all their stupidity it was a well planned and executed attack. You can't help but wonder if maybe they had some help.'

'I can't imagine anyone willingly helping the Blues, especially to destroy the Cloud. It's destruction could hasten the end of all man-kind…to help the Blues would make one unpopular, at best, with all that is left of the human race…if such an action were to be dis-covered.'

'I think 'unpopular' is wishful thinking…ostracized or dead is more likely, don't you think?'

'Well, let us hope that the destruction of the Cloud was just the Blues acting in their usual manner and nothing more sinister. I would not want to have to deal with having an informer in our midst. It ccould undermine all that we are trying to achieve.'

'Agreed.'

'So, are you going to return as the leader of the Network once your wounds have healed? I believe neither Abe nor Emi relish taking up your position.'

'I'm surprised you should ask. I would have thought you would prefer Emi as leader now that you are engaged to her. You would be a very powerful couple.'

'Ah. So you had heard. I did wonder if you'd been informed.'

'My congratulations.'

'Thank you. I hope you're not too upset. I realize you two were… fond…of each other but she did think that you were dead. We all did. And you can not offer her what I can.'

'No, nor would I want to. I could only ever offer her myself…but apparently that didn't hold much weight. She certainly turned to you quickly enough after my supposed demise.'

'Yes, she was easily persuaded. Mind you, I'm sure nobody would willingly choose to return to living in a hut with barely enough to eat when safety, luxury and an abudance of food is offered to them for the taking. You would have to…well, as I said, she was easily persuaded.'

Dez turned his head to stare out of the window. He reutned his gaze to Edward's self-satisfied countenance once he'd managed to mask his pain.

'I'm sure you'll be very happy together. You'll have the world at your feet…providing you can still manage to save it that is.'

'Not to worry. The Blues will be dealt with and we will overcome this setback. Again, I say, I do hope you'll return to being leader of the Network. You're still needed.'

Dez looked at Edward perplexed. 'What about Emi?'

'I have other plans for her.'

Dez raised his eyebrows questioningly.

'Can't you guess?' Edward paused. 'The begetting of an heir. And not just one, but multiple, for safety sake.' Edward's smile was gloating and non-apologetic. 'Who knows, she may already be carrying my child.'

Edward's smirk made Dez feel like he was going to vomit. Why did the guy hate him so much? Was it just a battle over Emi? He returned his gaze to stare out of the window. 'I'm tired. Would you mind showing yourself out?'

Dez heard the door quietly glide shut.

———+———

A few weeks later it was Matthew's turn to confront Dez.

Dez was now healed and it was time for Matthew to sign his release papers and send him home. Dez's burns had been entirely eliminated — his new skin a one hundred per cent match to the surrounding skin thanks to the advanced technology of the burn unit and their skin regeneration machines. His bruising and swelling was gone and his cuts and abrasions were nothing but an unpleasant memory. Matthew's biggest concern was still for Dez's mental attitude.

'Ready to head home?' Matthew asked as he entered the bleak room that had been Dez's hide-away for the last few months. Matthew hated the hospital. He hated the smell, the clinical neatness, the hum of machines hooked to the prisoners within the four walls of their cells, and the sterile environment designed to heal people. It was what he found hardest about being a doctor — watching people in hospital heal physically and turn to mush mentally by the complete lack of stimulation in the surroundings that were inflicted upon them.

Dez shrugged.

'You look like your old self, minus the tan.' Matthew grinned, trying for cheer.

Dez looked down at himself. 'Yeah, thanks Doc,' he said, but without an accompanying smile.

'Ready to resume your leadership role?'

Dez gave him a flat stare but did not respond.

'You're needed Dez. Emi and Abe have tried to fill your role but they don't know what you know. They haven't spent the last few years travelling to the different Cloud sites and meeting with people here and in England. People know you; respect you! It would take them years to build the trust that you already have. You have to snap out of this self-righteous blame you're putting on yourself. Nobody else blames you for the destruction of the Cloud or the death of the guards. We need to look forward. If we don't we will all die as we are quickly running out of time. We have to try to get things back on track and you need to be part of that plan. I'm a doctor. I deal with physical healing, not mental, although I believe the two are linked. I've done all I can for you physically. It's up to you to heal yourself mentally. But you must do it.'

Dez continued to glare at Matthew until his speech came to an abrupt halt. 'Are you done lecturing me now? Can I go?'

Matthew shrugged, resigned, he let out a pent up sigh. There was nothing more he could do; it was up to Dez now. 'Yes, you're free to go. I hope you choose the right path.'

'The path I'm going to choose is to go and say goodbye to Jax before I go. Another person whose life I have managed to ruin. I at least owe him an apology,' he countered as he closed the door behind him.

Dez glanced around him. The way the Fringe lived had always made him uncomfortable. Everything was too meticulous, too planned. The hospital was the extreme of all that he disliked. The stark white walls, plain slab doors, the overly shiny light beige floor reflecting back the harsh light from the light-tubes overhead. Nobody smiled as they rushed by him. There seemed to be no visitors, only doctors and nurses. And there was little human conversation. The faint hum of machines behind closed doors the only noise Dez could detect in the featureless environment. It was almost as if the place was built to ensure your death rather than your cure.

Dez made his way down the hall to Jax's room and quietly opened the door, not wanting to disturb Jax if he was resting. He had not been able to see Jax until now and the person lying in the hospital bed before him brought an involuntary groan of despair from deep in his throat. He had been told that Jax had regained consciousness a few weeks ago but was still in rough shape. Dez could hardly believe he was still alive given how he looked. Jax was thin and pale, his eyes sunken in his head, his hair hung lank and lifeless although it was obvious he had been washed and cared for. He didn't look like he could survive.

As the door opened Jax opened his eyes and gave Dez a weak smile. 'Dez,' he whispered.

'Hey, Jax.'

'You're okay. That's good. You'll be needed…now more than ever.'

'So I keep being told. But look where my leadership got us,' said Dez, the bitterness coming through in his voice though he tried to suppress it. 'I'm sorry, Jax. I never wanted to see you like this.'

'You're not to blame. It's hardly your fault,' he rasped. 'You're a great leader…and like a big brother to me. Please, you have to fix things. Don't make my life be for nothing.'

'You're going to be okay, Jax. They healed me, they'll fix you too.'

Jax shook his head. 'Promise me…you have to save the planet. It could be a beautiful place.'

'How? The Cloud is destroyed. They're trying to re-build part of it but I don't think it will be enough. What else can we do?'

'I hid panels,' Jax whispered.

'You what?'

'Hid…extra panels. I…lied. On the days I helped with the panels I would say one had malfuncitioned and needed replacing…but I just hid the replacement. It wasn't often enough for anyone to notice. But over time, well, there are a few. And then when you had us order extra in case of emergency…I said they were miscounted…I don't know why…gut instinct I guess…but I put some where they couldn't be found…hidden in the storehouses.' Jax stopped talking to take a gasping breath.

'But we know about the ones in the storehouses.'

Jax shook his head again. 'No, there's a room, camouflaged at the back, in the rock…there are more in there. You need to get them and fix it. The Blues…they can't ruin all our hard work. Don't let them win, Dez.'

Dez felt the first stirrings of duty. His stomach contracted with what Jax was telling him. Jax had not trusted anyone else with the information; he had clung to life until he could relay the secret to him alone.

'I'll do my best Jax,' said Dez, swallowing the lump in his throat. Jax had been the little brother he'd never had. Letting him down wasn't an option. He reached for Jax's hand and gave his fingers a gentle squeeze. 'Your life won't be in vain. I promise.'

Jax nodded, a faint smile hovered at the corners of his mouth and then was gone.

'Sleep well little brother…I'll miss you,' said Dez, his breath catching in his throat. He hadn't expected his visit to Jax to be a final farewell.

Dez pushed open the door and headed for the hosipital roof and the waiting Hovercraft that would take him home. He didn't look back. He couldn't…he was blinded by tears.

# CHAPTER NINE

After having looked at nothing but a blank wall for the last few months Dez found the Hovercraft ride home overwhelming. He focused on the world outside the window. The concrete jungle that was New York City took him by surprise all over again. The height of the buildings, the vast array of food grown in Central Park, the sea wall that kept out the ocean that went to the distant horizon. He shook his head. People were so ingenious, so intelligent to be able to design and construct such a place and yet they were also stupid enough to destroy the world in the process.

As they left the city behind they flew over the New York Cloud which was efficiently emitting its puffy clouds into the clear blue sky. At least it was operating at 100% capacity. Then they were onto the grasslands. The endless swaying yellow that dominated most of the landscape — the only crop able to grow and thrive in the toxic soil. It had no nutritional value. How were they ever going to re-gain all that had been lost? Dez pressed his head to the window, trying to not give way to despair. He'd promised Jax.

Finally, the green swath that was his valley, his home, came into view. It felt like a lifetime since he'd last been there. Yet it had only been a matter of a few months. What would his welcome be like? Would people be happy to see him back or would he be blamed for all that had gone wrong? He didn't know but he was about to find out. He took a big breath and sat back from the window as the Hovercraft landed on the village green.

Abe, with Lea and Fie in tow, were there to greet him as he emerged from the belly of the Hovercraft.

As Dez walked down the ramp Abe could hardly believe his eyes. 'You look as good as new,' he exclaimed as he threw an arm over Dez's shoulders. 'Welcome home.'

'Thanks.'

'We cleaned your place and brought over some food and picked some flowers for you and put the bouquet on your table,' babbled Lea and Fie, tripping over each other's words, each taking a part of a sentence to unfold the story. 'The flowers are from the new seeds The Fringe gave us to plant because they said they attract bees. The flowers are called Sunflowers, and Coneflowers and Hyssop.'

'Thank you both of you. Don't know what I would do without you,' said Dez as he reached out to ruffle their wavy red hair.

Fie pulled at Dez's shirt, wanting his undivided attention. 'Have you seen bees? Matthew brought us some. He said that now that we have better soil and better crops in the valley that they might survive if we don't run out of water. They're really cute. They have black and yellow stripes and they are small and kind of fuzzy,' said Fie excitedly, wanting to tell him all her news since he'd been gone. 'But...you don't want to touch their bums because then you get a sting in your finger...and it really hurts,' she added, her voice reduced to a whisper, sure that her news was very important and probably a big secret.

'I've occasionally seen bees. They have them in New York.' Dez smiled. 'They are pretty cute but I've never tried to pat one. I'll make sure I don't.'

'And the honey they make is delicious,' added Lea, not to be outdone by her sister in the story telling.

'Did you bring me some honey?' he asked seriously.

Fie nodded, her eyes as big as saucers, her grin lighting up her face.

'This is quite a welcome,' said Dez. He smiled over their heads and gave Abe a wink.

Abe smiled back, hoping that the girl's charm and enthusiastic welcome might help restore some of Dez's old self.

'How are things?' asked Dez as he looked around.

'Alright, given the circumstances,' shrugged Abe.

Dez noted the subdued response and observed his surroundings a little more carefully as they walked back to his place. In the weeks he'd been in hospital it appeared that things had gotten worse. Whether they actually had or he was unaccustomed to the environment after being inside for so long was hard to say. Certainly he felt acutely aware of his surroundings.

The valley was unusually quiet. The chirping of birds and the scurrying of rabbits and squirrels were not as he remembered. The fields and trees, though still green, had a whithered look, as if they were patiently waiting for someone to notice they were in desperate need of a drink. His footsteps stirred up swirls of dust that reached for his knees, covering his lower limbs in a fine film of grit. He supposed this was how it had been before Cloud III had started to offer them some relief from the heat, but in his memory it had never seemed this oppressive.

'Have we had any natural rainfall since the destruction of Cloud III put an end to the artificial rain?' asked Dez, his mouth turned down in a frown.

'Very little,' replied Abe. 'Less than normal for this time of year.' The girls had run ahead, so he added, 'and the river is down quite a bit.'

Dez glanced sharply at Abe. The river had never been down in all the years they had lived there. It was not good news.

'I've started to notice small changes here and there…less rain, fewer animals around, it feels hot — not just warm — at night now, and some of the crops are not doing as well as I would like given that the soil is now completely toxin free, and then there's the river…if the river is down it means things have changed at its source.'

They'd reached his cabin, the girls opened the door, ushering him in, excited to show off all their hard work. The place was spotless, the dust outside had not been allowed indoors, or if it had, it had been very thoroughly removed. Packages of food were neatly arranged on his shelf in the kitchen along with containers lined up like soldiers with labels that read, 'oats', 'lentils', 'beans', 'flour', 'sugar.' The far reaching tentacles of the Fringe even reached here into his home with the goodly supply of food all nicely presented and labeled. A bouquet of flowers, placed in the center of his coffee table, cheerily had pride of place, defying the problems they were all facing.

'Thanks girls, the place looks great,' Dez looked down at them, trying to instill an enthusiasm into his response that he was far from feeling.

'Come on girls. Let's let Dez get settled,' said Abe. 'I'm glad you're back. We need you,' he added, knowing that now was not the time to lecture, but at the same time Dez could not be allowed to continue to wallow in the place he had been.

Time was precious and it was beginning to run out.

———

A few days later Dez made his way down to his old swimming hole, feeling the need to restore his soul at his favourite spot. As he made his way through the trees he noted that there were more leaves under foot and fewer on the overhanging canopy, making the filtered sunlight more intense than he liked. His footsteps crunched as he walked — the fallen leaves no longer a soft mulch. His mouth turned down at the edges. Could things change so quickly? He'd never known the surrounding landscape beyond the valley to be anything but dry and barren. The use of chemical sprays and genetically modified crops had long since wiped out the fertility of the soil. The barren crops and barren soil had in their turn decimated the wildlife. And without seasons — they now had the hot season and the even hotter season — the cycle of life was under constant threat. But the few valleys, pockets that had withstood the harsh new reality of a polluted world, had been a place of refuge. Could it too be taken from them?

He clambered over the rocks that hid the waterhole from view. 'You've got to be kidding me,' he uttered aloud, his face falling as he saw how much the water level had dropped. 'We can't survive without the river,' he muttered. Running a hand through his hair he slowly lowered himself onto the rocky shelf and stared. *What were they going to do? How could they change things? Could they still change things or was it too late?* He removed his sandals and, stripping off his shirt, dove in. But the shock of hitting the water was not because it was refreshing but because it was noticeably warmer than it had ever been. It was certainly not as cool and pleasant as he remembered.

'Crap!' he came up out of the water and rolled over on to his back to float. Staring up into the serene blue sky he recalled his times here with Emi. The beginning of their attraction to one another, teaching her to swim, the time just spent enjoying one another's company and finally their commitment to each other and their plans to marry. How could it all go so wrong? He knew Emi loved him, so why had she given up so easily and agreed to marry Edward? Abe was right — she must have had a good reason and not that she'd thought him dead. It had to be something else. Surely she would have wanted time to mourn him. If you loved someone you didn't agree to marry someone else immediately after learning your fiance had been killed.

He took a big breath and dove down into the cooler depths of the rock pool. Returning to the surface he brushed the water from his eyes and began to swim back and forth across the waterhole. Though the water was not as refreshing as it had once been he still felt his soul return to him and his mind clear. Abe, Emi, Charlotte, Matthew, Jax — they were right. He couldn't sacrifice all they had tried to achieve because he felt sorry for himself or that somehow he had failed. He would only fail if he refused to try.

He returned to floating on his back, a slight smile hovering at the edges of his mouth. 'I will not quit. We have to save what we have,' he vowed into the silence.

Only the trees witnessed his vow as they shed a few more leaves into the stillness.

———————

'Hey, Abe, how's it going?' Dez asked as he approached Abe who was working in his garden at the back of his shelter.

Abe had built a rock retaining wall around the perimeter of his vegetable plot to keep animals out. Within the walls were neat rows of a variety of vegetables — carrots, potatoes, beans, squash, tomatoes — as well as some fruit trees and edible flowers which attracted the bees that had been re-introduced to the valley. The soil within the enclosure was dark and rich — enhanced by earth brought in by the Fringe — in complete contrast to the dry, barren dirt that surrounded the valley, where the grasslands had taken over.

'Dez.' Abe turned in surprise at seeing Dez purposefully walking toward him. 'It's good to have you back.'

'Good to be back. I think that sterile hospital room almost did my head in,' Dez stated.

'So, you've decided to step up? Return to the land of the living?' asked Abe hesitantly.

'Yeah. Before it's too late.'

Abe let out a sigh as he stretched and cracked his back. He'd been working in his vegetable garden for a couple of hours and was happy to be interrupted. 'Thank goodness. Didn't know what I was going to do otherwise. There's no way I can take on what you do and I don't know how Emi would cope without your support.'

Dez nodded, acknowledging all that Abe was leaving unspoken, thankful for his friendship and his unfailing support. 'Care to fill me in on what's been going on while I've been out of commission?'

Abe relayed all that had been happening, catching Dez up on the details. As he came to the end of his monologue he ran his hand through the dirt just outside of the vegetable garden. 'Look at this,' he said, the dismay clearly evident in his voice as the dry soil slid through his fingers. 'The girls want to expand the garden and plant more vegetables but I don't know if we can. It's like the weather patterns have shifted again. The heat is more intense, the rain less. The seeds we have from The Fringe are pure and most of the soil in the valley is not toxic…but without rain…' Abe trailed off. 'I have enough well-water to keep what I have alive but I don't know if we have enough to plant anything else.'

Dez gazed at the parched soil as it slowly seeped through Abe's splayed fingers. 'I can't believe it has gotten so much worse in a few short months.'

'Yeah. Quite truthfully, even with using water from the well to irrigate this small plot of veggies, it's getting hard to keep up,' said Abe, despairingly. 'The Fringe did warn us we didn't have much time to turn things around. Guess they weren't exaggerating.'

'But the other Cloud structures are working. I can't believe just having one not operational can throw the entire plan off.'

'Maybe it hasn't but Cloud III was nearest to us. It was making a difference but now…' he shrugged his shoulders, running his hand back through the dirt, letting it blow away in the warm breeze. 'I hope nothing else goes wrong or we're likely to be the last generation left alive on the planet.'

'Not if I can help it,' said Dez, as he felt some of his old resilience and determination take hold.

CHAPTER NINE

# CHAPTER TEN

'**W**hat on earth are you doing here?' asked Dez, returning home to find Emi resolutely perched on his doorstep.

'I need to talk to you.'

'Well, what do you want?'

*You*, thought Emi, but she couldn't bring herself to say the one simple word out loud. She felt her resolve weaken and her soul cringe at Dez's hostility. She desperately wanted to throw herself into his arms and not let go. She never seemed to have a choice…what she could do and what she wanted to do always seemed to be at odds. She heaved a sigh and in as conciliatory a voice as possible said, 'Can we just talk, please?'

Dez stared at her long and hard then, shrugging his shoulders, he pushed open his front door and waved her in. 'After you.'

His shelter was as she remembered it. Sparse and masculine but clean and neat. The white timber walls combined with the natural timber finish of the floor and the grass mats and woven seating gave it a homey feel. She averted her eyes from the bed that could be seen through the open door to his room. Emi quickly blinked back tears. The last time she had been in Dez's cabin they had been making plans for their future, plans to get married and possibly move to England where Dez said the hills in the far north were still mostly green and the sun was not quite so scorching. Their plans lay in ruins, just like the world around them, she thought bitterly.

Heaving another great sigh, she plunged in. 'You need to take up your role as leader again,' she said bluntly.

'No.'

Emi blinked, not expecting such a straight rebuttal. He obviously didn't want to make it easy on her. She had abandoned him, left him for dead and turned to Edward within days of his 'death'. She was sure that had hurt him more than he wanted to express but was he now going to let her beg and force her to bear the burden of being leader? 'Why not? You're back in perfect health, back in your home, surrounded by our people who love and respect you…'

'I don't deserve their love or their respect.'

'Well, you have it none the less,' retaliated Emi, her frustration making her angry at his stubbornness.

'It'll pass in time,' he said calmly.

'It won't. Nobody blames you for what happened.'

'You just don't get it do you?' asked Dez scathingly. 'I was leader and my people were killed and The Cloud destroyed…our one chance at saving the planet and all of the human race. I failed. Don't ask me to be leader again.'

'But I can't do your job. I don't know what you know…The Cloud, the people, New York, England, here…' Emi trailed off, sensing that she had taken the wrong tack.

'I get it. This is really all about you.'

'What? No, I…'

'Trust me, you'll be just fine. You have the all powerful Edward Black to help you,' he spat out the words, his eyes glinted with barely suppressed fury.

Emi looked down and pulled at her loose shirt, trying to conceal her baby bump. 'I…' What did she say now? She had no idea how to defend herself. Her own actions were terrible in her eyes. She couldn't justify them. 'I…I thought you were dead,' she whispered.

'Well, guess what…I'm not,' Dez said vehemently as he gestured to his body with his hands to prove his point. 'And you sure didn't wait long to throw yourself into the arms of Edward Black, did you?'

'I had no choice,' Emi said quietly, attempting to choke back the tears that threatened to overwhelm her, as her emotions roller-coastered between despair and anger.

'Don't give me that 'I had no choice' crap. You didn't even wait to hear if I was alive or dead. You just assumed and then ran to Edward. All those times you told me there was nothing to be jealous of…and I believed you. I'm such an idiot,' he ground out. He slammed his hand into the wall as he moved away from her to pace the confined space between them, feeling the need for distance. Then he turned and came to an abrupt halt in front of her, his hostility palpable in the quiet room. 'You need to…'

Emi pulled at her shirt again, a solitary tear escaped from her eyes to splatter alone on the floor.

Dez's gaze rested angrily on her. Noting her gesture, his eyes shifted to her midriff, to her rounded belly hidden by the baggy shirt.

The loan tear darkening the floorboards, proclaiming emotions just barely held in check, began to evaporate.

Emi looked up in time to notice as shock registered in Dez's eyes.

'What the hell! You're pregnant? You're carrying his baby. No wonder you don't want to be leader. How inconvenient for you and your happy little family,' he yelled. Pain eminated from Dez, the hurt evident in every word uttered.

Emi stood still, not knowing what to say or do. She shook her head, the tears finally having their way and escaping unchecked from her eyes. She stared at Dez, unable to look away, unable to put together a coherent thought.

Dez glared back at her.

'It's…it's not his…' she whispered quietly, her words barely audible.

Dez choked, his eyes wide with surprise. 'What?'

'Edward…Edward is not the father.'

Dez's gaze travelled to her well concealed bump and back up to Emi's forlorn face as realization hit him, stealing his breath away.

'It's…it's mine?'

Emi nodded as the tears continued to slide quietly down her cheeks.

'But…but…' Dez slumped to the couch, his gaze riveted to the floorboards — if they had come to life and danced before his eyes he would have been less shocked. He ran his hands through his hair and continued to stare at the floor. The silence lengthened.

By the set of his shoulders Emi could only guess that he was too stunned for thought. 'Dez…Please.'

He shook his head and rested his elbows on his knees. His hands remained grasping his hair as his eyes stayed firmly fixed on the floor.

'Dez. I thought you were dead, that there was no hope. The Cloud was destroyed and The Blues…killing…life was going to become so much harder. I needed protection for our baby…and I thought… if…if I was with Edward I would be able to help our people. I had no time…to think.'

'Does Edward know about the baby?' asked Dez, finally looking up and meeting Emi's eyes.

Emi nodded.

'And he's okay about it?'

'I let him think it's his. I had to.'

'Oh God,' exclaimed Dez as he ran his fingers through his already ruffled hair.

'You don't know what he's like.'

'What do you mean?'

'He's…he's so possessive. If he thought it was yours. I dread to think.'

'You're serious?'

Emi nodded.

'And how do you plan to pass off the baby as his once it's born?'

'It'll only be a month early as far as he's concerned. It's not that uncommon.'

'And what if it grows to look like me?' Dez asked, arching his eyebrows questioningly.

'You…you look similar.'

'What did you just say?' asked Dez, his head snapped up from rubbing his hand across his forehead.

'You look…you look similar enough.'

# CHAPTER ELEVEN

'Right, any last questions?' asked Peter, his expression grim as he looked at the nine other pilots standing before him.

They shook their heads in response, looking equally grim, but asking no questions.

'You're all up to date with the plan and the part each of you plays in it?' Peter asked for confirmation.

This time they all nodded their agreement, uttering 'yes, sir' in unison.

'Right. Let's go.' Peter forced himself to stride purposefully toward his waiting Hovercraft before changing his mind and disobeying orders became more than just a passing thought.

The ten Hovercrafts rose into the air with their fatal cargo and headed south toward the coordinates that Edward had ordered them to obliterate. As they left the New York skyline behind they flew out across where the New York Cloud was fully operational, emitting its white puffy clouds into the otherwise clear blue sky. They could see the shadows cast by the clouds floating across the parched land, offering the shade and slightly cooler temperatures they all longed for.

Edward is right, thought Peter as he looked down at the cloud formations below, we can't have The Blues destroy everything — all our plans over the last hundred years and all our hope for the future.

He breathed deeply, steadying his nerves, resolved now to do his duty and ensure the survival of the planet and the rest of humanity.

As they flew further south, beyond the distant perimeter of the New York Cloud, the comforting sight of clouds being emitted into the atmosphere disappeared. The landscape below became an ocean of dry, yellow grasslands and grey forests filled with brittle, dead trees. Nothing moved on the surface of the earth. Animals could not survive out this far, away from the few remaining green valleys that The Network had claimed as their own.

Their flight path took them over the destruction of Cloud III. Peter could see people moving around below like tiny ants, trying to restore the structure and do their bit to help save what was left of the planet and its few surviving species. He wondered if all their efforts would be in vain. So much of the world was uninhabitable — whether due to heat, Hyperstorms, toxic soil or higher ocean levels — that he questioned if all that they were trying to do was a few decades too late, maybe even a couple of centuries too late. He knew the timing and the efficiency of The Cloud structures dotted around the planet were vital to their existence. If they could wipe The Blues from the planet and fix at least a portion of Cloud III, would it be enough? Only if nothing else goes wrong was the thought that came unbidden to his mind. He grimaced as he left Cloud III behind and carried on past The Network valleys out into the wilderness beyond.

It didn't take long in the Hovercrafts to cover the distance between Cloud III and the outskirts of the ruined city The Blues were known to inhabit. As they neared the city they descended to a lower altitude, switched on their heat-activated motion sensors, and broke into formation to scan the suburbs as they flew over. The city below was nothing like New York. The grid like formation of the streets was still discernable from above, but where there had once been neat, orderly tree lined avenues there was now crumbling tarmac consumed by weeds and lined with broken, dead trees. A few houses remained standing, but most had long since fallen to pieces, their rooves caved in, gaping holes exposing the floors below. As they flew past the surrounding suburbs to the city center the buildings changed and became jarring segments of concrete with rebar reaching for the sky. One could see the shimmering waves of heat rising from the surface where portions of black bitumen still existed. There was little movement between the buildings. The Blues were known to inhabit the tunnels of ancient subway systems and underground parking garages.

As Peter flew low over the city he kept an eye on his motion censor, noting the locations where he detected movement. 'We only have one shot at this. If we don't succeed The Blues will surely move and then plan to retaliate,' he said through his radio to the other pilots as they spread out across the city.

He looked up to watch the flight paths of the other Hovercrafts. Each pilot had been given a different segment of the city to destroy.

'All right everyone, do your two fly-bys, trying to find as many Blues as you can and then on our third time around we unleash our cargo. We don't expect to get everyone, but the hope is there will be too few of them left to retaliate and they will be too terrified to do so.'

Glancing at his monitor he saw that his cameras had picked up the image of some immense, blue people emerging from one of the less destroyed shelters. Though his cameras were set to zoom, the image was still not clear and was quickly past — yet they were quite a site. To think that obesity and tattoo imprints had become hereditary traits even if one didn't get enough to eat and didn't ever have a needle full of dye injected into your skin.

'I guess you've never seen a Hovercraft before, have you?' he said aloud to those gathered on the ground.

———

Shade rubbed her belly. She was nearing her time and felt immense as her skin, stretched to a lighter shade of blue, held the life growing inside her. The baby kicked at her hand and she took her finger and poked it back. At first she had been angry at the thought of having a child to care for; life was so harsh and she dreaded having another mouth to feed. But once she'd felt the baby move, her feelings had changed. She enjoyed their daily game of poking at one another — the little feet pressing on her stomach, her fingers prodding at its heels. And given how swollen her breasts were she didn't think feeding the baby would be too difficult, she looked forward to it, hoping that once the baby suckled her the discomfort of her engorged breasts would lessen.

She turned her head to look at Spike, snoring loudly beside her, and gave him a shove. He rolled over and the snoring stopped. As her gaze wandered back to the grimy, broken window her forehead puckered in a frown. Now that the snoring had ceased she could hear a strange sound coming from outside. Shade rolled over on to her hands and knees to push herself upright and stretch her back before lumbering over to the filthy glass. She tried to peer out through the broken pane, the glass being too dirty to actually see out of, but could only see a sliver of the endless blue sky. Pausing, she tilted her head. Whatever it was, the sound was getting louder.

'Hey, Spike,' she said, giving him a kick with her foot to wake him up. 'There's something outside. Spike, wake-up you idiot. There's something coming.'

'What the hell? Don't kick me you stupid cow,' moaned Spike, snorting his way back to consciousness. 'What the hell are you on about now?'

'Listen. It's coming from outside…from the sky.'

'What are you talking about? Nothing comes from the sky except for bird shit and…' Spike stopped to listen as a whirring, thudding sound filled the air overhead. 'What the hell is that?' he asked, pushing himself to his feet to stand beside Shade and gaze out through the shattered glass. The hole was too small to see out of so he tried wiping one of the panes with the bottom of his shirt. 'Can't see nothin' out of this. I'm goin' outside, see what the hell's goin' on,' he said angrily before heading to the stairs and out into the blinding daylight.

'Fuck it's hot. What d'you go and have to wake me up for? It's too damn hot to be outside in the day,' he complained loudly so he could be heard over the strange noise that was progressively gaining in volume.

Shade turned to look behind her as the enormous machine responsible for the deafening noise appeared beyond the shell of their building. Her mouth gaped open and her eyes boggled as she stared upward at the terrifying sight. 'What…is it?' she asked.

Spike shook his head, never having seen anything like it. As they stood staring upward, the machine flew over and carried on past them. The others began to emerge from the building. They stood in a group watching as the enormous black monster turned to circle over them again.

As it flew past, Shade noticed a few more black demons flying over different areas of the city. 'Maybe they're from The Fringe… or from the guy who had you do the raid…they're looking for us… maybe they are bringing the food they promised us,' she said hopefully, smiling at Spike.

'I don't know,' said Spike, his guts twisting at the thought of being found by the guy who had ordered him to do the raid. 'We were only supposed to kill the guards. He might be pissed that we smashed things….' he trailed off as the black machine came back around for a third time. 'I don't know. I don't like this. Come on. Hide. We gotta go,' he pulled at Shade as he turned to flee from the approaching demon.

This time around the menacing looking metal bird was higher off the ground and travelling more quickly. As it neared the spot where they were grouped together — faces turned to the sky, mouths hanging open — the hatch doors in the bottom of the craft opened up and packages rained down on them from the belly of the monster.

Spike glanced over his shoulder, but nobody else had moved. They were rooted to the spot in awe. They had not followed him, not even Shade. Maybe it is food, thought Spike, with relief as the packages fell within their midst.

'Food,' said Shade, as the package detonated in front of them and wiped them forever from the face of the earth.

The metallic bird turned to regroup with the others of its kind and make its way back home to safety.

———————

Peter watched the section below him as the moving red dots on his heat detection screen emerged out into the street. First one, then two. Glancing back at his camera it looked like a guy and a girl...but it was difficult to be sure. Their blue, tattooed faces were turned toward him, their mouths gaping open. The girl had her hand covering her stomach. He'd recognize that particular motion anywhere — the gesture of a mother protecting her offspring. The girl wasn't just obese, she was pregnant! God, he'd never thought of one of them being pregnant, of bringing a child into the world. His stomach lurched at the thought of what he was about to do. He wished he hadn't flown so low — low enough that his camera on maximum zoom could bring them into focus — low enough that they became people with lives...lives he was about to extinguish.

'Damn, why did I have to be given this assignment?' he said to himself in the empty aircraft. 'Damn it.'

On his second pass there were others coming in a steady stream from the derelict building they obviously called home. 'Well, Edward's coordinates weren't wrong,' he muttered aloud. 'Very, very accurate actually,' he added, his eyebrows drawing down as the thought churned in his mind.

He finished his second pass before taking the Hovercraft to a higher altitude. Scanning the sky he noted that everyone was turning for the third and final pass. 'Ready?' he asked into the headset.

'Affirmative,' was repeated back to him nine times.

'Open and fire when ready,' he instructed as he hit the button to open the doors in the bottom of the Hovercraft.

He flew for the third and last time over his target, unleashing his deadly cargo. As he flew overhead he caught a glimpse of all the up-turned faces. The camera mounted on the bottom of his craft brought their faces into clear resolution on the console screen. He could swear that the girl looked like she was smiling and had mouthed the word 'food' before the explosion obliterated her and her baby from the face of the earth forever as he flew past to safety.

———

Chi, Tom and Liz looked up as they were surrounded by the whirring sound of Hovercrafts. They counted as ten of the black jets flew past overhead.

'What are The Fringe doing here?' asked Liz, clambering over a pile of rubble that had once been a house.

'Looks like they're heading for the city,' observed Tom as he stopped in his tracks. Covering his eyes from the glare of the sun, he watched the aircraft continue on their way south, toward the city that they were on the outskirts of.

Chi looked at the other two. 'I don't like the looks of this!' she stated, worry furrowing her brow. 'Why would The Fringe send Hovercrafts to the place known to be inhabited by The Blues?'

Liz glanced at her with eyes that mirrored the concern etched on Chi's face. 'I don't know. Do you think they've come to round up those that destroyed The Cloud?' she suggested.

Chi shook her head. 'I don't see how they would know who had done it. It's not like anyone saw them, except for Dez and Jax maybe, and they don't seem to remember much.'

As they continued their treck further into the derelict outer suburb, the Hovercrafts circled back around, flying low over different parts of the city.

'It's like they're looking for something,' said Tom.

'Can we pick up the pace a bit. I would like to have our little chat with The Blues, if we can find them, and get out of here,' said Liz as the hairs rose on her arms and a shudder coursed through her body.

'Yeah, I agree,' said Chi. 'I have a funny feeling…' she added, scanning the sky.

'Or we could leave it. Trying to convince The Blues that not attacking us is in their best interest is *not* going to be easy. I barely understand the plans The Fringe have, never mind trying to explain it to the likes of The Blues,' suggested Tom.

'We can't go back now. We've come so far and we're almost there,' said Chi.

Tom and Liz exchanged glances. It had been Chi's idea to come, to try and talk The Blues into leaving them alone so they could all live in peace. Neither of them felt like they had the right to veto what she wanted to do when they were this close to their goal.

'All right. We'll see if we can find anyone in these buildings coming up…but I don't think we should go into the main city…we just don't know how many there are or what to expect,' said Tom.

'Come on then,' said Liz, 'let's get this over with.'

As they walked down the street, picking their way over slabs of concrete, pushed up at odd angels by the weeds growing below, they stayed close to what remained of the walls of buildings, not wanting to be seen before they were ready in case The Blues were just as hostile when in their own territory. A few blocks ahead they could see some buildings that were in better shape. They watched as two Blues emerged from a building that still had a couple of intact stories…a guy and an enormous girl. They flattened themselves against the wall unnoticed by The Blues whose faces were turned skyward.

They watched as the Hovercraft flew low overhead and then turned to circle back again. More people emerged from the concrete structure and poured out onto the street, all of them looking upwards, mouths agape.

'They must not have ever seen a Hovercraft before,' Liz said to Tom as Chi continued slowly edging her way along the shattered wall toward where the group of Blues were gathered.

Tom shook his head and glanced at Liz. 'No, I would imagine not. But we found them…as soon as the Hovercrafts are gone we'll try to talk to this lot and then get out of here.'

Chi, who was a bit further along the street, stopped to wave them forward just as Tom and Liz turned to watch the Hovercraft circle back around for a third time.

'Here they come again,' said Tom. 'They must be on an exploration mission or something.'

'They're higher this time,' observed Liz. 'Look, the hatch doors are opening. What could they be delivering at that speed?' Liz's eyes boggled as realization dawned. 'Chi, run!' she yelled as loudly as she could before the deadly load was unleashed from the sky.

Life suddenly went into slow motion as chaos reigned. It was as if she had instantly lost her sight and her hearing except that the noise was deafening. An invisible force shoved her hard in the chest as her feet went out from under her and she was thrown backwards. Liz's mind was a jumble as she tried to comprehend what was happening. Her body flew through the air before coming to a sudden halt. Darkness enveloped her.

As Liz slowly came to, she could hear nothing beyond the ringing in her ears. She brought her hand to her face, wiping the dust from her eyes before blinking open her eyelids to observe the devastation surrounding her. Tentatively feeling for injuries she found nothing to alarm her other than being covered in a fine layer of dust and debris. As her mind recovered from the shock and began to function she became aware that she was lying on something soft and warm. Rolling over she found Tom beneath her. He blinked his eyes open and stared at her.

'What happened?' he asked, slowly sitting up and spitting out a mouthful of debris.

'They bombed them.'

Tom gradually absorbed the scene of horror encompassing them. The bomb must have hit on the far side of where The Blues had been gathered. As the dust cleared he could see that their building was flattened. The couple stories of concrete that had been home to The Blues were now a burial mound of slabs over where they had been standing gaping skywards. The blast had thrown he and Liz backwards, but at least they had been spared being buried under the rubble..

'Are you okay?' he asked.

'I think so. My ears are ringing.' She shrugged. You?'

'I...I think so,' he said, running his hands over his head. 'Dust, but no blood,' he added, gazing at his hands. 'Where's Chi?' asked Tom, looking around.

Liz turned her head in the direction of where they had last seen Chi standing, waving them forward, before the Hovercraft dropped its load with deadly accuracy.

'Oh God!'

Tom followed the direction of her gaze. 'No!' he uttered in denial, taking in the slab of wall that Chi had flattened herself up against that was now in pieces on the ground.

They hauled themselves to their feet and picked their way as carefully as they could in their haste around the devastation to where they had last seen Chi alive. The solid walls were now in remnants — some a few feet across, others, the size of a fist. Dust floated through the air, continuously re-coating their hair, making them sneeze and causing their eyes to feel dry and gritty.

'Oh God!' said Liz once more as she threw her pack to the ground. She choked, swallowing the lump in her throat as a moan of anguish escaped from the core of her being. 'Bloody damn Fringe. What have they done?' she cried, taking a gasping breath and then beginning to choke in earnest as the dust filled her lungs.

'Chi, Chi,' yelled Tom, 'can you hear us?' He crouched by the rubble, peering into the dark space between two small slabs of concrete.

A groan was emitted from beneath the pile of rubble.

'Oh God, she's alive under there,' whispered Liz in disbelief. 'We have to get her out.'

They both started scrabbling at the mountain of concrete, careless of the endless clouds of dust permeating their eyes or the abrasions to their skin. They worked furiously, hurling aside the chunks of concrete that were small and heaving on the ones that were larger, working together on the pieces that were too big to manage on their own. Time came to a standstill and stretched before them into eternity.

'We'll never get through this,' groaned Liz.

'We will. We have to,' Tom said in definance, uttering an animal grunt as he hurled aside a massive piece of Chi's burial mound.

Gradually they reduced the mound until they were left with only a couple of large pieces, fallen against each other like a tent, from which Chi's arm protruded.

'Chi?' whispered Liz, holding her breath as she waited for a response. They hadn't heard any sounds from beneath the pile of rubble for a while.

Another groan broke the silence.

'Oh, thank God,' said Liz, closing her eyes as relief washed through her. 'We almost have you Chi. Hang on.'

'How on earth are we going to move these two slabs? If we move one the other will fall and crush her. I don't even know if we have the strength to move them...they're too big,' said Tom quietly, not wanting to alarm Chi if she could hear them and was aware of what was going on.

'We'll have to find something to brace one and then we'll push or pry on the other. We have to try,' said Liz, her voice sounding frantic as her eyes darted back and forth, taking in the surrounding devastation, desperate to find something that could brace the slabs of concrete.

'Don't,' said Chi weakly from beneath her concrete prison.

'Chi.' Liz hunched down, the fine hair at the base of her neck prickling as she tried to peer in to see her friend. Her matted hair flopped into her eyes and she pushed in aside in frustration as she uttered Chi's name once more. 'Chi?'

'Don't...bother.'

'We're *not* going to leave you here Chi,' said Tom, trying to instill some degree of hope into his voice.

'The rebar…it's gone through me…and…,' whispered Chi. 'No point.'

Tom and Liz looked at each other over top of the slabs of Chi's tomb. Dust mixed with sweat caused dark rivers to flow down their faces, making the despair written on their features more harrowing. The bleakness shadowing their eyes seemed opaque.

'We have to try Chi. Get you back to Matthew. He can fix you,' said Liz, desperately wanting to instill Chi with the will to survive.

'No. He can't. Give my…love…to Abe…he's a good guy,' said Chi in a breathless whisper.

'Chi?' said Liz, holding her breath.

There was no response.

Liz moaned and covered her eyes. 'We should never have come. Why did we let her talk us into this?'

Tom shook his head. 'We didn't know they were going to attack.'

Liz's head snapped up. 'What did you say?'

'We didn't know….'

'No, before that.'

'Nothing, why?'

'I thought I heard something.'

They both stopped to listen, ears pricked. Then they heard it — a faint 'help'.

# CHAPTER TWELVE

Liz turned her gaze in horror toward the pile of rubble where The Blues had stood before they were obliterated from the earth.

'No. There can't possibly be someone alive beneath *that*,' stated Tom incredulously.

'There must be.'

They climbed their way over the debris littering what had once been a beautiful tree lined avenue and slowly approached the massive pile of concrete. Their eyes scanned the mountain of slabs, trying to figure out a spot where someone might be trapped without being crushed.

'Hello,' Liz called out tentatively.

'Help,' came the cry from one side of the pile.

Tom and Liz moved forward toward the desperate plea. One huge slab was resting at an angle, jammed up against the rest. Peering in, Tom could see that within the pile the one slab made a hollow beneath it.

'I think if we move some of these bits at the front we may be able to get to whoever is in there,' said Tom.

Liz didn't answer; she just started shifting hunks of concrete. Tom joined her until they had formed an opening beneath the massive slab.

'Help.'

They saw a hand move beneath the bodies, pebbles and dust. Looking at Liz, Tom whispered, 'We're going to have to try and pull him free.'

Liz nodded. Grasping the hand, they tried to haul the Blue from beneath the body lying on top which had cushioned them from certain instant death. Slowly, inch by inch they managed to free the upper part of the person. When they could finally get their hands beneath the arms they both pulled with all the strength they had left.

'My baby…save my baby. It's coming.'

Tom and Liz looked at each other in consternation. It was the pregnant Blue girl they had glimpsed before the bombing.

'We can't deliver a baby,' croaked Tom.

'I…I don't know how…' said Liz, shaking her head and looking at Tom, her face frozen with fear.

'You have to…before it's too late,' rasped the girl, grasping Liz's arm, her eyes dilated with pain, '…please.'

---

'Mission accomplished,' stated Peter grimly into his headset. 'Time to head home.'

The ten Hovercrafts turned to head back to New York. Silence reigned. As they flew back across the city they could see the charred ruins of where the charges had detonated. Blackened, gaping holes, crumbled buildings, smoldering remains of trees long since dead, and who knew how many bodies buried beneath the destruction. The Fringe were known for being peaceful — their mandate to restore the planet to its former beauty and try to save all species, including the human race. That they had just wiped out a portion of humanity did not sit easily upon the shoulders of the pilots who had obeyed the directive they'd been given.

Peter glanced down at his control panel and noticed a couple red dots of movement on his heat detection radar screen. Could someone have lived through the bombing in the area he had just decimated? It was one thing to instantly kill someone when they had no time to think about it, it was quite another to think of leaving someone to slowly bleed to death in intolerable pain and surrounded by bodies.

'The rest of you carry on to New York. I'll catch up. I need to check something on the ground,' Peter instructed into his headset.

He slowly did another loop around, flying low to the ground. There were definitely two, if not three, people still alive down there. He looked more closely at his monitor then punched the controls to maximize zoom on his cameras. The figures came into sharper focus — they didn't appear to be blue or obese. Did he recognize the upturned faces? Crap, who else could be in this area? And today of all days. His stomach knotted. He didn't like the feeling of this. Setting down in a clearing that must have once have been a park, and was now just long, dry grass with a few half dead trees around the perimeter, he grabbed his emergency supply bag, a knife for protection, and headed in the direction of the smoldering buildings.

Making his way over the uprooted slabs of concrete, past dead trees and crumbling buildings, he kept a watch out for anything that moved, ready to defend himself if need be. He passed derelict mounds of rusted metal with smashed out windows and rotted seats within. Stopping momentarily to peer into one of the heaps he realized from the panel at the front that it must have been a mode of transportation at one time. He had a book which had pictures of cars that had been used up until about 2050 — before 'hover' technology had taken over the world. He looked around mesmerized. He had previously only left New York to deliver supplies to other Fringe sites or to make contact with The Network in their villages… and they were nothing like this. Fringe sites were always meticulous and the Network villages might not be much, but they were neat and orderly, and the people in The Network tried to maintain things as best they could with what they had. He was surprised to find himself choking up at the thought of this massive city, now a crumbling ruin, once being alive with life. At one time it must have been like New York, before toxic oceans and soil and the resulting extreme weather wiped out the world's food supply and caused the deaths of most of the human race. He shook his head, never really having given quite enough thought to how the world used to be and how they'd got to this point. He had known the story intellectually but never personally. He had flown above the surface of the world, looking down on the devestation, but had never set foot in the destroyed cities or endless yellow grasslands. Until he'd had contact with The Network he hadn't concerned himself with how others around the world survived. How The Blues survived in a desolate ruin such as this he could not imagine. It was no wonder they raided for food. And it was no wonder they were angry and killed those who had the food, not thinking beyond wanting the sustenance for themselves. He pulled a length of pipe from beneath the debris. Extra protection. Though it was blistering hot out, a shiver coursed through his body.

He carried on toward the blackened ruin that he'd created. Treading carefully, trying to be quiet. Glancing left and right, and occasionally over his shoulder, he made his way through the ever-worsening piles of debris to his destination. Skirting around one last mountainous pile he stopped still in shock.

He gasped, choking on the inhaled dust, and rubbed at his eyes, hardly believing the scene unfolding before him. The moving red dots he had seen on his screen were from The Network and there on the ground in front of them was an enormous girl, a Blue, surrounded by a pool of blood.

The two Network members looked up at him as he approached, a riot of emotions running across their faces.

CHAPTER TWELVE

'Peter!' gasped the girl, incredulous.

'Liz? Tom? What the hell are you doing here?'

Liz just shook her head, too shocked and drained to form a coherent thought to explain their current situation.

'What are you holding?' asked Peter as he gazed at the bundle in her arms.

Liz looked down and then back up at Peter. 'A baby.'

'A...what's going on? Why are you here when we're bombing the place?'

'We didn't know,' said Tom, jumping in to the halting conversation.

Peter glanced at Tom. 'You weren't warned?'

They both shook their heads in denial.

'No, of course not. Why would you be?'

'Chi...she wanted to come and try talking to the Blues. We came with her...to convince them to leave us alone and explain what we're attempting to do — to save the planet. But then...' explained Tom, trailing off, not able to voice the rest of what happened.

'Where's Chi?' asked Peter, a frown creasing his forehead as he gazed around at the destruction he'd caused.

Tom pointed to the arm protruding from the nearby pile of rubble. 'She didn't make it. We...we tried to get her out but...'

'Oh God!' said Peter as he turned to stare at where Tom was pointing, his head falling forward into his hand as his fingers covered his eyes, not wanting to witness the death sentence he'd been instructed to carry out. *What had he done?*

'Can you take us home?' asked Liz. Her shoulders slumped as all the adreneline left her body. She looked completely exhausted and filled with despair. 'We can't get back all that way on the Hoverboards with...with the baby. It would take too long and she'll need feeding.'

Peter gazed at Liz — the fact that she was holding a baby finally registering in the thoughts swirling through his mind. 'Whose? Where'd the baby come from?' His words trailed off as he remembered the gesture of the Blue girl he had seen on his monitor.

'It's hers,' said Liz, indicating the Blue lying on the ground before them with a nod of her head. 'We pulled her from the rubble...alive...and...and delivered the baby. I thought she was going to live. The whole time she was ranting...about being promised food. But then she died. Maybe I did something wrong. We can't just leave it,' said Liz, the horror of it all making her speech come out in punctuated, clipped bursts.

'Shit. Edward has a lot to answer for,' Peter muttered under his breath. 'Come on then, let's get you out of here,' he said aloud to Liz and Tom.

They stood to follow Peter back to the Hovercraft — taking a last glance at the arm of their friend sticking out from the deadly pile of concrete — leaving behind the sorrow and devastation. There was nothing else they could do.

'Actually, can you take us to Sector A? We need to see Abe.'

———————

Abe opened his front door and took a quick intake of breath. His eyes widened at the sight before him. 'There's been another raid,' he moaned, his eyes scrunching closed to shut out the visions of horror.

'No, no...not that,' said Tom quickly.

'Oh...but...' He opened the door wider, waving his arm for them to enter. 'But...what happened? You're all bloody...and your clothes...' he trailed off as he moved aside so they could come in. Their clothes were torn and filthy, covered in what looked like a mix of dust, blood and soot. Their hair was matted and their faces had black smudges mixed with sweat and dirt. They wore expressions of abject misery and exhaustion and neither seemed capable of uttering a word. 'What's that?' he motioned to the bundle in Liz's arms, thinking to ask something that had a more simple response in the hope of eliciting a reply.

Tom and Liz slumped onto the chairs either side of the little kitchen table as Abe placed a jug of water and some cups before them. Noting their exhaustion, he rummaged around for some bread and jam before sitting down next to them. Eyebrows raised questioningly, he waited for them to respond.

Tom and Liz looked at each other across the table, unsure of where to start.

Tom cleared his throat and reiterated their story to Abe, who sat as if turned to stone, incredulous at what he was hearing. Tom, nearing the end of his diatribe, glanced at Liz, not wanting to share the last part of the story with Abe. 'Talking to The Blues, trying to get them to leave us alone, it was Chi's idea — we need peace to all survive.'

Abe stared at Tom, his forehead puckered, his eyebrows drawing together in a scowl as he asked, 'Where's Chi?'

'When they bombed the city, she had moved further in than us… the blast came…the wall collapsed…we couldn't get her out.'

Abe stared from one to the other. 'Killed? The Fringe killed her?'

Liz and Tom didn't answer, their expressions told Abe all he needed to know.

'Her last words were to give you…her love,' said Liz.

Abe's head sank into his hands, he stared unseeingly at the tabletop. His shoulders heaved as he took great gasping breaths. Then his hands balled into fists and slammed into the table causing the water in the glasses to slop over the edge and Liz and Tom to jump in their seats. He shook his head from side to side like an animal caught in a trap and then jammed the palms of his fists into his eyes.

Liz and Tom remained quiet, staring at eachother over Abe's bent head. Liz, tentatively reached out and put her hand on Abe's shoulder. Abe put his hand over hers and took a final heaving sigh before raising his head and looking Tom and Liz in the eyes. His expression was bleak. Finally, Liz glanced at Tom, who gave a slight nod of his head, before she took up the last part of the tale. 'One of The Blues was still alive under the rubble. We pulled her out…and delivered her baby,' she said as she pulled aside the bit of fabric, revealing the light blue face of the tiny girl.

Abe's eyes boggled with surprise as he sucked in his breath before letting it out on a slow exhale but remained speechless.

'The mom died, we had to…take her,' said Liz, looking down at the tiny bundle in her arms. 'Then Peter found us and brought us here.'

'Peter! Peter was one of The Fringe that did the bombing!' expostulated Abe, so shocked that his thoughts finally converged into uttering a sentence. 'I knew they were talking about it, but he didn't want to go…didn't agree. I thought he might change Edward's mind, or get out of it, or…send someone else.'

Liz nodded in affirmation as she started to rock the baby who was beginning to fuss. 'I got the feeling that he wasn't too…thrilled… about it.' Liz glanced over at Tom. 'It wasn't only him. There were a bunch of them. The Blues didn't stand a chance.'

'We figured he was following orders,' stated Tom.

Abe nodded in understanding at all that was being implied but not said. 'And what are you going to do with the baby?' asked Abe, focusing on the practical in an attempt to reign in the emotions that threatened to overwhelm him.

'I really don't know,' said Liz, looking down at the tiny bundle in her arms. After a pause she added, 'But she'll need feeding soon.'

'I'll take her.'

'But she's a Blue,' stated Tom and Liz in unison, hardly believing that Abe would want to care for any one of the Blues, regardless of how young they might be, given that they had slaughtered his entire family.

'She's a baby,' answered Abe.

'But how will you care for her?'

'My neighbour just had a baby…if she won't nurse her…I have a goat. The girls can help and Matthew can give her the vaccine…see if it works…helps,' he said in a rush, thinking out loud.

'I guess,' said Liz. 'We don't have any better ideas.'

Liz handed the baby to Abe who pulled aside the fabric and stared at the little face. 'I wonder what colour she'd be if she wasn't blue,' he said aloud.

# CHAPTER THIRTEEN

'Oh my God. That's it!' exclaimed Dez, his eyes widening with shock.

'What's it?' asked Emi, not following his line of reasoning.

'Edward. It's always eluded me until now. But that's it.'

'What *are* you talking about?' asked Emi in exasperation. The conversation had taken a lot of twists she hadn't planned on when showing up unexpectedly at his cabin.

'Edward…he's the one who set up the attacks on Sectors C and D…and on The Cloud.'

'What? You can't be serious,' Emi sqeaked, the colour draining from her countenance. 'What on earth makes you say that? Why would he do such a thing?'

Dez shook his head. 'I…I don't know. But Sam, he tried to warn me when he was dying and then The Blue…he thought I was the guy who gave him the tip off…which must mean that I look like him,' said Dez slowly, trying to formulate his thoughts.

'But it doesn't make *any* sense. Edward helped us save people and sent supplies to Sectors C and D and he's put his whole life into having The Cloud built. Why destroy everything?' Emi sat down next to Dez on the couch, trying to gather her thoughts. 'It's not logical,' she whispered, putting her hand out to touch Dez's hand where it lay resting on his knee, hoping he wouldn't flinch away.

He didn't flinch. Suddenly he was all over her — his hands in her hair, his mouth on hers, then his arms went around her, pulling her to him as he buried his face in her neck. 'Oh God, Emi, you've no idea the hell I've been going through.'

His mouth descended on hers once more making speech impossible. Winding her arms around his neck she kissed him back with a longing made more powerful by the thought that she had almost lost him…could still lose him…had lost him. 'I love you,' she murmmered against his mouth.

'You can't go back to him Emi. He's dangerous. You're in danger. You can't go,' said Dez vehemently, crushing her to him.

'Dez, I have to. He…loves me,' said Emi, pulling away. 'And I've promised. I can't just disappear. And he's jealous…jealous of you. He won't take it well if I don't return,' she said, shaking her head. 'And I'm sorry, but I just don't buy it…your theory. It's not logical. His family, his people, The Fringe…they've spent the last century trying to figure out how to save us all. He craves power. He wants to rule the world but that doesn't make him evil. Why would he destroy all that he's spent his life creating? It makes no sense. You need proof. Maybe Sam was just ranting, or meant something else, when he was dying.'

'I know it sounds ludicrous. But my gut instincts tell me I'm right,' Dez shook his head and ran his hands through his hair.

The familiar gesture brought a smile to Emi's countenance. But it was fleeting and then gone.

'I don't want him near you, touching you. Please, Emi.'

Emi stared at Dez, perplexed. She didn't know how to move forward.

'We need time. Time to figure things out. We need to know if I'm right or not,' he said, running his hands through his touseled hair once again. 'You're right…I need proof. I don't know where to start. I'll figure something out. But I can't stand the thought of you being with him.'

Emi let out a pent up sigh. 'I'll…I'll tell him I'm bleeding. He won't want to risk losing the baby…it's his heir,' she shrugged, putting her hand protectively over her rounded stomach. 'But I have to return. It's hard to explain but somehow my presense helps him to focus. And right now we need him to figure out how to fix the mess we are in.'

Dez turned grey at the thought. 'Emi, you can't.'

'I have to.'

Dez groaned. His stomach knotted, sensing that argument would be futile. She had to go back — for now. He sucked in his breath and exhaled loudly into the quiet room. His gaze rested on Emi's troubled countenance as he swallowed the lump in his throat. 'Okay, maybe now is not the time. But we need to think, focus, figure something out.' He was sure he was right. 'Before he kills us all,' he muttered.

Emi reached up and ran her hand through his hair trying to restore it to order. She leaned in and kissed him briefly on the mouth. That two men could love her so intensely still surprised her. No matter what she did someone was going to get hurt.

Their irrational jealousy made sorting the truth from imagination extremely challenging.

———+———

Emi returned to New York — returned to Edward. Attempting to behave as though nothing had changed was the biggest performance of her life. She told him she was bleeding and he was nothing but concerned and overly caring of her. Now that Dez wanted to rekindle things she found Edward's care more annoying than comforting. She knew it was her own attitude that had changed and she had to steel herself to not cringe at his touch, even a simple kiss as he left for meetings — meetings she was now banned from as he demanded that she rest.

'How am I going to extract us from this mess I've made,' she asked aloud of the tiny life gently kicking at her abdomen.

She washed her coffee cup and headed for the bedroom to make the bed. Edward's nightstand was stacked with E-manuals. He never trusted storing vital information at his office so he kept the discs at home. Since his apartment could only be accessed by retina and thumbprint recognition on the screen at the front door, only he and Emi had the ability to enter. Although, if the scanner failed then they could enter a code manually into the security system. He had told Emi that it was his name spelled backwards, with the E still a capital, and the apartment number the correct way around. His thought process he had explained was that to make everything backwards was too obvious. He considered his apartment to be his safe haven.

If Dez was right and Edward was the one to have planned the attacks on Sectors C and D, and on The Cloud, would he keep any record of it? Surely it would be the height of stupidity to keep any proof, but if Dez were right she had to at least look. She was the only one who could. And not even The Fringe would back Edward if he was the one behind the destruction of The Cloud. They might not care about the attacks on Sectors C and D but arranging to have Cloud III smashed by The Blues could be the final straw — the one that brought about the annihilation of the entire planet.

She shook her head and sighed. She doubted Edward would do such horrific things. He was powerful, controlling, possessive and jealous but she had never seen him as evil. His whole life had been dedicated to saving the planet and the human race. That he wanted to be ruler she had no doubt. There seemed no logical reason to back Dez's theory. Still, she had to find some proof one way or the other. 'Where to start?' she asked the empty room, putting her hand on her bump in a protective gesture.

Picking up an E-manual she inserted the disc into her reader. A blank screen stared back at her. Even in the secure environment of their apartment, Edward did not leave anything lying around without the need for some form of clearance. What would he use? A password of some sort was the most obvious answer. But what would his password be? Did she really know him well enough to be able to figure out a high security code? How many chances would she have before she was blocked — two, maybe three at best. She stared around the room — what was he so absorbed with that he would use it as a password for his personal life? She stared at the wall, her forehead furrowed in thought. Then her gaze shifted to the nightstand, the hair on her arms prickled — she felt like she was being watched. Slowly she looked over her shoulder at the open doorway to the bedroom, but there was nobody there. Her eyes once more slid back to the nightstand — she was being watched by her own photo. She picked up the screen that she smiled out from and turned it over; on the back there was a digital inscription which simply said her name and the date: Emi — May 17, 2194. The date he'd proposed. The date she had said 'yes'. She was his obsession. Would some form of her name and this date be the code? It was worth a try.

She had to think carefully. The PIN had to have an uppercase letter, more than one lowercase letter, more than one number and at least one symbol. Her name and the date would fulfill the basic requirements…but in what order? Just as it was on the frame either forward or backward would be too obvious. But would Edward care? Nobody was going to come looking for his journals. They couldn't even get into the apartment. And who would bother to look at the frame and think of using the date as a code? Absolutely nobody until Dez had put doubts into her mind and she felt like she had to find the truth. Would the too obvious actually work? Maybe. She typed in Emi-May.17.2194 — and held her breath. A red error message blinked back at her. Nope. Damn. Of course he would never make it *that* easy. She had two more tries at best. Staring at her name and the date she tried to figure out what would make the code less obvious. Backwards would also be too simple. Leave some of the numbers for the date out and still use her name? Replace May with a 5? Hmm. Maybe? She typed it in — Emi-51794. A red error message. Damn. Last chance. More complicated. Less obvious. One chance. Think. What would Edward use? Something he would remember but impossible for anyone to guess or decipher. The same reasoning as the code for the apartment. The name backwards and still with E as a capital and the date in its logical format? But which should she put first...her name or the date? She had a 50-50 chance. Could it work? Slowly she typed in 51794-imE and hit enter. The screen blinked open. She stared and let out the breath that she hadn't realized she'd been holding. It worked! She couldn't believe it. She did know him well enough. Although she was elated, a knot of dread cramped her stomach. The E-reader would record the last log-in date. Would he remember? Did Edward keep a record? Too late now! She had to look. She had to know, to have no doubt — one way or the other. A multitude of calculations popped up on her screen; the mathematical formulas for the workings of The Cloud. She scrolled through but without a better understanding of the workings of The Cloud the numbers meant little to her. She removed the E-manual and inserted the next. She tried the same code. Again it worked. She scrolled through each disc, not knowing what she was looking for but hoping it would jump out at her when she found what she needed.

She rubbed at her eyes, weary from looking at the screen for so long. One more and she would go for a walk, see if Charlotte was available for lunch. She inserted the second to last E-manual and began to swipe the screen to scroll through. Then she stopped — this one seemed to be of a more personal nature — a list of appointments and times to meet with people. Some were spelled out clearly but others just had initials.

She heard the click of the front door.

Hastily she removed the E-manual, put the stack back as it was before and lay down on top of the bed. She breathed slowly in and out, trying to subdue her heart rate, sure that its loud thumping could be heard in the too quiet room.

'Emi?'

'In here,' she replied, attempting to make her voice sound sleepy.

'Are you okay?' asked Edward, coming to sit on the edge of the bed.

'Yes. I was just tidying up but felt tired.' She covered her mouth and faked a yawn. 'I thought I would read for a bit but dozed off.' She rubbed her eyes and stretched.

'How's our little guy?' he asked, putting his hand on her stomach.

'Fine,' she grinned up at him, pretending a calm she was far from feeling, hoping he couldn't hear the loud thumping of her heart. 'He's been kicking me a lot this morning.'

'I thought we could go out for lunch,' he suggested, brushing her hair back from her forehead and kissing her gently on the mouth.

A shudder ran through her body as she wound her arms around Edward's neck. How could she doubt this man when he had spent his life trying to save the planet? He loved her and had given her so much and yet she was going through his personal things trying to find evidence to convict him of hideous crimes. Did she doubt him because she wanted to doubt him? If he had set-up the raids then she would be free to be with Dez. Was it just wishful thinking?

For now she must let him think her shudder was of desire — it was part of her performance.

# CHAPTER FOURTEEN

Spike groaned. *What the hell had happened?* The world had turned black. He shook his head to rid himself of the ringing in his ears. Rolling over he spat out a mouthful of grit and blood and then pushing himself to a sitting position he tried to make sense of his surroundings. Behind him were the charred remains of the derelict building he'd called home. He couldn't see beyond the concrete stairwell on the outside of the building that must have protected him from the blast. It alone appeared to be intact. Where the street used to be there was now a smoking crater. Straining his ears for the sound of the demons from the sky he was met with silence. Complete silence — there were no sounds of either demons or people or birds. *Had he alone survived?*

'Shade?'

He waited but there was no reply — no nagging or bitching. Just complete stillness.

'Shade?' he yelled, louder this time, choking on the layer of dust that felt like it was lodged at the back of his throat.

Still nothing.

Pushing himself to his feet he stood still to regain his balance and let the dizzy sensation pass. Cautiously he put one foot infront of the other, returning to the spot where he thought he had last seen

Shade…gazing at the demons, hoping for a food-drop. There was no food. Instead he found a tent of concrete slabs and the body of Shade laying in a pool of blood, her clothes torn from her torso by the blast. He lay his hand on her protruding stomach but there was no movement, no kick. It was better this way — life was too hard, pointless — and now that he had made an enemy of The Fringe it would only be worse.

He turned to go. There was nothing for him here anymore. He would make his way back to the stream and the fruit trees until he could figure out where to go and what to do. At least he would have food and water. As he spun around he noticed an arm sticking out from beneath another pile of rubble but the arm was different — it was not blue. He lumbered over to take a closer look. It looked like the arm of a child, small, thin with a light skin tone. Why would anyone other than a Blue be in the city? He reached down to touch the hand, fascinated. The fingers closed over his. He yanked his hand away and fell back. Could they still be alive under there? He looked at the rubble and the concrete slabs. It looked like someone had tried to get the person out and given up — the last two slabs looked heavy and almost impossible to move.

He heard a faint groan.

'You okay?'

'Mmm-mmm.'

He doubted there was another person left alive in the entire city. The demons had obviously come to destroy all that they could. He had to get her out, even if she were not a Blue. Someone was better than nobody at all. Looking at the angle of the slabs he thought he would just be able to wedge himself under the concrete and if he shoved at both with all his bulk he might be able to shift them at the same time without one or the other falling inwards and crushing the person beneath…maybe.

'I'm gonna try to get you out. Hang on.'

Wedging himself between the two concrete slabs, with a massive roar that contained all his pent up anger and frustration, he heaved himself upwards, pushing the slabs outwards and hoping he didn't kill the person beneath in the process. The slabs fell with a heart-rending crash.

Spike held his breath and closed his eyes…waiting for the dust to clear and waiting to see what state he would find the person in.

'Aaahhhhh.'

Spike looked down into the upturned face of a young woman. Brown eyes gazed back at him reflecting immense pain. Her straight black hair was covered in a fine layer of dust and her slight form was curled in a ball as if she had been trying to protect herself when the blast came. A single piece of rebar protruded from her arm.

'My…pack,' she whispered.

Spike looked around. Then he saw it. There, just below her shoulder, was the corner of her pack. If it wasn't for the pack the rebar would have gone through her chest instead of her arm. He knelt down beside her and tried to remove the pack from under her.

The girl groaned in pain. 'No.' She whispered the single word on an unsteady exhale.

The pack had been slung over her shoulder and without cutting the strap he would not be able to get it around the rebar that impaled her arm.

She looked him in the eye and then glanced toward her legs. 'Knife.'

Spike's forehead furrowed before noticing the handle of a knife protruding from a sheath strapped to her thigh. He slid the knife from its case and started cutting at the strap of the pack.

The girl groaned and then closed her eyes and clenched her jaw. With one last slice he was through the strap. As gently as he could he pulled the pack from beneath her shoulder and lowered her to the ground.

'The first-aid kit…alcohol and bandages,' she whispered. 'You'll have to remove the rebar.'

Spike shook his head. 'I can't. Don't know how.'

'I'll die otherwise. Have to stop the bleeding. If you do it wrong… it doesn't matter…I'll die anyway.'

Spike stared hard at Chi and then nodded and rummaged around in the pack until he found the container holding the first-aid kit. He looked at Chi questioningly.

'I need something to bite down on. Then tie off my arm and remove the rebar. I might pass out. Pour alcohol over the wound and wrap my arm with the bandage,' she croaked, her voice, barely audible, was ragged with pain. 'Got it?'

Spike nodded. He found a stick and put it between Chi's teeth and then proceeded to pour the alcohol over the area where the rebar protruded from her arm.

Chi bit down on the stick and closed her eyes but managed to refrain from screaming as the alcohol permeated the wound. She opened her eyes and looking directly at Spike gave him a small nod as he prepared to pull the rebar from her arm.

He grabbed hold of the end of the rough metal, pinned her arm with his other hand and pulled.

Chi bit down hard on the stick and screamed at the back of her throat as the pain shot through her body. She let the stick fall from her mouth, panting, trying to regain control and focus her mind so that she might survive. 'The bandage…and more alcohol,' she instucted, her fists clenched, her nails biting into her palms. She whimpered as Spike did as he was asked. The ordeal was over. She lay still with her eyes closed.

'Are you dead?'

Chi opened one eye, before closing it again and giving Spike a glimmer of a smile. 'No, not yet. Better luck next time.'

'Humph,' Spike snorted in laughter. 'Yeah. Guess I normally kill people from the Network, not 'elp them.'

'Quite.'

'You okay?'

'Not sure. We'll have to wait and see.'

'Now what?'

'I don't know. I just need to…lay here for a bit.'

Spike looked Chi up and down. 'You're small. I could carry you. Know a spot with shade and water and some trees that grow food. Be better than here,' he said looking around at the destroyed city.

'Why are you helping me?' asked Chi, once again peeking through one eye before her eyelid drifted down, the small effort almost too much to bear.

'Dunno. But there's nobody else,' stated Spike, looking across to where everyone else he had ever known was buried beneath the rubble of the building that had been their home. He glanced back at Chi, not wanting to look at the pool of blood that surrounded Shade and the unborn baby that he would now never get to see.

'They're all dead?'

'Yeah.'

A groan of despair escaped from Chi as she realized she was the reason for the deaths of Tom and Liz. If it wasn't for her wanting to come and talk to the Blues they would not have been here when The Fringe struck. She gazed at Spike, the only person in the world who knew that she was still alive and could help her. 'Let's go to these trees of yours. We can figure out what to do from there. We…can't stay here.'

Spike nodded and picked Chi up effortlessly. He couldn't bring himself to glance back.

———✦———

Very few people knew about the firepower of the Fringe and fewer still thought it would ever be used against anyone. Outright warfare was a thing of the past and unleashing bombs on defenceless people was unthinkable. Even though the resources of the world were minimal, there were so few people left on the planet, the Fringe had long since decided that isolation and self-reliance was the best policy. If others lived or died it was up to them.

But when the Blues destroyed the Cloud — decades of planning and hard work — Edward felt the need for retaliation. He could not control and rule over such an unreliable and aggressive group of people. They had taken things into their own hands. They were too dangerous. And so he had unleashed his fury.

Word soon spread. Most shrugged their shoulders. It meant less mouths to feed. The Blues didn't have long life spans anyway. The Network would be safe from further raids. The obliteration of the Blues mattered little to most people. But others felt unnerved by the action. Who would be targeted next? If you displeased the ruling elite would you be permanently silenced? Who would defend you? If they managed to save the planet would you have a voice in the new world order?

When Dez learned of the bombing he was furious…and scared. Abe had arrived at his front door carrying a Blue baby in his arms.

'Abe. What the…?'

'Have you heard?'

Dez looked at Abe, his forehead scrunched. He raised one eyebrow and ran his hand through his hair. 'Hmm. Somehow I don't think so.' He opened the door wider so Abe could enter. They sat at the kitchen table. 'Care to fill me in?'

'You're not going to like it.'

'Why am I not surprised. Go on.'

'Peter just dropped Liz and Tom off at my place. Liz, Tom and Chi had gone to try and talk to the Blues and convince them to leave us alone. Explain things to them. But while they were there Peter, along with nine other Hovercraft pilots, bombed the city.'

'They did what?'

'Bombed them. Wiped the Blues from the face of the earth.'

Dez shook his head, his mouth curved down in a frown. He ran his hands through his already dishevelled hair. 'But...' He stopped and drew a big breath, his mind in turmoil. 'Crap. I didn't know they had weapons nevermind would actually use them. Their prime directive is to save the planet, the human race, the rest of the species we have left and to live at peace.'

'Yeah. I know.'

'So, are we going to be wiped out when we displease them or are no longer useful?'

Abe shrugged his shoulders and shook his head. He didn't have an answer. 'I know Peter was not pleased about following the orders he had been given.'

'Orders?' Dez raised his eyebrows questioningly. 'So it wasn't a committe decision.'

'I guess not.'

'Edward?'

'That's my understanding.'

'So we're living in a dictatorship now.'

'I told you you weren't going to like it.'

'You got that right.'

Abe glanced down at the little bundle in his arms. The baby was just starting to stir. Woken by the voices.

Dez's gaze followed Abe's. The baby finally registering with him after the shock of Abe's news.

'Why do you have a Blue baby?'

'Tom and Liz delivered her after the bombing. The mom lived just long enough to give birth.'

'But how did you end up with him?'

'Her.' Abe gave Dez a hint of a smile. 'I offered to take her. Peter dropped Tom and Liz off at my place so they could tell me about… Chi.' Abe swallowed, too choked up to say more. He ran his hands across his eyes and took a deep breath.

'Chi! What about Chi?'

'She died in the bombing.'

'Chi. Chi is dead!' Dez shook his head. He didn't want to hear any more. Didn't want to know any more of this dreadful story. 'How?'

'She was ahead of Tom and Liz. Closer to the bomb site. Tom and Liz tried to save her but couldn't.'

'Oh God.' Dez rested his elbows on the table and dropped his head into his hands.

'I wanted to tell you so you didn't just hear about it.'

Dez nodded. Then his head snapped up. 'It's time I confronted Edward. We can't go on like this.'

'Yeah. That was my thought. If you didn't want to face up to him then I was going to. I'll go with you. Just say when.'

———⋅———

Edward was alone in his office. It was late in the evening and most people had gone home for the day. He looked up with a frown when he heard the door opening.

'Dez! Abe! To what do I owe the honour?' He paused. 'A pleasant surprise to see you back up and about, Dez.' Edward smiled but it was a thin smile which did not reach his eyes.

Dez and Abe glanced around. The office was immaculate. Not a pen or notepad was out of place. Every surface gleamed. The old-fashioned, heavy desk was huge — a barrier between Edward and whoever might have the courage to sit in one of the two seats on the other side of the desk. The view out of the floor-to-ceiling windows was of Central Park. That every inch of the park was perfectly planned and cultivated to grow the food they so desperately needed was obvious from this vantage point. It was a place for Edward to plan and to enjoy witnessing the fruits of his labours. His ancestors had left him in charge of a world they could still save, which they planned to save, and which he would rule over.

Edward's smile turned to a frown as Dez and Abe entered and availed themselves of the two chairs opposite him. 'What can I do for you? I'm rather busy.' He swallowed. He did not intimidate easily but Dez and Abe had a hostile air about them. And he was accustomed to seeing Abe outside; inside he seemed to fill the entire room.

'You bombed them,' stated Abe.

'Ahh. That is what this is about. Yes, I did. It was imperitive to our survival. Yours as well as mine.'

'And you killed Chi,' Abe added. The accusation came out as a growl and Abe almost choked as he uttered Chi's name.

'Chi?'

'She was a vital part of the Network and our friend. She was working hard to further your cause and help save the planet. She was caught in the bombing,' explained Dez. The glint in his eye showed his hostility at the fact that Edward could so easily forget a key member of the Network.

'Must have been an unhappy accident. Wrong place at the wrong time. I certainly did not intend to harm any Network members.' Edward shrugged. 'My sincerest apologies.'

Abe clenched his hands into fists where they rested on the arms of the chair.

'Since when do the Fringe go around bombing people? Your prime directive is to live in peace. Warfare was outlawed long ago.'

'This was not warfare.'

'You got that right. They didn't stand a chance of defending themselves.'

'Exactly,' agreed Edward with a smile. 'They destroyed the Cloud. They might have just finished us all off. The Cloud is our last hope of survival. We've spent decades planning and years constucting it. I cannot leave our survival to chance — hoping the Blues do not attack again. They had to be eliminated.' Edward was completely unrepentant.

'We should have been included in the decision making. Had a meeting. Taken a vote,' said Dez. 'The Fringe and the Network working together...it is not a dictatorship...or is it?'

'Ahh. So that is the real reason for this visit. Your feelings were hurt. You weren't consulted and your position as leader of the Network was threatened by my action. Well, might I remind you that it was you who lay in hospital not wanting to be leader anymore. So don't come whining to me now.'

Dez turned an angry shade of red. 'No, that is not what this is about.'

'We don't feel illiminating whole groups of people solves anything. Especially before trying to converse with them first,' Abe interjected.

'Yes, I gathered that but it's too late now. The deed is done.' Edward looked from one to the other.

'Everything is going exactly as you planned isn't it? Years of planning. Right back to having Sectors C and D attacked so you could then offer us help and we would be obliged to help you in return. Be your workforce. Under your authority.' Dez's voice rose and octave and came out almost as a growl. His eyes flashed with anger. He paused. His mouth a thin hard line. He couldn't contain his suspicions any longer. 'Did you have the Blues destroy the Cloud so that you have a reason to wipe out the segment of society you do not wish to provide for in your new world? You can use their actions as an excuse to have things all your own way,' challenged Dez, looking Edward straight in the eyes, daring him to to contradict his theory. 'And the icing on the cake, I just happened to be a guard on the day in question…so you kill me off as well…the only real threat to your dictatorship.'

Edward froze. His face blanched. But it was a momentary lapse. The expression so fleeting that if Dez had not been looking directly at Edward he would have missed it. He had hit a nerve with his accusations. But how much of it was true…or was all of it the truth?

'You may as well leave. You've had your say.' Edward stated coldly. 'I'm not going to engage in conversation over such rediculous accusations. I've spent my life preparing for the Cloud. It's not something I'm willing to have destroyed. Thus my decision to have the Blues killed.' Edward paused. 'Please leave.'

Abe looked at Dez who looked like he was about to launch himself over the desk and beat the truth out of Edward.

'Come on, Dez, let's go. There's no point,' Abe said. He needed to get Dez away before things turned really ugly.

Dez glanced in Abe's direction. He looked startled, almost as if he hadn't known Abe was there. Dez heaved a sigh and nodded at Abe.

They turned to go.

Abe was through the door, heaving a sigh of relief that they had escaped before things escalated further. Dez was following Abe out of the office when Edward quietly issued a parting jibe…almost under his breath.

'Or maybe this is actually about Emi. About the fact that she chose me over you and is now carrying my child.'

Dez froze. He turned slowly back to Edward. 'You have no idea what you are talking about.' He clamped his mouth shut. He could not reveal the truth about Emi. It could put her in danger. He spun on his heel and left, leaving the door wide open and Edward with a look of uncertainty on his face.

What did Dez mean that he had no idea what he was talking about?

# CHAPTER FIFTEEN

The weather had been unusually oppressive for so long now. There hadn't been a breath of wind, the sky remained a resolute blue, the sun beat down relentlessly — it was eerily quiet. The calm before the storm.

Emi felt as if she were suffocating — physically, emotionally, mentally. Just as there was no reprieve from the heat there was also no escaping the daily turmoil of her life. Edward was unfailingly kind to her with a carefulness of her wellbeing that she found smothering. He loved her with an intensity that still surprised her and his excitement over the baby was heart-wrenching, especially since she was deceiving him. She dreaded his reaction if he ever found out the truth. He still preferred she not attend the meetings, saying it was best that she rest and not stress herself but she wondered if his true motives were to prevent her from questioning his authority. His ability to conceal his need for power and control beneath the calm exterior of charm never failed to amaze her. She had yet to find any proof to back Dez's theory but as time marched on and Edward's true colours began to appear from beneath his charming veneer within their private lives, she began to question if perhaps he did have the ability to sacrifice the world for his own motives. Except there were no motives! She racked her brain, going around in circles, but always coming back to the conclusion that it was in Edward's best interest to work together with The Network to save the planet. If he craved power and control then surely ruling the world would give him those things in abundance. She could never see how his motives would differ from anyone else's.

She gazed out at the distant horizon from the balcony of their 70th floor penthouse suite, her hand resting protectively on her rounded belly. The baby kicked in response to her caress, bringing a smile to her face. Most of the time it seemed that the life growing within her was the only bit of joy she had left in the world. Somehow she had to find a way forward — to lead The Network in her own way without being controlled by Edward and to fix the mess she had made of her life. But finding a way through eluded her. She felt a desperate need to see Dez again but now that he was fully recovered, and back in Sector A, it was much more difficult to arrange.

Emi stood on the balcony, lost in thought. She didn't noticed the sun's disappearance. A gust of wind whipped her hair across her face bringing her out of her reverie. Pushing the hair out of her eyes she glanced over her shoulder. A shudder ran through her body as she gasped, hardly believing what she was seeing. The calm before the storm was over — the Hyperstorm had arrived. Black-green clouds on the distant horizon were being pushed by gale force winds in the direction of New York, toward the spot where she stood. She watched in mounting horror as the sky gradually turned black and the wind picked up momentum, sucking the breath from her body.

Ducking back inside, she battled to close the glass door as a mighty gust of wind suddenly hit with terrifying force, rattling the glass and forcing the bi-fold door back against her. It was as if some-one bigger and stronger than she was pushing against it, not wanting her to close the door, wanting entrance to her apartment so as to unleash havoc within. Using all of her body weight, and with the adrenaline that comes from fear, she began to inch the door closed — but not before the rain started. Within seconds the wood floor was awash, the puddle spilling inwards, making the floor slick underfoot. She fell to her knees, keeping a grip on the handle of the door for support against the onslaught of the storm. The rain poured in, soaking her to the skin. She grabbed the trim around the doorframe and with herculean effort pushed the door the last few inches until there was a faint click. She gasped. Locking the door, and latching the bolts for extra security, she sucked in a shuddering breath before turning to watch as the sky above continued to darken and the wind became a continuous howl.

Her pupils dilated in fright as the hail started. Not all Hyperstorms had hail. Usually they were just ferocious winds and an abundance of torrential rain — things that The Fringe in New York had prepared the city for. But the Hyperstorms that had hail were deadly and destructive.

At first the hail was nothing more than stones the size of pebbles; she drew a breath of relief as the tiny stones pinged on the balcony, bouncing back up to hit the glass — small stones were just an inconvenience; they did little damage other than stinging one's body if you were unlucky enough to be caught outside when they started. She watched in fascination as the balcony became a sheet of white, glistening ice. But soon her relief turned to dread as she noticed them gaining in size — becoming the size of a fist before turning into stones the size of which she had never seen before and hadn't thought possible. She covered her ears to drown out the furious screech as the wind rattled the door, on its way past to rain terror down on whoever was left outside. She shook herself out of her stupor. She had to initiate emergency lockdown. She ran the length of the hall to Edward's office. An ocean of monitors, instrument panels and buttons confronted her. She hit the red button for Central Park first and prayed she was in time. She watched the monitors as the blast shields slowly slid into place above the park, protecting their food supply. Obviously Edward was not at his office, the meeting must be over, as surely someone would have already activated the shields if they were there.

Next she hit the Hyperstorm covers for the apartment and waited in terror for the storm to pass. She'd never felt more alone.

———·———

Dez was at the New York Cloud conducting a routine inspection. Since the close call with the freak hail storm last year, and then the destruction of Cloud III near Sector A, it had been decided that having the relays operate independently of each other was probably a good idea. Moving forward, if there were any unforeseen troubles in the future, they should now be able to salvage a portion of a Cloud structure and be able to work on individual rows without shutting down the entire operation. They were currently in the process of connecting individual circuits for each relay to the control panel. The engineers were gradually making headway with re-configuring the entire panel. It would take a few more weeks to complete but they were making good progress.

Dez was out in the field checking over the new configuration when a shiver ran up his back. He felt as if he were being watched. He turned but nobody was there. Then he heard it. Ducking out from beneath the panel he saw black-green clouds filling the horizon. He felt the first gust of wind catch at his breath as it sent spirals of dust eddying about his feet. Grimacing, he swore under his breath. The last thing they needed right now was a Hyperstorm. He studied the distant horizon — it was definitely coming this way. 'Damn,' he said aloud as he surveyed the Cloud site. Most of the panels were facing the sun, providing power to the condensers which emitted puffy white clouds into the sky, reflecting the suns warmth back into space, away from the troubled planet. But the effect of the wind turbines, which blew the clouds to certain locations, was suddenly rendered void as the gusts from the approaching storm took over.

'Crap,' he said angrily to the menacing storm. He was at the far end of the Cloud, away from the control room. He knew the other technicians would also be at the far end of the relays as they were all working their way in toward the control room from the farthest points. Scanning the area around him he couldn't see anyone else who was close enough to the control room to punch the buttons to spin the panels to the vertical position in case the storm brought hail with it.

He turned back to the looming clouds, building quickly, extinguishing the sunlight, their dark shadows blanketing the ground as they headed his way. 'Shit!' The oath was torn from his lungs by the strengthening wind. He sprinted for the control room knowing that a delay of a minute could be the difference between life and death. As he ran the length of the row of panels, his breathing coming in ragged gasps as the sudden force of the wind made it difficult to draw breath, the heavy rain started and quickly turned to icy pellets of hail. 'Damn, damn and damn! Not again!' he yelled in frustration. Yanking open the door of the control room, he hurled himself inside just as the hail turned into a pounding cascade of fist-sized stones. 'No!' he muttered in disbelief as he listened to the din of the massive stones hitting the roof of the shelter. 'No, no, no,' he yelled, the unfairness of life making him irate. Looking around frantically he found that there was no one else there. He cringed at the enslaught of sound and emitted another cry of despair. The guard should have already started turning the panels if they were to save The Cloud. Where could he have gone? Dez launched himself at the control panel and hit the first of the red emergency buttons, which would turn the panels to the vertical position and hopefully protect them from being pummeled by the massive hailstones. With the relays now being on separate circuits there were more buttons to hit and the process took longer than he liked — longer than he had. Yet it was only a matter of seconds to hit all nine buttons.

Time had come to a standstill and the few seconds felt like eternity. He punched the ninth button — the one that still controlled most of The Cloud. He glanced out the window. Nothing had happened. 'Damn.' It must have been disabled in favour of the manual override while they were working on reconfiguring the rows of panels. He turned to the instrument panel behind him and pulled the manual override lever before turning back to look out the open door. 'Oh, God, no!' he exclaimed. He could barely make out the shape of the panels in the gathering darkness. The newly configured rows were almost vertical but the majority of The Cloud had only just begun to move from the horizontal position when the hail turned from fist-sized stones to stones the size of his head. 'No...please...' his cry a mix of anger, frustration and utter, hopeless despair as he watched the horizontal surfaces submit to the destructive power of the oncoming hailstones.

He moved the few short steps to behind the open door and used all his strength to fight the door closed against the rising wind before hitting the manual override to bring down the protective shields outside. There was nothing more he could do and he didn't have Emi for comfort this time. He slid down the door, with knees bent he rested his head in his hands and listened as the enormous hailstones pummeled their last hope of existence into the ground.

———

Edward was walking across Central Park on his way home when the storm hit.

The breeze felt good after the stillness of the last month or so, even if the air was warm. He lifted his shirt to allow the wind access to his sweaty back. The leaves danced around his feet and swirled in front of his face. He plucked one from the air and threw it even higher overhead, happy to watch the ballet being played out before him, happy to be going home to Emi and his unborn child…his heir…leader of The Fringe and all of The Network. He grinned as he watched the leaves play about his head. He and his panel of experts had just finished the calculations for cooling the earth according to the new configuration of Cloud III. The projections were promising. They may still have time even with only half of Cloud III in operation. He couldn't wait to tell Emi. There was still time to save the world — and he and Emi would rule it together and one day pass it over to their son. The idiotic Blues hadn't got the best of him. When he got home they would celebrate…the best wine, a meal at The Top Floor, maybe a dance or two before returning home together.

He quickened his pace, anxious to see Emi and share his news. His grin split his face from ear to ear and his eyes gleamed in anticipation as the gust of wind picked up and a few drops of hail bounced off the path at his feet. He increased his pace, wanting to get beneath the trees in case the hail increased in size or intensity. Glancing over his shoulder he was snapped out of his pleasant reverie by the realization that the storm was gaining momentum. The clouds had turned greenish-black. He groaned, covering his eyes with his hand — a Hyperstorm. They seemed to come out of nowhere and struck with a ferocity that was terrifying. Furrowing his forehead he finally glanced around and noticed that everyone else had already disappeared. Instead of daydreaming they had run for cover. He was the only one in the park. 'Shit,' he exclaimed aloud. He started to run.

The hail turned from pebbles to fist-sized stones. He was nearing the trees when one hit him directly on the head, making him feel as if his head had been split in two. 'Damn,' he yelled in pain, raising his arms above his head to try and protect himself against the onslaught. A couple more hailstones slammed into his shoulders and a few smacked into the backs of his legs. The ground underneath his feet became an ice-rink — but not a smooth ice-rink but rather an uneven, rocky, moving ice-rink. He went down with a groan as another hailstone smashed into his forehead. Keeping his arms raised to protect his head he knew he only had moments to try to reach the safety of the trees and their overhanging canopy. They were only a few feet away. Sluggishly pushing himself to his feet he had barely started to take his first step when the fist-size stones suddenly tripled in size and were unleashed in a torrent from the angry sky. Just when he thought he was a dead man the blast shields that were built to protect the park in case of a Hyperstorm began to slowly close overhead. He looked up through the blood pouring into his eyes from his head wound, praising whoever had the sense to push the park-shield emergency button in time, as a massive hailstone slammed straight into his upturned face. He slumped unconscious to the ground beneath the trees as the blast shields closed over the park.

———————

Peter had just boarded his Hovercraft and was conducting safety checks. He was planning to take the last of the panels they had to the Cloud III site.

Sitting in his Hovercraft in the hangar, waiting for another pilot to return before he had clearance to leave, he scowled at his instrument panel. 'Crap, why didn't we get this fixed properly?' he exclaimed, pointlessly tapping at the screen that was his weather radar. He could get the wind speed and outside temperature but the rest of the gages remained inoperative. They hadn't managed to get the early weather warning buoys repaired since the last Hyperstorm had damaged them and he didn't like the feel in the atmosphere today. The excessive heat and stillness put him on edge. Tapping again at his instrument panel, knowing it would do no good, he lifted his gaze to the horizon. Still no sign of the other pilot. She was late. 'Damn, I'll run out of daylight before I unload the cargo at this rate!' Where was the incoming pilot? His gaze shifted to his left. Surely it couldn't be getting dark already? The hairs on the nape of his neck rose as he felt the Hovercraft shudder. What the hell! Glancing down at the instrument panel he noted that the wind speed had suddenly increased. Almost 60km per hour. Could that be right? He was not moving. The wind gusts were coming straight-on through the massive hangar doors. 'Damn, I can't go now, this isn't looking good,' he said to the empty Hovercraft. 'Bloody new pilots, always late.' He muttered then he paused and scrunched his forehead. *I hope she's okay out there in this. Did she have the sense to land somewhere out of harms way?* He'd wait to make sure she was okay — it had been her first solo flight. Unless he was scheduled for a flight himself, like today, he usually preferred to be on hand when his trainees returned.

Peter slowly pushed the control lever and rolled his Hovercraft into its customary parking spot in the hangar and turned off his instrument panel. Exiting the Hovercraft, he was pushed by the wind as he climbed the stairs to the observation deck. The thick glass partition that separated the observation deck from the hangar below was a godsend. He heaved a sigh of relief as the automatic door slid shut behind him.

Scanning the distant horizon he saw a black smudge of clouds in the blue sky and the lights of a Hovercraft highlighted before them. Damn, looked like it was going to be a pretty good storm. He hoped the new pilot could outrun it as he hated the thought of having to lower the blast doors before she got here if the storm picked up. The thought remained as the wind entering the hangar turned into a howl. Peter scowled and swore under his breath.

He watched the Hovercraft racing before the storm. It was as if he could read the pilot's thoughts. The need to stay ahead of the gathering doom, to outmaneuver it, to get back to the hangar and close the doors on the life-threatening Hyperstorm. The thought of landing and taking your chances waiting it out on the ground was

CHAPTER FIFTEEN

not a natural response. One wanted to flee, to escape. But did she have time? The black-green clouds, with what could only be sheets of hail cascading from them, were gaining in intensity, and quickly. He could have sworn it only took a moment before the Hyperstorm took over his senses. The temperature plummeted causing his skin to break out in goosebumps, his ears rang with the roar of the wind, and his pupils dilated with fear as all the light was sucked from the building. He watched in horror as the massive hailstones being driven before the storm by the gale force winds pummeled the approaching Hovercraft to the ground. There had been no moment in which the new recruit could have escaped. His stomach contracted as he witnessed her plummet to her firey death as the Hovercraft exploded. He blinked, hardly believing the suddenness of the events unfolding before him. The wind entering the hangar turned into a screech, the like of which he had never heard before. He looked down at his remote and pushed the button to close the hangar doors. Then he pushed the red emergency button for the blast shields.

He waited in the cacophony of noise, as the Category 10 Hyperstorm, the worst to ever hit New York, unleashed its fury on the city and the surrounding area.

# CHAPTER SIXTEEN

T hree days later the storm clouds cleared and the landscape became dazzlingly white. The sun's rays reflected off the icy sheet of hailstones.

As Peter retracted the blast shields he squinted, raising his hand to cover his eyes as the hangar filled with the intense, bright light of the wintery landscape. He headed for the office to retrieve his sunglasses before returning to the observation deck to stare out at the new world. It was blue and white and blinding.

His gaze travelled to where the New York Cloud usually emitted its puffy white clouds into the endless blue sky. There were no clouds today — he hoped it meant that somebody had managed to turn the panels in time and shut down the operation and not that it was damaged by the hailstones. The loss of another Cloud would surely spell their doom.

Off to his left he could see the buildings of the city reaching for the sky. They seemed dark and menacing against the stark white landscape. He grimaced, knowing he would not be able to get back into the city for a while yet — not until the ice melted — he couldn't risk trying to land a Hovercraft on a roof. He prayed Elizabeth was safe and had been indoors when the storm hit.

He tried his Satcomm and managed to get a signal.

Elizabeth answered, 'Hello.'

'Oh, thank God you're okay.'

'Peter. I was so terrified. I had no idea where you were...if you had left yet. I...I saw a Hovercraft go down...exploded.'

'Sorry, I couldn't get the Satcomm to work before now. I'm at the hangar. The Hovercraft was the new pilot, on her way back...I watched as well.'

'Oh God. Poor girl. But the Hyperstorm, it was so sudden. I'm sure we'll hear of more deaths before this day is out. I'd just left the meeting at Edward's office. Barely made it home before the storm hit. Never been so thankful to live so close to the office. I hope the others found shelter because I don't think some of them would have made it all the way home...' Elizabeth trailed off, not wanting to think about what they might have to face over the next few days as the ice melted.

'I'm going to try flying out to the Cloud, see if anyone needs help and if everything is okay. I can't fly into the city yet. Landing on a roof would be impossible. I'm hoping I can land near the Cloud... if I can get out of here that is. I'll be home as soon as I can but it'll probably depend on what I find when I get there.'

'Yes, okay. Stay safe. I love you.'

'I love you too,' said Peter as he hung up and headed for his Hovercraft.

It was going to be a tricky business to get out of the hangar. With the blanket of ice hard up against the doors it meant that he would not be able to roll out to the launch pad. He hit the button to open the hangar doors and watched as they rolled out of the way. A groan escaped his lips as he took in the space he had. The ice was at least three feet deep — worse than he'd been expecting. Damn. But waiting for it to melt was not an option. The devastation must be horrific and he was sure to be needed. He should still be able to clear the doors if he raised the Hovercraft a few feet into the air before heading outside — but there wasn't much room for error. Thank God the doors were immense — they had to be at least four times the height of the hovercraft. He's flown in tighter spaces.

He took a big breath to steady his nerves and pressed his thumb against the scanner to activate his control panel. The lights came on and the engine hummed. Pushing the lever he rolled the Hovercraft forward before coming to a stop in front of the thick carpet of ice. Keeping his eyes glued to the screen, he gently raised the Hovercraft into the air a few feet and then pushed the lever forward once more to head out into the featureless landscape. He held his breath as he manoeuvered between the ice sheet and the top of the door. One miniscule motion of his wrist too far up or down at the wrong moment and he would also end as a firery explosion. He kept his eyes fixed to the screen, unblinking, as he passed through the open doors. Exhaling loudly he escaped into the blinding daylight.

Flying toward the Cloud, the landscape below seemed like a barren wasteland. It was as if all the colours had been sucked from the world — the only one that remained was blue, the blue of the sky and the blue of the ocean. Everything else was a glittering, deadly white.

As he neared the Cloud it appeared to have shrunk in size. A few rows petruded from the ice in their vertical position — obviously someone had managed to initiate the emergency shutdown — but the rest of the Cloud seemed to be missing. As he gazed at the ground below it slowly dawned on him that the rest of the panels must be buried under the destructive sheet of ice, not even their remnants were visible.

Whoever had tried to save the Cloud had failed.

Peter felt sick to his stomach as he lowered the Hovercraft, grabbed up his emergency supply kit and went to see what, or who, he could find.

Dez opened the door to find Peter crouched before him. There was at least four feet of hailstones blown up against the door and congealed into a solid icy wall. Peter, perched on top of the ice, slithered his way into the control room between the glittering blanket and the top of the doorframe.

'Peter! I didn't think anyone would be able to get out here so soon,' exclaimed Dez in disbelief.

'It was a bit dicey, I must admit. Trying to get out of the hangar was near impossible and then trying to walk across the bloody ice to get to here…I must have wiped out at least twenty times between the Hovercraft and here,' he said rubbing his backside.

'I'm the only one…the only one who made it to safety. I don't know where the guard went. I tried to turn the panels but then…,' Dez trailed off, unable to finish his explanation. His shoulders slumped and he ran his hand across his face, trying to dispell the exhaustion. He had dark circles under his eyes and his hair stood on end as if he had been gripping it in his fists.

'I see that. A few rows remain standing, but the rest…it's like it never existed. Completely buried beneath the blanket of white.'

'That's it then. With Cloud III only partially operational and this one destroyed…we don't stand a chance.'

Peter stared at Dez, shaking his head. He was a bit surprised Dez could be so calm after he had just spent the last few years of his life overseeing the building The Cloud, and had volunteered all of his people to help with the task. But he suspected Dez was probably too drained at this point to have any energy to spare for emotions. 'No, it seems unlikely at best. So now what?'

Dez ran his hand through his hair and looked around. 'I don't know exactly but can you give me a few hours?'

'Sure, I'm in no hurry. What are you thinking?'

'I need to double check that the control panel is working and reboot the power for the individual rows. I'll also need to make sure that the few rows remaining can operate with most of The Cloud beneath a blanket of ice. They are meant to…I mean that is what we were working on…but the work wasn't complete yet and…and we weren't expecting a storm of that magnitude. There are spare parts in the storeroom. I should be able to at least get the relays that are still intact functional…I hope. Our survival is hanging by a thread and if these few rows are that thread then I have to try.' Dez exhaled loudly. 'I feel as if I am re-living my life…or a nightmare. Deja-vu. How could we have not had better foresight…better emergency backup? The main shutdown didn't work. I don't know… was it offline because of the engineers reconfiguring the panels or did it freeze…and by the time I turned to the manual override…it was moments too late.' Dez shrugged and ran his hand through his already tousled hair.

'I don't know. But our backups to the system certainly failed and catastrophically by the looks of it out there,' Peter said, not trying to sugarcoat the truth. 'Come on, I'll give you a hand.'

Dez nodded his thanks and went to get the parts he thought he might need from the storeroom. He and Peter worked for hours in the cold, concrete room checking over every inch of the control panel and fixing connections. Finally, Dez thought they had repaired enough that the few remaining relays would work even if the rest of The Cloud was buried beneath the ice. He tried turning them on one at a time and then stood at the open doorway with Peter, peering overtop of the wall of ice, waiting to see if the panels would turn to face the sun.

They heard a hum and waited with baited breath to see if the panels could turn or whether they were also damaged beyond repair.

Slowly, they came online and returned to their horizontal position. 'Woohoo,' exclaimed Dez, slapping hands in a high-five with Peter, thankful for the small victory. 'Can you fly me back to Sector A?' asked Dez.

'Sure, there's nothing else we can do here for the moment,' agreed Peter. 'But be prepared for a treacherous walk back to the Hovercraft,' he added, his lips twitching up on one side.

———————

As they left the New York Cloud behind and flew southwest the ice field gradually lessened until they reached the outer limit of the storm's reach. The landscape slowly changed from blinding white to the endless sea of tall yellow grasslands they were accustomed to. Eventually they reached the green valley of Sector A and were happy to note that the repaired half of Cloud III was still functioning, emitting its puffy white clouds into the atmosphere, casting cooling shadows across the ground below.

Somehow, irrational though it was, Dez had envisioned the Hyperstorm wiping out Cloud III as well. The knots in his stomach lessened as he watched the white masses drift across the serene blue sky. His spirits lifted. The Fringe had been so ingenious to invent such a thing in the first place that one Hyperstorm could not possibly destroy all their efforts. The Cloud structures could put out great, billowing amounts of cloud when at full capacity that surely they could increase the output of the others to make up for the one in New York now buried beneath the ice.

'Where do you want me to set her down?' asked Peter.

'I need to see Abe, so maybe in the village green,' suggested Dez. 'Care to join me? I could use the help,' he added.

Peter raised his eyebrow but refrained from asking questions and nodded his head in agreement. Landing the Hovercraft, he followed Dez to Abe's place.

'Peter, Dez, come on in,' said Abe, opening the door for them to enter. 'What are you doing here?' asked Abe, looking at Dez, his forehead furrowed in surprise at seeing the two of them on his doorstep. 'I thought you were working on the New York Cloud and then going on the city to try and see Emi.'

'There's been a Hyperstorm,' stated Dez bluntly. 'It's destroyed.'

'What's destroyed?'

'The New York Cloud. Hail the size of my head. I managed to save the first few rows but I didn't get to the manual override to turn most of The Cloud before the hailstones were immense. The rest is under a sheet of ice.'

Abe stared from one to the other his face registering his horror at such unwelcome news. 'Hail. The size of your head,' he parroted in stunned disbelief as he gestured for them to sit around his kitchen table.

'Never seen anything like it.'

'We should never have built a Cloud so close to New York,' stated Peter, collapsing into a chair. 'But the storms didn't used to be so intense and we thought it would save us time being close to the factory. We were wrong. Didn't forsee the weather patterns shifting again. It was a mistake,' he said, shaking his head at their folly.

'It would have been fine...well, maybe not fine, but at least salvagable...if I could have turned the panels. But it's too late now to dwell on the 'what-ifs',' countered Dez.

'True,' agreed Peter. 'I've never witnessed a Hyperstorm of that intensity before. They're getting worse,' he said, looking grim.

'So, can we salvage anything?' asked Abe, looking from one to the other.

'In New York…no,' said Dez emphatically, shaking his head. 'But Jax told me of some panels he hid. I haven't mentioned it to you before because…well, he took a lot of blows to the head and I thought he might be…muddled up, thinking of the ones we had kept in the storehouses in case of emergency. He said there's a room…hidden at the back of the storehouses…camouflauged. I've tried looking… haven't asked for help until now as I didn't want to get anyone's hopes up. But the Hyperstorm has changed things. If there's a room, and more panels, we need to find them and increase the capacity of Cloud III to its maximum potential…depending on how many panels Jax has hidden.' Dez stopped talking as his gaze rested on his dumbfounded audience.

'Are you serious?'

'Yep. I know. I had the same reaction when Jax told me. Wasn't sure if he was serious or just confused from the beating he took. Either way, I need help to look. If there's a room, it's *very* well concealed. Maybe there isn't one, but we at least need to rule out the possibility.'

'I don't see how he could move those panels without help. They're not light,' stated Abe doubtfully.

'He might have had help. I don't know.'

'I still don't see how there could be a secret room and more panels without anyone knowing about it. Sounds more like he was… delusional.'

'That's what I thought. But given our new circumstances…I need to be sure.'

'Alright. There's no harm in looking and no time like the present. Let's go,' said Abe.

'Where are you going?' asked Fie, as her and Lea poked their heads into the room.

Abe looked at Dez, unsure of what to tell them.

Dez turned his head toward the girls, his mind racing — maybe a child's mind, a mind that liked to build forts and hidey-holes, that liked to play hide and seek, would think to look for things that they missed. 'We're going to look for a secret room. Do you want to come and help us?' asked Dez.

The girls nodded their heads enthusiastically. Abe left the baby with his neighbour and then they headed off to the storehouse.

Abe pushed aside the vines that hid the storehouse from prying eyes. Jax had the storehouse built and camouflaged so that if they were raided by The Blues at least they would still have a back-up supply of basic foodstuffs until they could get on their feet again.

'Jax did this?' asked Peter, incredulously.

'He did, yes,' answered Dez with a smile. 'He was very proud of it.'

'I would imagine,' said Peter, taking in the vast cave that had been converted to a room full of shelves with various foods and necessities stored within. It was amazingly dry and relatively cool, a perfect place to store food. The entrance, hidden behind trees and an over-hanging canopy of vines would have gone unnoticed unless you were purposefully looking for it.

'So much food,' said Lea in astonishment, her eyes like saucers.

Dez's lips twitched up as he looked at Lea. 'Yes, neither Jax nor I ever wanted to watch anyone else die from starvation after The Blues took all our food.'

Lea nodded in understanding.

'And Jax said there is another room hidden within this one?' asked Peter, looking around.

'Apparently.'

'Jax would want the extra assurance that he'd done all he could to ensure The Blues never got all our food again, even if they found this first room,' said Abe. Turning to Peter he elaborated, 'Jax's parents were killed by The Blues. He and his three siblings survived. Jax was the youngest but the best at scavening and hunting. He tried to help but could never get enough food and watched them all die slowly from starvation. When we found this valley his goal was to make sure we always saved some food, stored it, hid it. I think the hidden room is his back up plan of his back up plan.'

'But why wouldn't he tell anyone about it?' asked Peter.

'I don't know,' replied Dez, running his hand through his hair. 'I really don't. But, in the end, he did hold on to life until he could tell me, which was miraculous given the state he was in. Shall we spread out and start the search?'

They made their way further into the massive cave, the filtered light coming through the vines giving the cave an eerie green glow. The torches they held cast shadows, the beams of brightness in the surrounding dimness causing their silhouettes to walk in strange patterns along the rough floor.

Dez held his light up to the rockface, which was the rear wall of the storehouse. The ceiling of the storehouse was lower back here, only just above his head, as the rock curved down to end in the undulating wall at the back. Running his hand over the surface, above the shelves, he felt a bit foolish. It was solid rock and nothing more — maybe he had misunderstood Jax. He wished he had continued to look on his own rather than gathering others to help. He didn't know what he was looking for, but as he continued to run his hand along the rock surface he was certain he was not finding it.

He came to the end of the rock, to where it met the timber wall that Jax had built out of trees and branches. He had planted live vines and bushes in front of the wall to disguise it from the outside. Lea and Fie were poking around in the corner.

'This reminds me of building forts in the forest when I was a kid,' said Dez to the girls.

Lea looking up at Dez, a smile lighting her face in the glow of the torches, she whispered, 'I think we found something.'

'What? Really?'

'Here, see. The rock, it carries on. We think you can push these branches and vines aside and get through to the other side…but they're too heavy…can you try?'

Dez looked at the girls, astounded. Of course the rock carried on — why hadn't he realized? He pulled at the vines, the girls holding them to one side as he surveyed the wall of branches.

'Look there, see, that branch, it goes across the others, like a latch, pull on it, see what happens,' said Lea excitedly.

Dez looked down at the branch that Lea was pointing to. Pulling on one side, away from the rock, the branch slid back and the wall of branches sprang open, revealing itself to be a door, an opening into the cave beyond.

'We did it, we found it,' said Lea and Fie together, their excitement bubbling over.

Dez grinned at the girls. 'Glad I brought you two along…I would have never found this on my own.'

'We found it, we found it,' Lea called to Abe and Peter.

They pushed open the door and entered into the room on the other side. The cave went much further back into the hillside. It was impossible to see the scale of it in the darkness. Holding their torches high, the area immediately in front of them was illuminated and there before them were the spare panels for The Cloud.

'There's enough here for another few rows…at least…maybe more. We could get most of Cloud III operational again,' said Dez in awe.

'How did Jax manage to store so many? Surely they would have been accounted for?' asked Peter.

'I wish I knew. He helped with unloading quite often. The only thing I can figure is that he reported panels as damaged in transport and put in orders for more, doubling up without anyone the wiser,' said Dez, thinking out loud.

'But how did he get them here without anyone knowing? He must have had help. It would be a long way to pull one of the trolleys that the panels are moved in,' said Abe.

'Whoever it was kept pretty quiet about it,' observed Dez. 'We may never know.'

'I have the feeling it might have been Chi,' said Abe, with a catch in his throat. 'So you're right…we'll probably never know.'

'This might just be our salvation,' said Dez. 'Good job girls,' he added, ruffling their red hair. He hoped it would be enough. He squashed his lingering doubts, knowing they needed a miracle to survive now that both the New York Cloud and Cloud III were only partially operational.

'And it will restore the shade and rain we need to grow our crops,' added Abe, looking down at the girls upturned faces.

Dez had to smile. Knowing Abe he was probably more thrilled with being able to cultivate the vegetables the girls had planted than with the thought that they might now still have a slight chance of saving the planet.

'I guess the next task is how to get them out of here and over to The Cloud,' said Dez, running his hands through his hair as he voiced his thoughts aloud. 'I really wish I knew how Jax got them in here. It's probably something ingenious and would come in very handy right about now.'

'Unfortunately the Hovercraft won't be of any use, there is no place nearby to land. The village green is about as close as I can get,' said Peter.

'Abe, what's this?' called Lea, who had wandered further into the darkness. 'It looks like a Hover…something.'

Dez looked at Abe, eyebrows arched. Of course Jax would have hidden his mode of transport as well.

'Oh, can I have a ride…please,' exclaimed Fie in excitement as her gaze took in what could only be described as a Hover-wagon.

Abe grinned down at her. 'I'm sure that can be arranged after all your help,' he said affectionately. 'How about we get it out of here first and see how it works.'

They pulled the contraption out into the daylight and stood looking at it. One of the trolleys used for transporting Cloud panels had been strapped to a series of Hoverboards that had been joined together. There were platforms at the front and back of the trolley so that two people could stand and hold on to the panel as they manouvered the Hoverboards over the ground. The handle of the trolley looked like it could be used to pull the whole contraption over the ground on its wheels or be used to help steer if Hovering. The panels were longer than they were wide, so if they were placed lengthwise the Hoverwagon would not be top heavy.

'Jax really outdid himself this time,' said Dez in admiration.

'It must have taken a bit of practice to master hovering together with a panel to hold on to,' said Abe, shaking his head.

'Can I have a ride? Can I have a ride?' asked Fie, jumping up and down and tugging on Abe's shirt. 'Please.'

Dez grinned down at her indulgently. 'I think Abe and I will try it out without any cargo first and then you two can be our first passengers,' he replied, winking at Abe.

# CHAPTER SEVENTEEN

E mi hit the button to raise the shields over the windows. Outside the balcony was covered in a two-foot thick solid block of ice. The top glistened as the sun's warmth began to melt the mass of hail-stones. The surrounding rooftops were covered in smashed green-houses and decimated plants where people had not been able to get to their emergency shields in time.

Looking down, at street level, she could see fragments of build-ings, branches and a few broken bodies scattered randomly across the white, icy blanket. The shields were still over Central Park. Thank goodness she had got to the emergency shutdown in time. To lose the food supplied by the park would make life in New York infinitely more difficult for everyone. She couldn't retract the shields yet, not until the ice had melted off of them. As the sun rose to its zenith in the endless blue sky the glistening hailstones became blinding. Emi turned away from the window, unable to look into the glare and not wanting to contemplate the number of bodies scattered below. Any-body caught in that storm would not have had a hope of surviving.

Her thoughts turned to those who had been at the meeting at Edward's office — Edward, Charlotte, Elizabeth and all the engi-neers. Had the meeting still been in progress when the storm hit or had they been on their way home? She picked up the Satcomm, breathing a sigh of relief as it was now working again…Hyperstorms always interfered with the signal making it impossible to use when in an emergency and most needed. She tried to get through to Edward's office but there was no answer. Next she tried Charlotte's apartment.

'Hello.'

'Charlotte. You're okay.'

'Emi. Yes, I just made it home in time. Never been so terrified. I had no idea Hyperstorms could get like that. I mean we usually don't get anything too intense here. That was…that was like all the demons from hell unleashed. I've never been in anything like it.'

'No. Me neither. The destruction. Looking out my window is unbelievable. There are…bodies…down on the street. And the debris. And the greenhouses — all smashed — people's food.' She paused and took a breath. ' And the glare — it's blinding out there. I can't tell you how thankful I am that I was home. But what about the others at the meeting — had they left?'

'Yes, we all left at about the same time. Why?' Charlotte paused and then on an intake of breath she asked, 'Edward…he didn't make it back yet?'

'No. He's not here.'

'Oh God. That's not good. Maybe he knew he wouldn't make it home and found shelter somewhere close by.'

'Yeah. He wouldn't be able to make it back yet anyway. Until the ice melts it would be lethal to try walking out there.'

'It shouldn't take too long. It looks like the sun is already back to scorching and the drains will soon take the water away. I'm sure he's fine.'

'I'll let you know if I hear anything. I better go in case he's trying to get through.'

Emi hung up and waited. There was nothing she could do until the streets were free from the ice. She wondered what the end result of the Hyperstorm would be. Did she want Edward to return to her and be okay? If he was the person who had orchestrated the attacks then the world was better off without him. But if it wasn't him, if he was just a powerful man, who felt the need to maintain control to ensure the survival of the planet and the human race — a man who loved her — then she could not wish him dead even though she desperately wanted to be with Dez.

---

The ice melted and the water dissipated. All the Hyperstorm shields had been retracted and people were venturing out to start the unwelcome job of cleaning up the city.

The first task was identifying and then burning all the bodies of those caught out in the storm. Fortunately the deaths were not as numerous as expected as most had managed to find shelter once the initial blast of hail had started.

The removal of the debris would take longer. Rooftop greenhouses were smashed; plants and trees had been ripped out of the ground by the wind or decimated by the icy cold hailstones; segments of buildings had been torn off and scattered all over the city, and many areas were a saturated, muddy mess. The sea-wall had withstood the pounding high tides, but many areas close to the ocean had been lashed by the massive waves. It had been the worst Hyperstorm ever recorded in the vicinity of New York. Hyperstorms were a rarity in the area and the fact that it had been so sudden and so devastating was not a good sign. The planet would not be able to sustain life for very much longer.

Emi met Charlotte outside her apartment building.

'What a mess,' she stated, staring around at the dripping buildings and the steaming streets littered with every object imaginable — anything that had not been securely fastened down.

'I hope this is not the beginning of a new era.' Charlotte's eyes were shadowed with misery.

Emi glanced sideways at Charlotte, her eyebrows drawing down in concern. 'No, it would be impossible to live here if Hyperstorms became a regular occurrence.'

'They used to not reach us. New York was too far north…but it seems like the weather patterns are changing again…and becoming more severe.'

'If The Cloud structures don't start making a difference soon it seems like we won't have anywhere left to go.'

'No, I don't suppose we will,' agreed Charlotte, moving a tree branch from her path. 'So, what's the plan? Where do you want to look for Edward?' asked Charlotte, abruptly changing the subject and concentrating on the task at hand. 'It's not good that he hasn't contacted you yet.'

'No, I know. We should head to the office, cutting through Central Park. It's the shortest route,' suggested Emi. 'Maybe he's just helping out somewhere and is immersed in what he's doing. Although it really is strange that he hasn't called. But I managed to get the shields over the park so if he was walking home that way at the time then he should be okay.'

They made their way down the street toward the park, picking their way over branches, broken tables and chairs from outdoor cafes, children's toys blown out of back gardens, felled trees and numerous unidentifiable objects. They stopped at each body they came across, making sure that the person was not still living and needing help, and was not Edward. It was a grisly walk. Emy pulled her headband that was meant to keep the sweat from her eyes, down over her mouth and nose to stop herself from gagging.

They headed into the park, taking the most logical, direct path toward Edward's office. Emi breathed a sigh of relief as the park was in great shape compared to the surrounding streets. Thank goodness she'd managed to raise the protective sheilds before the massive hailstones had started. The trees still stood, providing shade as well as food as they had not been stripped bare by the winds. The surrounding landscape of herbs and vegetation was almost undisturbed. The strength of the sheilds and the protection they offered was nothing short of miraculous. Emi returned her headband to her forehead and inhaled deeply — the heady aroma of the prolific herbs of Central Park was a welcome relief.

'I hope Edward was here somewhere. It looks like there's hardly been a storm. But where could he possibly be that he hasn't managed to get home or even get in touch. I don't like it,' said Charlotte, scanning left and right. 'Did you know we'd run the calculations again. It looked like The Cloud might still have the capacity to alter the atmosphere in time, even with Cloud III damaged...as long as the repairs go according to plan. Edward was so happy to be going home to share the news with you. He was thrilled. I hadn't seen him that happy in quite some time.'

'Really! That's the best news I've had in a while. What a relief. I was struggling to come to terms with the idea that this would be the last generation,' Emi said, rubbing her hand across her rounded stomach. 'I couldn't reconcile myself to the kind of conditions that he, or she, would have to live with. It's almost impossible to imagine things being any worse...' Emi trailed off as she realized that Charlotte had stopped dead in her tracks.

Charlotte stood as if turned to stone; her hand covering her mouth, her eyes wide with horror. 'Oh God,' she moaned, turning onto the intersecting path and beginning to run.

Emi's eyes followed her, finally coming to rest on the heap on the ground that Charlotte had almost reached. She recognized the shirt. Gagging, hand to her mouth, she stumbled after Charlotte until she reached the still form lying on the ground. Lowering her eyelids, bringing her hand to her eyes to shut out the sight, she turned, gasping in lungsful of air until she could bring herself to look back at Edward. She didn't love Edward, but she didn't wish this on him. She hadn't closed the shields in time. He must have been looking up when the hailstone hit. His face was barely recognizable. He was covered in blood.

'Is he…is he alive?' she whispered.

Charlotte put her ear to his chest. 'He's still breathing and I'm getting a heartbeat…but it's weak and his breathing seems shallow.'

'I'll get Matthew,' said Emi as she turned and ran through the park in the direction of Matthew's apartment.

---

Matthew had brought the collapsible stretcher he kept at his place in case of emergencies. They managed to load Edward onto the stretcher and, using the hover mechanism, they gently elevated him off the ground and headed to the hospital.

Charlotte and Emi sat in the waiting room as Matthew took Edward to emergency to examine him. Time stood still. Emi could think of nothing to say as her mind flitted from Edward, to wondering what Dez was doing and then to how they were ever supposed to save the planet when they seemed to have one disasterous problem after another.

Finally, Matthew emerged looking grim.

'He took some blows to his legs, which are minor, and some to his torso, one of which has cracked his collarbone. There's no easy way to say this next part but he's had multiple blows to the head. He must have been hit several times by the fist size hail before taking a direct hit to the face by one of the largest stones,' he paused, before taking a deep breath and adding, 'His skull is fractured, putting pressure on the brain. The fluid buildup has also caused swelling in the brain. I'm not sure if there is permanent brain damage or not at this point. Time will tell.'

'Can you do anything for him?'

'I've hooked him up to life support…in case he forgets to breathe, or his heart forgets to pump…but I can't operate until he is in a more stable condition.'

'So, we just have to wait?'

'I'm afraid so.'

'For how long?'

'I really don't know and I don't want to guess. But he is strong and determined. He loves you,' Matthew said, looking directly into Emi's eyes, 'and he is dedicated to saving the planet…two things that keep him anchored to this world. The fact that he survived laying on the ground in that condition while the storm raged is a miracle in itself.'

Emi nodded. Matthew seemed a long way away, as if he was talking to her from the end of a tunnel. The waiting room wavered, shrinking from view and then becoming overly bright. She closed her eyes and took a deep breath. 'Thanks, Matthew,' she managed to utter as she opened her eyes, focusing on his face. She took another steadying breath and turned to go, Charlotte following after her. Her thoughts were in turmoil. Life was full of twists and turns. Even if they managed to save the planet, life was so fragile; things could change in an instant.

As Charlotte and Emi emerged from the hospital the heat hit them like a blast of steam from a kettle. During the few hours of waiting in the hospital things had changed drastically outside. The harsh sunlight beating down on the dripping city had turned the melting ice to water vapour. The air was thick, stifling. Within seconds Emi's clothes were glued to her body and she was dripping with sweat.

'Uhgg,' said Charlotte, wiping the perspiration from her forehead, 'I feel like I can't breathe in properly.'

'This is worse than dry heat,' agreed Emi, pulling at her sweat-drenched shirt. 'I don't see how we'll ever survive these kind of conditions. Even with the reconditioned soil, the organic seeds, and the seaweed cleaning the oceans, we still need cooler temperatures for most crops to thrive.'

'The Cloud should have made more of a difference by now.'

'Do you think that Cloud III being out of commission and now only partially functional has slowed the outcome more than expected?'

'I don't know. I know the calculations were very precise. The tipping point between working and not working was a very fine line. Edward seemed to think it was still going to be okay. Maybe the rest of the world is doing better. Maybe the Hyperstorm was just a one-off and won't happen again. Who knows?' said Charlotte, rambling, thinking her thoughts out loud, not really having an answer.

'Yes, who knows,' agreed Emi but she was not convinced.

———✦———

Emi returned to the apartment, changed out of her saturated clothes and put her feet up, her hand resting protectively on her stomach. The stifling humidity had taken it out of her and she felt slightly ill. It seemed strange to be living in Edward's apartment now that he was not around. The place was too opulent for her, not comfortable. When she thought that Dez was dead and had agreed to marry Edward, it seemed the only way to protect her people and her baby. She'd regretted the decision every moment since she'd made it. It had been made in desperation with no time to consider. Now she must stop and think. So much had changed. She needed to find a way forward. She didn't want to live the rest of her life in regret. But she could not abandon Edward in his current state.

How had life gotten so complicated?

She was pregnant with Dez's baby. Dez had survived and still wanted to be with her even though she'd abandoned him. Edward thought the baby was his but he was now injured and may or may not recover. Cloud III was still only partially functional which meant that they all may or may not survive. Edward might be the person responsible for the destruction of Cloud III but the only evidence was some Blue saying that Dez looked like the guy who had given a tip off about something…and that evidence was from when Dez had been injured and who knows in what kind of shape mentally. If Edward survived what kind of shape would he be in? And if he survived and she left him to be with Dez would Dez's life be in danger…was Edward capable of killing others to get his own way? Why would she even think such a thing?

With her thoughts spinning out of control she knew that the only way forward for her, and possibly for the world at large, was to know with certainty what kind of man Edward was. She swung her feet to the floor. There had to be some kind of a clue here somewhere. Second-guessing and chasing red-herrings was not going to get her any of the answers she needed. Because if it wasn't Edward who was behind the attacks then they still needed to know who was.

Or had The Blues attacked just because they were Blues — they were violent and aggressive and destroying things and killing people is what they did.

———

Peter was sitting at her kitchen counter while she made them tea. 'You haven't changed the place much,' he commented, observing the opulent but very masculine apartment. 'I thought you might have added a touch of your own by now,' he added as he took the tea from her.

Emi smiled. 'No, I still think of it as Edward's place. And with everything else that's been happening I just haven't felt very bothered,' she shrugged her shoulders, looking around at the now familiar, well organized, gleaming kitchen that was open to the living room and the view of the city beyond.

'Yeah, I can imagine,' agreed Peter. He took a big breath before getting to what he had come to see her about. 'Charlotte just informed me that Edward was injured in the Hyperstorm.'

'Yes, he's on life support at the hospital. He was coming home through the park when a massive hailstone hit him directly on the head. I…I didn't get the shields closed in time. It's too early to tell if he'll be okay or not.' Emi choked and cleared her throat.

'Life seems as if it's one disaster after another lately,' commented Peter, 'but it's not your fault you know. You were the first one to hit the emergency lock-down…you got to it faster than anyone else who had access. And the storm was very sudden,' said Peter, offering what little comfort he could. 'And it was the worst storm I've ever encountered.'

'It did take me by surprise…the suddeness and the ferocity. I was alone here. It was terrifying.'

'I hate to be the bearer of more bad news but…have you heard that The Cloud was damaged?'

'Cloud III…I thought it was getting repaired.'

'No, not Cloud III. The New York Cloud. The control panel… they were working on it…reconfiguring the rows. The manual override had to be used and…Dez couldn't turn the panels in time. Most of it was smashed by the hail.'

'But…but there are still clouds on the horizon…ones from The Cloud.'

'Yes, we managed to get part of it functioning, but most of it is completely destroyed.'

'So, that's it then. There's no hope of survival,' said Emi, her voice filled with despair as the realization dawned that the Hyperstorm had spelled their doom. The massive hailstones had literally destroyed their last chance. With two of the Cloud structures only partially functional there was no room for hope.

'There's still some hope,' said Peter, sensing where the logical line of reasoning would take her thoughts.

'There is?'

'Yes. We found more panels. Jax had them stored…hidden. We're planning on bringing more…if not all…of Cloud III online. I've come back to get some parts and a couple of the engineers. But I was also hoping to take you out to Sector A with me. Abe, he's adopted a little Blue baby and he wants her to have the vaccine. I thought you could come with me to administer it.'

There was silence.

'Emi?'

Emi felt too stunned to respond to the last part of Peter's hurried speech, but at last she gasped, 'Abe has a Blue baby. But they killed his entire family. I can't believe he would want to raise…a Blue.'

'I guess he figures this little girl hasn't done anything wrong and he's hoping the vaccine will cure her of most of her hereditary genetic imprints before they cause her permanent mental problems.'

'How did Abe come to have a Blue baby?'

'It's a long story. I'll tell you on the trip out to Sector A.'

'Yes, alright. I'll pick up some vaccine from Matthew and meet you at the hangar. We have a lot to catch up on obviously.'

———

As the Hovercraft left the hangar Emi and Peter and the engineers flew out across the end of New York City. The tops of the tall buildings peeked out above the veil of white — steam billowed and rolled along the streets, caught between the skyscrapers. Some of Central Park showed through as a green expanse where light breezes shifted the sultry air.

'How are we to live like this Peter? Our apartment is on the seventieth floor, so it is almost bearable, but at ground level the conditions are impossible,' said Emi, her face plastered against the window watching the continuously shifting landscape below.

'I don't know. I really don't.'

'Do you think the Cloud structures have caused weather patterns to shift…sending more Hyperstorms our way?'

Peter glanced at Emi out of the corner of his eye. 'I don't think so,' he said hesitantly. 'I sure hope not. Weather patterns were part of the calculations. Maybe with Cloud III being damaged it has thrown things off but it's more likely to be from the continuous worsening of our planets atmoshpere that has been going on for the last few hundred years. The Cloud structures haven't been operational long enough yet to make enough of a difference on a global scale. Factor 10 Hyperstorms were sure to happen at some point…I had just hoped that point would have been later…and that we would have had time to change things so that they never happened.' Peter trailed off. He sighed and, trying for a more optimistic note, said, 'Still, the sauna-like conditions shouldn't last too long.'

'No, but if we get more Hyperstorms these conditions will be unlivable.'

'True but hopefully they will be infrequent at best and now that we know how severe they are we can be better prepared for…the…next…one.' His voice was husky with distress. He shook his head, his mouth a pinched line. 'We'll have to wait and see, I guess.'

'But with the New York Cloud damaged as well…' Emi gasped and trailed off as they neared the site, giving her her first glimpse of the devastation. 'Look at that. There's almost nothing left,' she whispered as they flew directly over the New York Cloud. Only a few rows were intact, pushing their harmless white clouds into the sky around them. Everything else had been smashed into a million pieces and scattered across the landscape by the ferocious winds. Emi could see that even the superstructure was a mangled wreck in parts where the weight and the continuous pounding of the massive hailstones had crushed the metal as if it was made out of nothing more than tissue.

'So long to build and so quickly destoyed,' said Emi.

'At least part of it is functioning. Depending on how many extra panels were stored, and how much of Cloud III we can restore, all may not yet be lost,' commented one of the engineers.

'But life in New York will definitely be more challenging until the Cloud structures have an overall effect and lower the earth's temperature. With two only partially operational it will all take longer than planned. The next few years will not be easy,' stated the other engineer, not believing in sugar-coating the truth.

Emi glanced at them and nodded her head. She had the feeling her life was going to be one tough choice after another and the choices she made would no longer effect only her.

'And what of this Blue baby, Peter?' asked Emi, wanting to change the subject.

Peter filled her in on what had happened.

'You…you annihilated an entire city?' questionned Emi, when he came to the end of his monologue.

Peter nodded as he glanced sideways at her, his expression grim.

'But…I thought just a small group had been killed…as a warning,' stated Emi, feeling confused and foolish for being duped so easily.

'I wish it were so. But no, it was an entire city. Edward's orders. We had little choice. The Blues will no longer be a concern in the region.'

'Couldn't we have tried talking to them first? Killing them makes us little better than them,' she vented, anger causing her eyes to glint dangerously. She did not appreciate being kept in the dark and manipulated. If The Fringe — if Edward — was going to start annihilating people then what would become of The Network once their useful purpose was fulfilled? She shuddered.

'Yes, that is what Elizabeth believes and it must have been what Chi thought as she died trying.'

'What?' said Emi, her voice rising an octave as she turned to stare at Peter. Her eyes filled with tears.

'You didn't know…of course you didn't know. What was I thinking? Shit, sorry.' He watched as she brushed away her tears.

Emi shook her head.

'I wouldn't have said that so abruptly had I thought. Chi was caught in the bombing. She had gone to try to talk to The Blues…a building collapsed on her. Tom and Liz tried to get her out but they couldn't. I brought them back to Sector A with the Blue baby.'

'Oh, Peter, life is so…unfair.'

'I'm sorry, Emi. Really I am. Bombing the Blues was bad enough, but the fact that Chi was caught in it makes it infinitely worse. My guilt knows no bounds.' Peter's mouth turned down in a grimace.

'It's not your fault anymore than the Cloud being smashed when Dez was on guard duty is his fault,' said Emi forlornly, still mopping up her tears. 'But it sure feels like the world is conspiring against us lately. No matter how hard we try something else seems to go wrong.'

'Don't give up just yet. As horrible as detonating the city was, it does mean we don't have to live in fear of what The Blues will do anymore and we do have a bunch of panels to restore Cloud III with. What will become of New York, I can't say. But you and Dez are good leaders…I'm sure you'll figure something out.'

'Thanks Peter. I don't know if I feel like I deserve having that much confidence placed in me, but…thank you,' responded Emi with a faint smile.

The Hovercraft touched down in the village green and Emi headed for Abe's place. As she walked she noted that Sector A didn't seem as lush and abundant with life as it used to. The greens weren't quite as green, the paths were more dusty, the rabbits and squirrels not as numerous. There were fewer bird sounds. If felt as if death were just around the corner and everything was holding its breath, waiting for it to strike in whatever manner it so chose. Her mouth curved down at the edges. If New York was getting more Hyperstorms as the weather patterns shifted it appeared as though Sector A was heading toward drought-like conditions. They definitely needed the artificial rain from Cloud III…and soon.

When she knocked on the door of the cottage, Abe answered holding a little bundle. A tiny blue face peeked out from the light cotton wrap.

'Good heavens. It's hard to believe until you actually see it for yourself,' exclaimed Emi. 'I've never thought of The Blues as babies, only as violent adults who kill and pillage for the sake of a handful of food.'

Abe grinned at her. 'I know.'

'It's a bit startling.'

'I know.'

'I've brought the vaccine…the new one that Matthew made for those with deeper imprints,' Emi said, coughing and clearing her throat. Sal had been the accidental sacrifice needed to figure out that a stronger vaccine was necessary for some. 'Do you want me to give it to her now?'

'I don't see why not. I'm hoping if she gets it early then she won't have to grow up with all the toxins in her body…and maybe she'll be okay.'

Emi nodded. 'From a medical point of view it's an interesting experiment. One I never thought to do.'

'Yeah. That's what Matthew said too. He called just after you left New York to fly here. He wanted to come out but he's needed in New York with the storm and all.'

'Yes, New York is a mess. If Hyperstorms become a regular thing then it won't be a good place to live.'

'If we don't get some rain soon then here won't be good either.'

'I noticed,' said Emi, her forehead creased with worry. Hope for a better future, or any future at all, seemed to be in diminishing supply. 'Well, here goes. I expect the results will take a month like they did with everyone else. Not sure what to expect really given that she is blue all over and doesn't just have an imprint in one specific spot. What have you named her?'

'Gigi.'

Emi looked up at Abe and smiled. 'It suits her. I like it. Well, Gigi, without making you into an experiment, it will be fascinating to watch you grow up…if we can sort out the mess the world is in so you have a chance of growing up, that is.'

'I think we may have enough panels to get most, if not all, of Cloud III operational again. So it gives us some hope. Except, I guess we've just exchanged Cloud III not working to capacity for the New York Cloud not working fully. Only time will tell…' said Abe, shrugging his shoulders, before taking the little bundle back from Emi, as Gigi let out a hollar from being suddenly poked with a needle.

'Yeah, it's too bad we don't have a stockpile of panels, but they take so long to make and other sites in the world still have faulty panels that need replacing so we never seem to have extras. Even if we did, the frame of the New York Cloud is destroyed. The weight of the hailstones on the panels that couldn't be turned bent the frame. I think trying to re-build it would take longer than the original construction. Plus it is too close to the current route Hyperstorms seem to be taking…so it's all too risky to waste the time and resources on.'

'Has anyone come up with any other solutions that might help make up for the shortfall?'

'No, not yet. I'm going to go and talk to Dez and see if we can think of anything with our combined knowledge. He's travelled a lot, knows The Fringe, knows The Network and the workings of The Cloud. I've sat in on many of the meetings to do with our current state of affairs and have heard numerous ideas thrown about. Maybe we can come up with something. We have to.'

'Whatever I can do to help. Let me know.'

'For now the focus will be getting Cloud III restored to full operation. It will at least alleviate the drought conditions you seem to be facing.'

'True. But I feel like in the overall scheme of things that it is just a drop in the bucket and won't be enough to make the difference we need.'

'You're probably right…but I hope you're wrong,' said Emi, her lips twitching up in an attempt at a smile.

---

'Emi.'

'Hey.'

Dez opened the door wide, pulled her inside, pushed the door shut and drew Emi into his arms, burying his face in her hair.

'I'm happy to see you too,' she murmured into his shoulder, wrapping her arms around his waist.

'Thank God you're okay. I had no idea. I was at the New York Cloud when the Hyperstorm hit. You were all I could think about.'

Emi pulled away to look into Dez's eyes. 'I was at the apartment — safe,' she replied, running her hands through his mussed up hair, trying to bring its unruliness into some semblence of order. 'I...I managed to get the shields over Central Park just as the massive hailstones started, but...Edward was walking through the park at the time...he took a direct hit to the head and is on life support in the hospital.'

'Oh!' said Dez, the emotions flitting across his face the only evidence of the internal struggle he was having between hoping that Edward was finally out of the picture and knowing that it would still be hard on Emi since, even if she didn't love Edward, she still had some emotional connection to him.

Emi pulled further away. 'I'll sit in on all the committee meetings now...until he recovers. Dez, we're part of the leadership. Not just of The Network but of The Fringe as well. We need to, have to, try and figure out a way to save the planet before it's too late. Maybe it's already too late...but still, we have to try. There must be something we're overlooking. We've been so focused on The Cloud...and The Blues. We need to look elsewhere. The Blues are no longer an immediate threat and The Cloud...it is what it is. There has to be something else that can make up the difference we need.'

Her impassioned plea shook Dez out of the euphoria he was feeling at knowing she was okay. He led her to the kitchen and then set about making coffee. After placing everything on the table, he sat next to her and looking her in the eyes asked, 'What are you thinking?'

'I don't know. The meetings were always focused on The Cloud. If a board member tried to mention anything else, Edward shut them down. It was like The Cloud was his baby and he couldn't see beyond it. Now we have no choice, we have to look beyond. We have to figure out something else that will make up the difference of the New York Cloud not being fully operational. And something that can work quickly.'

'Okay, well, let's go through all the other things we are doing to improve the planet and see if any of them can help lower the earth's temperature,' suggested Dez, pragmatically.

'Okay. We have new species being introduced from the saved DNA of extinct species.'

'Hmmm. That helps with ecological diversity and possibly a bigger variety of food in the long run…and pollination,' said Dez, thinking out loud. 'And pollination helps with plant diversity and health which in turns helps maintain the balance of what is emitted into the air and the soil…but I can't see it helping with temperature in the immediate futrue…or at least not enough.'

'What about plant and soil detoxification?'

'Hmmm. Well, we are certainly better off without all the toxins. The animals thrive when not exposed to chemical sprays and fertilizers that they used to use. The healthy crops replenish the soil and the soil then gives the plants the nutrients they need to grow,' said Dez, listing off the benefits on his fingers.

'As plants and soil are healthier we should have more green areas on the planet instead of the barren red, orange and yellow hot spots…providing we get enough rain…which The Cloud structures should supply in most places. But that will still take too long to make the difference we now need,' said Emi, her brain churning, trying to put her understanding of how the environment worked and how everything was connected into words.

'So, what else?'

'The oceans?' suggested Emi questioningly. 'I mean…they're even more vast than the land mass of the world. Surely we can use them somehow,' she said, her enthusiasm for brainstorming ideas causing her eyes to shine as hope returned.

'That's it,' said Dez, excitement lighting up his face. 'The oceans. Seaweed farms. I've seen some in my travels. There aren't many of them given the size of the oceans, but I had someone explain them to me once when I first saw one and wondered what they were doing.'

'I've never seen one but I have heard of them. How do they work?'

'They take the carbon from the air, reducing the temperature, and they bring the cooler water up from the bottom of the ocean to make the surface water more temperate,' Dez explained, keeping to the basics. 'They also help with providing a habitat for marine life and seaweed has multiple uses.'

'Of course,' agreed Emi, catching his enthusiasm. 'We've been so focused on the land and how hot it is that we've overlooked the importance of the oceans…well not overlooked exactly, but we haven't put the energy into maximizing the benefits they can provide. Seaweed farms…'

'We just need more of them…a lot more.'

'Yes, but we have the necessary workforce,' she said, reaching for his hand across the table and giving it a squeeze. 'Once we've finished re-building Cloud III we can put everyone on to producing seaweed farms.'

'And seaweed grows rapidly — something like two to three feet every day, if I remember correctly. It could work. It could make the difference we need in the time we have.' Dez leaned over and kissed Emi. 'You're brilliant.'

'It was your idea,' she countered. 'Edward, if he regains consciousness, is going to hate it.'

'Why? Because it is my idea…or ours?'

'Yep. Or at least because it was not his. But I'm not sure how much I care. We have to do something and I have not liked his ideas lately.'

'Hmm. Rebellious Emi. I think I like it.' Dez grinned at her.

She grinned back at him. 'We need to make a plan and put it into action.'

'Abe, Peter, the use of the Hovercrafts. Anyone who lives near a coastline should start planting seaweed. We need people to construct the platforms,' said Dez, continuing to think his thoughts aloud. 'I think I should go to England. I haven't been there in a while and they have plenty of coastline. I'll get them to focus on planting the seaweed wherever possible and send ambassadors from there to the rest of Europe. There are not many people left in the hotter parts of the world, like Africa, Australia and India, but maybe we can extend the seaweed farms further south by sending people temporarily to those areas…it could be the tipping point we so desperately need.'

'Oh God, Dez, we need this to work. I want to live, for our baby to live. To not have to struggle for every mouthful of food.'

'I know,' he said, pulling her into his lap as his hand caressed the mound of her stomach. He was rewarded with an almighty kick to his fingers.

Emi smiled. 'I'll go back to New York. Talk to the committee. I'm sure I can persuade them. I'll have them put the seaweed farms on the 3-D map and get them to calculate the temperature change when they are added to the Cloud's new configuration.'

'I'm sure it'll work. I just know it will. I feel it in my bones,' said Dez, holding her tight. 'But it will be nice to have an idea of how many we need and how long it might take to make a difference. It's easier to convince others when you have parameters and they know you've done the research behind the theory.'

Emi turned around in his embrace and put her arms around his neck, looking him in the eye, before stating, 'I'm also going to search the apartment for any evidence, one way or the other, of Edward's behaviour. He offered me salvation in my darkest hour, when I had lost all hope and could not see a way forward…it might have been for his own selfish needs…but still. I can't abandon him in his present state without proof of who he is. Either way, I want to be with you, but I would like to come to you with freedom and a clear conscience.'

Dez returned her gaze, his eyes filled with all the pain they had been through, all the times of just missing being with each other, of being manipulated by time or circumstance…or people. Their desire to have a future together had always been an elusive dream. Holding her tightly, running his hands through her long auburn hair he brought her mouth to his in a kiss of such longing — for all the things they had missed out on but were still potentially ahead of them.

He finally pulled back, leaving them both breathless. They had come to a crossroads — either Edward was a villain and Emi would be free to leave him, or Edward had spent his life trying to save humanity, was hideously injured and Emi would never truly be free of him, though she had not said as much. He stared at her, trying to drink her in, as she laid her head on his shoulder and he tightened his hold, both lost in their little cocoon, trying to ignore the harsh world for just a few more minutes.

# CHAPTER EIGHTEEN

E mi returned to New York. Her priority, to meet with the committee and get their new plans started. She was thankful that seaweed farming had been around for a long time, at least two hundred years, so she did not need to explain their intentions — it was a well developed industry and easily implemented.

Gathered around the conference table, she and the committee focused their attention on the 3-D map before them. First they brought up the map of the world from five years previously — before The Fringe and The Network had started working together to build The Cloud. Most of the world showed red, orange and yellow with only a few spots of green. Emi had them overlay the seaweed farms in operation at the time. Wherever there was a seaweed farm the air and water temperatures were slightly cooler — not a lot, but the results were consistent across the globe.

Next they brought up the map from just before the destruction of Cloud III. The overall temperature of the world was still too hot, but areas that had showed as red hot spots had turned to orange — a very bright orange — and those that were orange had turned to deep yellow, and there were a few more small green spots emerging. The Cloud structures had started to work though the change was still barely perceptible.

The third map they brought up was a few months after Cloud III had been destroyed. The immediate vicinity around Cloud III was noticeably warmer and drier and one could see how the increased heat in the one area to the southwest could draw the Hyperstorms more directly over New York. With the rest of the Cloud structures in operation the weather pattern had shifted and as soon as a Hyperstorm made landfall it unleashed its fury. New York had been the unintended victim.

The next map brought them to the hypothetical. The New York Cloud no longer functioning but Cloud III fully rebuilt. The New York Cloud had been the biggest in the world, with it out of commission, New York would become a hot spot and its own warmth would draw the Hyperstorms toward them. The area around Cloud III would be downgraded from red to yellow — able to grow crops and sustain life. But the overall picture was that with the New York Cloud no longer functioning, the planet as a whole would be too warm, most areas still in the orange zone with only the immediate districts around a Cloud structure being mitigated to yellow, or green if they were near a large body of water.

In all these maps they had not changed the seaweed farms. They had been maintained but not added to over the last couple decades — since The Fringe had started concentrating all of the energies and resources on the production of the parts necessary to build The Cloud.

Now Emi had them add in the extra seaweed farms that her and Dez had figured would be necessary and had them place them on the map in the designated spots. Then she waited with bated breath for the results to appear before her. The colours of the 3-D map slowly shifted and changed as the analysis of the results from different years appeared. After ten years the northern countries including much of Europe and the UK, would be almost green, large sectors around the equator would be more yellow than orange, and hot countries, currently uninhabitable, such as Australia and parts of Africa would fade from red to orange. After twenty years, New Zealand, Canada and parts of the USA would have some segments of green and after thirty years no red hot spots showed on the map — the hottest temperatures were only shown as orange.

'Oh my God…it's going to work,' said Emi, hardly daring to believe her eyes.

The room erupted into mayhem and noise as everyone exclaimed over the results, yelling in triumph, slapping backs and hugging one another.

As the room quieted down Emi added a disclaimer. 'I hate to rain on my own parade…but the results are based on Cloud III and the extra seaweed farms being operational immediately…which is obviously not going to be the case. Still, barring any more calamities it does at least offer us a way forward.'

'I wish we had thought of this earlier,' said Elizabeth. 'We were just so focused on The Cloud we couldn't see past it. Thank God for you and Dez and a fresh perspective.'

'Thanks, Elizabeth,' said Emi, smiling her appreciation at the vote of confidence.

Elizabeth nodded at Emi and then asked, 'Can I make a suggestion?'

'Of course.'

'Looking at the map it appears that New York will remain in an orange zone for at least the next few years, until our local seaweed farm is sufficiently large. The weather pattern shifts seem fairly permanent in the short term and it looks like Hyperstorms may be something we are going to have to contend with for some time to come. I would recommend moving The Fringe headquarters to somewhere else on the planet.'

The board members looked at Elizabeth in consternation and then returned their gaze to the map.

'She's right,' said William, one of the environmental engineers.

'But that will be a monumental undertaking,' said Cameron, a Cloud panel expert. 'And I can't see Edward ever approving such a move. He loves New York. His family have built this city. Transformed it into what it is and protected it. I just can't see moving as a reality.'

'We certainly can't just abandon New York to the mercy of the Hyperstorms,' said Emi. 'But we have to do what is best for the planet and the human race overall. So, I suggest a compromise. Some must stay here to activate the shields. And I can't see relocating the Cloud panel factory.... So any key workers would have to stay here. We could have some leaders here and some elsewhere. But everyone relocating...I can't see it.'

Elizabeth and a few others nodded in agreement.

Emi looked around the room. 'We also need to send people to where the seaweed farms are to be planted. We could give them the option of staying there if they want. I'm obviously not going anywhere with Edward in his current condition so I'll stay in New York for the time being. I think we should let others decide for themselves as long as they are not a key worker needed in a specific location,' said Emi. 'But first we need to put out a bulletin to the city, and to those in The Network, explain our plan to them, and then get started.'

'Consider it done,' offered Charlotte.

Emi nodded at Charlotte and took her leave, happy to give the details of the plan over to the experts in the room. She had other things on her mind.

———+———

Emi holed herself up in the apartment and started to meticulously go through things. She began with the E-manuals. Putting the one with his appointments into her reader she scrolled through. Mostly it was meetings with the Cloud engineers, some with Matthew about the vaccine and the occasional entry about one of the dinners that had been held to celebrate various accomplishments. Her name was documented a number of times and she realized that Edward had been interested in her long before she became aware of it. Some entries were just initials or a star on a page with no other reference. Almost like a code. But how to decipher what it meant?

She ejected the reader and stared out the window. She wasn't sure how she could figure out what the initials meant without something to reference them to. Even the dates didn't help much as they had not bothered to keep track of specific dates in The Network villages; one day was much like any other. She could roughly work out what had happened within a season a few years ago, but she would not be able to link a day in Edward's E-manual with a particular day in her life.

She continued to stare out the window at the bright daylight, certain that she was missing something. Some detail that was right in front of her but that she couldn't quite grasp. She drifted off, lulled by the peace and the warmth into an exhausted sleep.

The sun continued its path across the sky, the few clouds emitted by the New York Cloud were not enough to give the area much relief from the brutal heat. Those caught in the shadow of a passing cloud looked up and smiled as it went by. Clouds were a symbol of hope and every one was thankful to the ingenious minds of Edward and his committee, which had invented and built The Cloud.

As the day faded, Emi awoke with a jolt as her baby gave her a good swift kick. She smiled and put her hand to her stomach. He or she was the reason she wanted, needed, to help save the planet. Her mind wandered back over the last few years to learning about the trouble they were all in, the solution and all it entailed and her awe at what The Fringe had accomplished.

Her eyes snapped open and she took a quick intake of breath. That was it. The banquet — the first one she had gone to when she and Dez had come to New York with Elizabeth. The banquet had to be recorded in Edward's planner and the raid on Sectors C and D were right around that time — would there be a star or some initials? She leaned over and touched the solar-tube to turn on the lights. Picking up the E-manual she inserted it back into her reader and scrolled back to the time of the banquet. There it was:

*Banquet — welcome to Network leaders — Dez and Emi*
- *beginning of plans for construction of The Cloud*
- *collaboration with The Network*

*Sectors C and D raided by Blues*
- *send supplies*
- *send medical staff to help*

The events were documented. The information was so minimal it didn't help much. She scrolled further back. She couldn't remember how many days there had been between the attack and when they learned of it. Two or three, maybe — had it been that long in between? She continued to scroll. There was a star, a couple of days earlier. Was that the day of the attack? There was no other information, just the star. She continued to scroll back through time in the planner — another entry with just an initial this time — B. Did that mean meeting with a Blue or was it something else completely? She ejected the E-manual. Shaking her head, her forehead furrowed in concentration she headed for the kitchen to make a cup of tea. It didn't make any sense — if Edward needed the help of The Network why would he have them raided right at the time he needed to be-friend them? She let out an exasperated sigh. Maybe she was chasing red-herrings; imagining things that weren't there. It was all just based off of a couple words Sam uttered when on his death-bed and a solitary sentence from a Blue that Dez thought he had heard when he had been knocked almost unconscious. It wasn't much to go on and certainly nothing rational.

She sipped her tea and headed for the office.

# CHAPTER NINETEEN

**W**hile Emi concentrated on planning the seaweed farms and coordinating the labour force necessary for the undertaking, Abe and Dez focused all their energies on getting Cloud III back to full capacity. Time was running out and they all knew it. The predictions The Fringe had calculated were obviously accurate. The Cloud running at seventy per cent efficiency, as it currently was with both Cloud III and the New York Cloud damaged, was not enough to make the difference they so desperately needed to save the planet. With Cloud III back in full operation they would be at eighty five per cent efficiency. It would be up to Emi and the plans for the seaweed farms to make up the other fifteen percent they needed.

Dez's thoughts strayed to Emi frequently. She was fairly far along in her pregnancy now and he worried that the stress would be too much for her with her increased activity with the leadership committee, planning the seaweed farms, and trying to decipher whether Edward, the man she had agreed to marry, was in fact good or evil. If he recovered, and if it turned out he was the decent human being he appeared to be, would she stay with him? His mind went around in circles. An answer eluded him. He wasn't even sure what he wanted the answer to be. If Edward were indeed a good guy, then he couldn't wish him dead so that he could have Emi to himself. He felt like that would be winning by default. He wanted her to choose him freely.

The only way that was going to happen now was if Edward did recover and had nothing to do with the attacks.

'Hey, earth to Dez. Wanna actually lift your end? They're a bit heavy to move all by myself,' said Abe.

'Sorry.'

'Yeah me too. My arms have grown six inches longer since you became my panel placement partner.'

'Sorry,' grinned Dez, taking the good-natured reprimand in stride and focusing on the task at hand. 'Too much going on in my head.'

'Yeah, well, your mental energies aren't helping me none. It's your raw brawn that's needed at this precise moment,' said Abe. 'Keep the bigger ideas for saving the planet for later, when you're lying in your cot at night too exhausted to move. This place is going to become a dust bowl if we don't get the Cloud back up and running again soon.'

Abe was right. Dez looked down at his feet as they edged sideways to place the panel in its frame. The dust rose up in swirls, coating his legs to the top of his shins. There was no doubt the ground underfoot was drier, dustier. After sliding the panel into its frame he stretched and snapped his back, giving his lower back a massage with his fingertips. He sprayed his shirt with water from his canister before removing his bandana, wiping the sweat from his eyes and then dousing his head. The sun felt more glaring, the temperature slightly hotter — something he had not thought possible. Glancing up he noted there were no birds flying above and there had been few rabbits or squirrels running for cover as he had walked through the forest this morning — the wildlife was less, the river was down and even the wells for household water seemed to have a lower water table. The recent shift in weather patterns meant that their valley in Sector A, and the surrounding area, all the way to D, could no longer rely on natural rainfall. It was now essential for Cloud III to be fully operational. They needed the cloud cover and the rainfall it could produce when necessary. Dez sighed. Maybe they were all just wasting their time. Maybe he should take Emi to England and they could live out whatever time they had left together and forget about saving the planet. He hadn't been the one to create the mess they were in, why should he be the one to have to sacrifice his life to fix things? He shook his head. He knew he could never not try.

'Hey, earth to Dez.'

Dez looked up to find Abe staring at him, ready to lift the next panel into place.

'Sorry.'

Abe shook his head in response, rolling his eyes, but refrained from offering further comment.

———

Emi looked around the room. The office. Edward's sanctuary. She rarely came in here. In the centre stood his desk — neat, organized — the space of a man who was diligent, focused and had no time for mess or clutter. In front of it an open space where the 3-D map could be brought up with the colour codes of the planet — past, present and predictions for the future. The existence of the entire planet depended on Edward's predictions for the future being correct. On the wall to the right, a blank space, for the map to be projected in 2-D. The wall to the left was floor to ceiling windows with views out over Central Park. And on the far wall there was the control panel with all the buttons to activate the different Hyperstorm shields around New York. One screamed out at her — she hadn't got to it in time to prevent Edward from getting a massive hailstone to the head. He was in hospital on life support and it was her fault. Granted, when she had visited a couple days ago he looked better than he had. The swelling and bruising had gone and Matthew had re-set his nose. If she didn't know better she would have thought that he was just resting. But his vital signs were no different. He had not woken up. His internal injuries remained unchanged. And now she was in here because she doubted his character. Other than his possessiveness when it came to her, she had never had reason to doubt his intentions for saving the planet and the human race. Having the thought added to her sense of guilt.

The baby kicked her as she put her hand to her stomach and sighed. The only way forward for her personally was to not live with the indecision and the doubt. Last time she hadn't been able to bring herself to go through the office, to invade Edward's personal space while he was lying in hospital. This time she knew she must persevere or her own mind would drive her crazy.

She sat at the desk, brought up the screen and started going through the E-cards. The first one activated the 3-D and 2-D maps. Scrunching her forehead she looked for a designated year on the E-card. The maps had a lot of blue and green with some yellow and very few orange or red hot spots. Was this what they were striving toward, their goal for the planet? She doubted the projections were realistic. It must be their most hopeful scenario for the distant future. She swiped the screen to an earlier page and saw the year come up — 1920. She stared.

'Good God…it's how it used to be!'

She could hardly believe the world had been so perfect before they had destroyed it with overconsumption, chemicals and pollution. The planet had been alive and well for billions of years, and the human race had managed to decimate it in only a few hundred of those years. Maybe humanity should not be allowed to survive. Without the human race the world might find its own balance and another species, a better species, could live here.

The baby gave her another hard kick. She sighed and pushed the little heel to a more comfortable position — at least more comfortable for her.

'It's okay little one, I'll do all I can to make sure you have a home. I love you and your dad too much to not try.'

She ejected the E-card and inserted the next. Calculations. She rubbed her eyes and ejected the disk. She doubted there would be anything to answer her questions in the formulas. She barely understood them, never mind trying to find some hidden secret within them.

Inserting the next E-card she was confronted with what appeared to be nothing more than an alphabetical list of animals. Her eyebrows drew down and her forehead furrowed in confusion as she scrolled through the list — there were hundreds of animals listed. Why would Edward keep a list of animals? She slowed the scrolling motion of her fingers and stared at one screen. She realized she had never heard of most of the creatures listed — Pademelon, Panda, Panther, Patas Monkey, Penguin, Pied Tamarin, Platypus, Polar bear — and the list went on. She scrolled down a few more screens — Saola, Savannah Elephant, Sea Lions, Sea Turtles, Seals, Sharks, Skipjack Tuna, Sloth, Snow Leopard, South China Tiger, Sri Lankan Elephant, Sumatran Elephant, Sumatran Orangutan, Sumatran Rhino, Sumatran Tiger, Swift Fox. There was screen after screen of names of animals. The only one she recognized was a fox. She scrolled back to the beginning, gasping as she read the first page. It was a record of extinct species. The ones with DNA printed next to them meant they had the original DNA sample and could now reproduce the species. The ones with an X meant there were no DNA samples and none of that species left alive on the planet. Next to the animal name was also a single word, one of habitat, hunting, food, pesticide, pollution or plastic — the simple reason for their demise. Emi scrolled more slowly through the list. Baboons, Bees (with a long sub-list), Bengal

Tiger, Birds (with another long sub-list), Black Rhino, Blue Whale, Bluefin Tuna, Black Bear, Bonobo, Bornean Orangutan, Brown Bear. Tears sprang to her eyes — so many and most without DNA printed next to them.

'Baby bump, what are we to do? We can't turn back time,' said Emi. How had Edward lived with the burden of this knowledge? She felt heavy, as if she was being smothered with guilt for the careless-ness of her ancestors. Surely Edward would only ever want to work toward saving the planet and not undermine all their efforts to right the wrongs they had inflicted on the world and their fellow species. She shook her head and inserted the next E-card.

After going through the rest of the E-cards on the desk she leaned back in the chair and gave her tummy a rub. Her lips turned up at the edges in a halfhearted smile. The poor little thing had the hic-cups. 'Hold your breath little one and they'll go away.'

She opened the drawers of the desk until she came to the last one. It was locked.

# CHAPTER TWENTY

Peter and Elizabeth had joined Jon, Amy and Abe at one of the sites where the seaweed farms were being planted. Jon and Amy were in charge of The Network task force that were installing the massive farms off the coast. Peter, Elizabeth and Abe wanted to have a better understanding of how they were going to work with cleaning the air and the oceans.

'Having spent my life flying above the oceans, I'm keen to go beneath the surface and see what it's like,' said Peter as he zipped him self into his scuba suit.

Jon stared at Peter before smiling and winking at Amy. 'Hmmm, well, first off you have your suit on backwards. The zipper goes in the back not the front.'

Peter looked down. 'Damn! I thought it felt strange. Explains the pull cord attached to the zipper,' he said, laughing at himself. 'Glad I don't have to get into this every day to fly a Hovercraft,' he grinned as he stripped the suit back off.

'Hopefully, that is the only minor hiccup we have. The tanks are self-regulating so try to breathe normally and take your time diving to allow your body to adjust to the pressure difference. Everybody remember their lessons? Any questions?'

'Can we communicate once we're in the water?'

'Only by hand gestures. Try to stay together if you can…it's safer that way,' Jon instructed. 'Amy will remain in the boat. If you run into any troubles, return to the boat. And remember…bubbles rise.' He grinned. 'Ready?'

They all nodded before sitting on the side of the boat. One by one they fell backwards into the water. They were fairly far out to sea where there were no seaweed farms. Jon had wanted to show them the 'before' — what the ocean had been like before the seaweed farms were planted. It wasn't exact as all the surrounding ocean benefitted indirectly from the seaweed farms, but at least it gave them some idea.

As Peter dropped into the water in a myriad of bubbles he gazed around at the others, easily visible though the water was slightly murky. Giving Jon a thumbs-up he started to dive, letting Jon take the lead, following him down into the depths. As he headed away from the sunlight glinting off the surface of the water it became darker and harder to find the others around him. He switched on his headlight and took a few deep breaths — in and out, in and out — as Jon had instructed, trying to keep calm. Turning his head he could see further into the deep as his headlight reflected off a ledge along the ocean floor.

Jon swam up beside him and gave him a thumbs-up, the only way to ask if he was okay. He returned the gesture before following him to the shelf they were exploring. Jon pointed and gave him the thumbs-down gesture. The rocky outcrop on the ocean floor showed little signs of life. An occasional sea creature swam by — things that he had never seen before and had no knowledge with which to identify them. There were a few tendrils of seaweed here and there, but again, nothing of significance. If this is what all the oceans are like it was amazing that there was anything left alive in them at all. He knew the acidity level of the ocean had risen too high due to the chemicals that had run into it for hundreds of years and that plastics had killed off many types of sea creatures, but having never been beneath the oceans surface before he had not thought to imagine what the reality might look like. He shook his head in disgust.

He slowly realized he could no longer see any of the others. A rocky outcrop blocked his line of vision. He took a few deep breaths and closed his eyes for a moment. No need to panic. They would be close by. Kicking his feet and doing a breaststroke he pushed against the water, forcing himself upward, above the rocky ledge that hid him from view. A few good strokes and the rockface was beneath him. He glanced around, trying to shine his light into the murky depths. Not a soul. Crap, where could they be? He couldn't even see any other light beams shining in the area. How could they disappear so quickly? He took another three deep breaths and closed his eyes again. He definitely preferred being in a Hovercraft flying high above the earth than here, under the surface of the water. This was unfamiliar territory. He looked up. The hull of the boat was outlined against the brightness of the sunlight on the water. Up! He would surface and wait in the boat with Amy as Jon had suggested if they ran into trouble. He wasn't sure if this counted as trouble but he didn't like being down here on his own — it gave him the creeps.

He kicked vigorously and headed for the light of day remembering to exhale and pause as he went. It was a slow process. He most definitely preferred the speed of the Hovercraft. Emerging above the surface of the water he swam for the boat and hauled himself in with a helping hand from Amy.

'You okay?'

'Yeah, just lost sight of everyone.'

Amy nodded. 'It isn't the best feeling if you find yourself alone down there. Happened to me once. Now I volunteer to stay in the boat,' she grinned.

'Good thinking,' said Peter, a snort of laughter forced out of his nose in subtle agreement.

'They probably won't be much longer. There's not much to see here.'

'No, the lack of life is almost worse than on land. I never thought much about it before.'

'No. Me neither. We were so far from the ocean…it made little difference to us.' Amy paused. 'Never crossed my mind really.' She looked out to the distant horizon, her gaze troubled. 'I was always so caught up with how hot out it was and how to try and grow things in the depleted soil…didn't have time to think about something that I was barely aware existed.'

'Living in New York, I flew over the ocean all the time…I just thought it was too vast to do anything about,' Peter said, shaking his head. 'Like controling the weather and the air temperature is a smaller project. Funny the things we get caught up in and lose sight of all else.'

At that moment the other's heads bobbed above the surface of the water. Elizabeth, Jon and Abe joined them in the boat.

'You okay?' asked Elizabeth after she had removed her headgear.

'Yeah. Just lost sight of everyone,' said Peter.

'You alright to dive in the seaweed farms?' Jon asked. 'There's a bit more going on there so it's even easier to lose sight of one another.'

'Yeah. I'll be more careful of keeping an eye out.'

'Right, off we go then,' said Jon as he steered the boat inland, toward where the seaweed farms had been planted. Some had been established long ago and some were part of the new project. He manouevered the boat through a channel between the old and the new — the best place to get a sampling of the difference the farms made to the ocean's environment.

'Wow. I didn't realize you already had so many,' commented Abe. 'When you're in the middle of them like this you can't see where they end.'

Jon glanced at Abe. 'Yes, we've already added quite a few new ones but we'll need thousands more all over the world to make any kind of a difference. I know this seems like a lot but really…it's not.'

'Is that why they originally gave up on this project in favour of The Cloud? Were the numbers needed too overwhelming, especially before The Network agreed to help?'

'I think what happened was that as the soil became more toxic and the earth's temperature rose it became harder to produce food. The focus of The Fringe was to produce clean soil and be able to control rainfall. We didn't have the manpower to plant and maintain the seaweed. You can eat seaweed but it doesn't offer much variety,' said Peter with a grimace. 'And, as the population died off and sea levels rose, there were fewer people willing to live by the ocean and so even less who knew how to swim.'

'Emi started giving swimming lessons in Sector B before she moved to New York. We kept it up after she moved so there are quite a few of our people here,' said Amy.

'Here we are,' said Jon, as he slowed the boat before coming to a halt and allowing the boat to drift in the gentle swell. 'This one was planted not too long ago. It'll give you an idea of how quickly the stuff grows and changes the surrounding environment.'

They suited back up and fell into the water.

Peter was immediately struck by the differences. The seaweed hung in long lengths off the purpose-built platform, reaching downward into the depths rather than upward to the light as plants on land would do. As he dove beneath the ocean's surface he could feel the temperature of the water getting cooler, the cascading tendrils of seaweed stirring up the colder water below and bringing it to the surface. The seaweed grew almost a meter a day, so the abudance of it was astonishing. Schools of fish swam in and out between the strands, some of them swimming up to him and staring at him through his mask — as if they were on tour and he was the object of interest.

He turned on his light as he swam further down into the murky depths, checking that he still had sight of the others. He could see it would be easy to get lost here, surrounded by so much swaying plantlife. Jon gave him the thumbs-up and he returned the gesture. Then Jon pointed and they followed him to a different seaweed platform. This one was obviously older. The seaweed grew down to where the sunlight could no longer reach. The depths below seemed to be opaque, the lighter lengths of seaweed barely visible in the darkness. The sea creatures were prolific. Peter had no idea what they were, no way of identifying them, but the size of some of them was a shock. He had only ever thought of fish big enough to fit on a dinner plate as that was all that was raised at the fish farm in New York. He had never stopped to imagine creatures almost as big as himself.

He shone his light into the depths and dove lower. The swaying plantlife and the variety of creatures never seen before were fascinating. It was another world. His fear dissapated as his curiosity got the better of him. He shone his light around, extending his finger to poke at a friendly grey fish. Reaching out he tried to pick up a length of seaweed — it was heavy and slick, slithering through his grasp to sway in the gentle ocean current.

He shone his light around. Damn! He had lost sight of everyone again. He thought he could see a lamp shining dimmly in the gloom a ways off and started to swim toward it when he came to an abrupt halt by something tugging on his leg. He looked back. Seaweed was wrapped around his leg. How did that happen when the stuff was so slick? He pulled at it but it just slid through his hands. He grasped one small section with both hands and tried to tear it in half. It was too tough and too slippery. He moved his leg in a circle to loosen the seaweed and then pulled his leg upward but it held firm. He closed his eyes and breathed in and out, in and out, keeping panic at bay. Opening his eyes he pushed the length of seaweed down his leg and then, slowly, tried to unwind it from his ankle. The task was impossible. He stopped to breathe again — in, out, in, out. He looked about, shining his lamp into the murky water — water that was now teaming with life, blocking his vision and blocking any chance of being found.

He turned his head. The lamp he had seen before off in the distance was still there. Further away, barely visible, but there. How could he get their attention? He closed his eyes to concentrate for a moment and then realizing his stupidity, he opened his eyes — he couldn't lose sight of that lamp. His lamp, that was it, S.O.S., the age old code for help and in distress. He would signal using his hand over his headlamp and pray the other person would see it and understand. He raised his hand to infront of his lamp and made a pulsing motion hoping that from a distance the flickering light would look like a call for help. S.O.S was taught to pilots. Was it taught to others? He could only hope that it was clear enough and someone else knew the code. He waited, his eyes never straying from the distant light, his mind focused on signaling and breathing, not panicing. Time stood still. He felt as if he was caught alone on some distant, unfamiliar planet with no way to escape. In, out, in, out, breathe. Eyes focused. He could already feel himself getting weary. Treading water, under water, with the use of only one arm and one leg was not an endurance test he was accustomed to. If he ever got out of this he was sticking to flying. The ocean was not for him.

In, out, in, out, breathe.

# CHAPTER TWENTY-ONE

**L**ocked! She bent down to look more closely causing the baby to kick her violently and her insides to cramp. 'Sorry, little one. Didn't mean to squish you,' she said, rubbing at her stomach as she straightened back up. It was an old fashioned type of lock — one that required a key. She got up, stretching her back. The baby sat heavy in her today making her feel tired and uncomfortable. She sighed — not long to go now. She made her way to their bedroom and opening Edward's chest of drawers, felt around beneath his underwear — the one place most people would not dream of invading. Sure enough, there was a set of keys. Returning to the office she bent down and inserted the key that seemed to match the hole. There was a faint click and the drawer slid open. Journals! The kind that people used long ago — filled with paper and written by hand in ink.

She picked up the top one and flicked it open to the first page. She was pretty sure it was Edward's handwriting. Most of his writing was done by dictation into his E-files but she had seen him write a few things and it looked familiar. She licked her lips and exhaled loudly, not sure how she felt about invading the privacy of someone she was meant to marry who was currently critically injured in hospital. Her stomach knotted painfully as she thought about what she was doing — her doubts about Edward and her need to have answers at war with what she knew of him personally — his charm, his love for her, his dedication to saving the planet, his leadership abilities.

She swallowed and began to read. Most of it seemed quite mundane — meetings with various people, plans, his hopes for ruling over a better world — there was not much that she considered very personal or surprising. But then some paragraphs began to jump out at her.

*We are left with no choice — we must make contact with The Network and convince them to help us. I had hoped that we could create The Cloud on our own but the committee assures me that this is not a possibility given our time constraints. Not enough people within The Fringe can be taken from their jobs to build The Cloud in the little time we have left. Elizabeth believes she can make contact without alarming them, and has a plan to bring them to New York to show them our climate predictions and our accomplishments. She thinks that once they understand how dire the situation is that they cannot help but agree to cooperate. I am not so sure. Their ways are so different from ours — they seem happy with less and with living day to day. They may not care enough about the future to agree to become a workforce so that The Fringe can rule the planet. I feel I must have a back-up plan. There must be some way to ensure that they do not say 'no' to our proposition.*

Edward was very perceptive. What he wrote was exactly what Dez had thought when Elizabeth had first approached them. She kept reading, wondering if he had devised a back-up plan in the end or if he never ended up needing one.

*A lot has happened in the last few weeks. The Blues have raided Sectors C and D and The Network have agreed to help us. But*

CHAPTER TWENTY-ONE

*then how could they possibly refuse? The Blues killed many of*
*The Network people. I was not happy about this as it reduces the*
*workforce we need, but it is done, and everything has worked*
*out quite well in the end. I sent a medical team and provisions*
*to help after the raid…The Network could be nothing other*
*than obliged to help us in return.*

Emi lowered the journal, squeezing her eyes shut. She felt as
though an icy hand gripped her heart. Sitting slumped in the chair,
feelings of betrayal overwhelmed her…had he orchastrated the raid
or was he just happy at the timing of it all and how it fell in with his
plans? She had trusted this man, agreed to marry him and share his
future, had given up Dez for him, and all the while…the way it was
written…either he had been the one responsible for the deaths of so
many of her people or, at the very least, didn't seem to care too much.
She felt sick as her stomach contracted in a knot. She didn't want to
know anymore but yet, once again, she had no choice — she had to
keep reading.

*The Network people are not as toxic and uncivilized as I had*
*thought them to be. Unlike The Blues they only seem to have*
*trace amounts of toxins in their systems due to small inherited*
*imprints and the toxic crops they are still forced to survive on.*
*However, they have cleaned themselves up quite well and seem*
*to understand the association of toxins with health and mental*
*health. I am hoping that once they are used to our ways and our*
*food that they will yet become clean and more like the people of*
*The Fringe. There is one in particular that incites my interest*
*— her name is Emi and I have a hard time dispelling her from*
*my thoughts and even from my dreams. Yet, I know, I cannot*
*be captivated by one from The Network. I must remember they*

*are still toxic, they are not genetically pure. My heir must be*
*pure of blood.*

Emi inhaled and loudly exhaled out the pain. So calculated! There was no charm, no charisma, none of the Edward she knew in these words. It was all so planned out — except for falling for her and even that seemed almost cold. She had only become truly acceptable once the vaccine had made her pure. Again, the feeling of sickness made her want to gag as her stomach cramped with suppressed emotions. She cringed at the thought of reading further, but forced herself to pick the journal back up and carry on.

> *The vaccine has worked a miracle. I can hardly believe my good*
> *luck. Emi is now as pure as any Fringe member and I have been*
> *gently persuing her. She is new to the ways of the Fringe and I*
> *do not wish to push too hard in case she bolts. I feel I must go*
> *slow, yet I must have her.*
>
> *I happened to learn today, quite by accident, that she is in a*
> *relationship with Dez and that they may have plans to marry. I*
> *cannot even express in these pages how irate this made me. Yet, I*
> *am thankful that this knowledge came my way before it's too late.*
> *He has already taken my past, he cannot have my future too.*

The hair at the back of Emi's neck prickled and stood on end on her forearms. Her intuition that Dez had been in danger was not the fanciful workings of her mind. She knew without a doubt that she was not going to like what she had yet to read. How could Edward hide such animosity so well for so long?

> *The Blues have destroyed Cloud III. This puts us all at peril and*
> *I must act quickly to try and salvage the situation. I hope I can.*
> *I do not want to lose it all now as I have planned everything*

*so meticulously. The only good that came from the destruction of the Cloud is that it will, for a time, make life so much more difficult, which was a perfect reason for Emi to need my protection and all that I will be able to provide in this desolate world. Since Dez was one of the guards, he is missing and presumed dead. It was the perfect moment for me to step in. So, though all our lives are at risk, I cannot be wholly ungrateful.*

*I finally have revenge for the sins of my father.*

Tears finally escaped from her eyes. Had there ever been any love there or just a need to possess her? She'd given up her hopes and dreams to this man. How could she have been fooled for so long? She rested her hand on her distended belly. 'Thank God this man is not your father, little one. And never will be, even in name,' she said aloud, as her insides griped at her once again.

She looked back at the last entry. It was still ambiguous as to whether Edward planned the raids or they just conveniently worked in with his wishes. If only it was all stated more explicitly. But if Edward was a part of all that had transpired he would not give himself away…he had mearly recorded the history of the events and how they had benefitted his overall plans. Other than showing a man with a complete lack of empathy, it still did not point the finger at him. And what on earth did Edward mean by he finally had revenge for the sins of his father? She knew almost nothing about his parents or his childhood?

She reached down to pick up the last journal, causing her tummy to contract once again as her waters broke.

# CHAPTER TWENTY-TWO

**W**as the light getting nearer or was it just a trick of his mind and the ocean currents? Peter maintained the steady rhythm of his hand infront of his lamp and kept his eyes trained on the distant light. It was definitely closer, but was it coming to him? He closed his eyes momentarily, and focused all his energies on breathing. He felt like he was being smothered and drowned at the same time. He wanted nothing more than a breath of fresh air, to breathe normally and not have to think about it.

He opened his eyes and Abe was there before him. Oh, thank God. He pointed to his leg and gave the thumbs-down signal. Abe swam under him and producing a knife from a sheath strapped around his thigh, he slit the long length of seaweed that had Peter firmly in its grasp. The seaweed loosened and Abe pulled it away, freeing Peter from his tether. Abe signaled a thumbs-up to Peter and they headed for the surface.

'Everything alright?' asked Amy as they flopped themselves into the boat and removed their scuba gear.

'Peter got entangled in this here bit of seaweed,' said Abe, holding up the offending plant.

'You okay?' she asked, casting her concerned look upon Peter.

Peter nodded. 'A bit shaken in all honesty. Thank God for Abe and his knife or I don't know what I would have done.'

'The girls wanted me to bring them back some seaweed so they could see what it's like. Thus the knife,' responded Abe.

'You certainly have a knack for saving people,' said Peter, his thankfulness apparent in the tone of his voice. 'Those two little red-heads, then the Blue baby and now me,' Peter smiled his appreciation.

'Except I wasn't really planning on adopting you,' said Abe, giving Peter a friendly pat on the back.

Peter grinned at Abe. 'I'll stick to flying after this so hopefully you don't need to come to my rescue again.'

'Thank goodness you're okay,' said Amy.

'Yeah, I got distracted by all the marine life and lost sight of everyone again. Slow learner I guess,' said Peter. 'But honestly, the difference the seaweed makes is nothing short of a miracle.'

'It was a fantastic idea. Let's hope it makes the difference we're so desperately in need of.'

Jon and Elizabeth returned to the boat and hauled themselves aboard.

'Everyone alright?' asked Jon.

'Yeah, got tangled in a bit of seaweed and Abe came to my rescue with his knife,' said Peter as non-chalontly as possible, not wanting to frighten Elizabeth.

Jon cast a quick glance at Peter, picking up on his tone. 'Wouldn't have thought that was possible…the stuff is so slick,' said Jon, his brow furrowing as he thought about the implications. 'But good to know for future reference. Sounds like it might be a good idea to issue knives to all the workers,' he added.

'I think the extent of my involvement will be delivering supplies to build the platforms,' said Peter with a smile. 'Don't think I fancy another swim.'

'Well, we'll need a few more pilots and Hovercrafts pretty soon as we try to deliver supplies and workers to different sites,' said Jon.

'My girls are keen to train as pilots as soon as they're old enough,' said Abe.

'And I'd be delighted to train them,' said Peter. 'I certainly do *not* want to teach scuba diving.'

————

Peter and Elizabeth were happy to get back into the Hovercraft. They had to deliver Abe to Sector A before heading back to New York to report to the committee.

'Do you have time to stop in and say 'hi' to the girls?' asked Abe. 'Lea is heading on for sixteen, so she could start to train as a pilot in a couple years. She's really keen. I thought maybe if you had something she could study in the meantime…as preparation.'

Peter glanced at Abe. 'Sure. I have lots of info on how the Hovercrafts work — engines, air flow, propellars. Be good for her to know before taking control of one.'

'She'd love that,' said Abe before turning to stare out the window at the landscape below. Flying in a Hovercraft, and having a birds-eye view, still gave him a thrill. All his years in The Network it had never occurred to him that one day he would be able to soar above the earth's surface as if he too were a bird in the sky. He had seen pictures of planes from the twentieth century but he'd had no idea that flight still existed until The Fringe had made contact. One day he hoped to explore more of the world to reassure himself that it wasn't all just an endless sea of yellow grasslands.

The area they were currently flying over was different from anything he'd ever seen before. As sea levels rose, not all cities and towns were able to construct seawalls for protection. Some places did not have enough resources, manpower or both; other places were simply too flat and the engineering to design an adequate seawall was not thought worth the resources needed. As they flew along the coastline he could see where towns had once been, now beneath the ocean waves. The grid patterns of streets was still discernable and one could pick out the rubble of buildings washed away by the tides. Where the ocean was still most acidic, little plantlife had grown and the towns were more obvious…you could almost expect someone to walk out their front door and head down the underwater street.

Peter turned the Hovercraft west across the golden landscape that Abe was accustomed to, heading for Sector A. Even from this height he could see the tall, yellow grasses ripple in the wind. Grey, brittle forests, that once must have been green and vibrant, stood like sentinals here and there. There was little discernable movement other than the swaying of the long grasses. As they neared Sector A Abe could see where industrious souls had burned off and then cleared the invasive grass and obviously detoxified the soil with the micro-organism befor attempting to plant one of the new crops. There were a few squares of light green competing for their right to grow in the earth's unfriendly environment.

Would they win?

Eventually they came to Sector A, where Peter set the Hovercraft down, before they all headed to Abe's shelter. The two most popular red-heads in the village were at the door to greet them. Lea was holding a little black baby in her arms.

'Who's this?' asked Peter.

'This is Gigi,' said Abe, 'Don't you recognize her?' he asked, winking at Lea and Fie, while a look of false innocense played across his features.

Peter gave Abe a look of stunned disbelief. 'Good God, she's black,' he exclaimed, stating the obvious.

Abe grinned. 'She is.'

'She's adorable,' said Elizabeth. 'It's impossible to associate her with the Blues,' she added, reaching out her hand to touch the baby and finding her finger immediately grasped by Gigi's tiny fist.

'I...never...I never considered what...colour...race...the Blues might be if they weren't...blue,' stated Peter. 'I guess they must be a mix of races like the rest of us but it's startling to actually see.'

'No, neither had I. I doubt anyone gave it much thought,' said Abe. 'I could hardly believe my eyes when the blue started to fade and her skin slowly changed to the same colour as mine,' he said, pausing to look down at the tiny bundle that now resembled him, at least in the colour of her skin.

They followed the girls into the house and sat around the kitchen table. Fie put out a jug of water while Lea got busy chopping up a variety of fruit for them to nibble on — apples, melons and grapes that they had managed to grow themselves from the seeds The Fringe had given them.

'This seems to be a day for considering things I haven't thought about before,' said Peter, staring at Gigi, who Abe now held in his arms. 'I do know a number of other black people in New York, but you're right, proportionally they make up a small segment of the population. I guess, as a race overall, they tended to live in the warmer counties of the world and as the earth's temperature rose, and then the world famine hit, those countries had the highest death tolls.'

'We've always had a mix of races in New York,' stated Elizabeth, 'We took in quite a few refugees at first. But that didn't last long... not as supplies around the world ran out. I know that the parts of the world hardest hit by the droughts and toxic soil there were very few people who survived. Africa was almost devoid of people by the end of the famine. The countries that made up Africa weren't in great shape when it started thanks to corrupt governments and big business, so the people had little resilience and certainly no help. Mind you corrupt governments and greedy businesses were world wide. Africa certainly did not have a monopoly on them. And they were more than happy to sacrifice the many to protect the few.'

'So true,' agreed Peter, his mouth turned down at the edges.

'It's quite the coincidense that she turned out to be black and that you took her in,' Elizabeth smiled as she re-inserted her finger into the tiny waving fist.

'It'll be fascinating to see how growing up with no toxins in her system, as well as in a family where she can learn, will effect how she turns out. Now that we've obliterated the rest of her people from the face of the planet we will never know if we could have helped them or not,' said Peter bitterly.

'You shouldn't blame yourself, Peter. You were simply follow-ing orders. You had no choice and at least you've given Gigi here a chance,' said Abe. 'But I'll not let her become a science experiment for The Fringe. She's my little sister now and I'm going to make sure that, this time, I don't fail in protecting her.'

'You're a good guy, Abe,' said Peter as he reached out and taking a grape from the platter, popped it into his mouth. 'Now, to the task at hand…I hear you girls are quite serious about becoming pilots,' Peter beamed at them, taking in the looks of delight that suddenly registered on Lea and Fie's faces.

They both nodded, holding their breath, too excited to get a word out.

Peter laughed. 'Right, I'll take that as a 'yes' then,' he said. 'Fie, you'll have to be patient as you are a bit young to be flying but that doesn't mean you can't do some reading and learn what you can in the meantime. Lea, I'll give you some E-manuals to study and you can start coming with me on trips, whenever it works out logistically, as my co-pilot. You're still too young to be piloting, but in a couple years, when you're eighteen, you can be fully trained and be able to take control of a Hovercraft. How does that sound?'

'I thought I would have to wait years yet to start training. Thank you. I can't even begin to tell you how excited I am,' said Lea, a smile spliting her face from ear to ear.

'Oh, I think I can guess by the gleam in your eyes and that tiny smile hovering around your mouth,' teased Peter.

# CHAPTER TWENTY-THREE

Emi stared in horror at her soaked and bloody skirt as another wave of pain rolled through her. Was this amount of blood normal? She let out a groan, her hands gripping her distended stomach, as the pain intensified and she doubled over.

'Ahh!' she whimpered. She had to get help, and quick. The Sat-tcomm on the other side of the desk looked miles away. She forced herself to her feet, and using the desk for support, walked the few feet to the life saving instrument. She punched the number for Matthew and waited.

'Hello.'

'Matthew, it's Emi. The baby's coming. There's blood everywhere,' she said in a strangled voice before hanging up and falling to her knees.

She would never be able to clean up this mess. If Edward recovered he would find out that she had been going through his journals. Her mind contracted in fear at the thought. Matthew would be here soon. He would see the journals everywhere and the opened drawers. What would he think? But she couldn't move; couldn't do anything about it now.

Another pain ravaged her insides. Closing her eyes she focused on breathing. She felt like there wasn't the extra room in her body for the air she inhaled. The pain filled every cell of her being, it was impossible to breathe in, there was nowhere for the air to go. She gasped and exhaled. Where was Matthew? Surely it had been — she didn't even know how long — since she had called him. He had to be here soon. Please.

The Sattcomm buzzed loudly in the still room. Thank God Edward's Sattcomm was linked to the security for the building and she could use it to allow entry to the foyer.

Emi opened her eyes and pushed herself up so she was in a kneeling position. She lifted the Satcomm and without speaking buzzed Matthew in. 'Please let the front door be unlocked,' she whispered to the empty room.

'Oh my God. Emi!'

It was Charlotte. Charlotte was here. Emi closed her eyes in thankfulness. She had never been so happy to hear another human voice. She felt a hand rest lightly on her back, but even the slight touch made her insides scream in pain. She opened her eyes to find Charlotte's face inches from hers.

'Emi. We need to get you to the bed. I'll go get things ready and be back to help you in a minute. Are you okay for a minute?'

Emi nodded once.

'Matthew. Have you called for Matthew?'

Emi nodded again. Charlotte's face disappeared from view and she closed her eyes as another contraction took possession of her. Dez! She wanted Dez. She didn't want to do this alone. But he was so far away. Could they get him here in time? She gasped as another contraction ripped through her body. How long did this go on for? She had heard of women having to go through labor for a day or two with their first child. Could anyone endure this for a day or two? Was this amount of pain normal? Five seconds seemed enough for a lifetime. Surely she would die if she had to do this for an entire twenty-four hour period or more. She screamed.

Charlotte appeared on one side of her and Matthew on the other. When had Matthew arrived? They lifted her to her feet and managed to get her to the bedroom. It felt like the longest, most difficult hike of her life. She groaned as they lowered her onto the bed that Charlotte had made up in preparation for what was to come — whatever that might be.

Charlotte removed her sodden, bloody clothes and draped a sheet over her. Matthew bent to examine her.

'The baby is backwards,' she heard him say through the fog in her brain. 'Hang in there, Emi. We'll soon be putting your baby in your arms.'

'Dez,' she whispered.

Charlotte and Matthew looked at each other as Charlotte left the room to contact Peter and ask him to bring Dez to New York.

———

Abe answered the Sattcomm. 'Hello.'

'Abe, it's Charlotte. Is Peter there?'

'Yeah, he's here. Everything okay?'

'Emi's having the baby. We need Peter to bring Dez.'

'Is Emi okay?'

'I don't know. I think things are complicated. Matthew's here. But I've been trying to track down Peter for a while and I think it would really help if Dez were here,' Charlotte said in a hurry. 'She's been asking for him. We're at the apartment. We couldn't get her to the hospital.'

'I'll get ahold of Dez, let him know. And I'll tell Peter to land on the apartment roof then.'

'Thanks, Abe,' said Charlotte, the relief evident in her voice. 'I better get back. Matthew might need me.'

---

'Dez!'

'Hey, Abe.' Why did he suddenly feel like he had a knot in his stomach? Abe had only uttered his name. But it was the way he had said it. There was an edge to the simple greeting. His arm hair stood on end. Did he want to know the reason for the call? 'What's up?' he asked, closing his eyes, waiting for the reply.

'It's Emi. She's having the baby and is asking for you. Charlotte just called. Said things are complicated. Peter is here with me and can fly you out.'

Dez squeezed his eyes more tightly shut and took a big breath. 'What do you mean…'complicated'?'

'I don't know. She didn't say more than that. Matthew is there, but Charlotte sounded in a rush and needed to go help. That's all I know. Sorry.'

Dez ran his hands through his hair and swallowed the lump in his throat. He hadn't given much thought to how he might feel in this moment. He had subconsciously assumed he would feel joy but instead he felt only dread. He tried to breathe deeply. He inhaled and then exhaled loudly through pursed lips. He must quiet his fear — fear of losing Emi. He needed to be strong. He looked around. What to take? His dread turned to panic — panic at not arriving in time.

'Tell Peter I'll meet him at the Hovercraft. I'll be ready to go in a few minutes.'

'Right,' said Abe, 'and Dez…good luck. I hope everything goes okay. Give my love to Emi.'

'Yeah. Thanks.' He barely heard what Abe had said. He had no time to be polite. Abe would understand.

Dez jolted into action. He grabbed his satchel from the hook on the back of the door. What to take? Probably not much. He headed to the bedroom and threw a couple of changes of clothes into the bag. Looking around, his eyes fell on the little wooden truck that had been in his family for who knew how long. He mustn't panic. He took a big breath. All would be well. He had to be strong, to believe everything would be alright. A smile tried to hover at the corner of his mouth — time to pass the little wooden truck on to the next generation. Picking it up from the shelf, he spun the wheels and then gently placed it on top of his clothes. Throwing his bag over his shoulder he closed the front door behind him and didn't look back. One way or the other his future was before him — with Emi. The thought of losing her made him realize that that was not an option he wanted to live with. Whether Edward turned out to be a good guy or not, he had to win Emi back.

———‡———

Dez was almost out of the Hovercraft before it landed. He bolted for the apartment — the door was already unlocked as they were obviously expecting him. A bubble of hostility surfaced from deep within him as he pushed the door open. Entering the apartment that Emi had shared with Edward over the last few months was taxing his composure. Picturing them here together as a couple was a bit galling. He wanted to be with her, but the fact that she'd left him for dead so quickly and turned to Edward still rankled — even if her reasons were understandable. As he placed his bag by the front door and headed down the hall he heard a groan that made the hair at the base of his neck prickle. It was the groan of someone in intense pain. It had taken him hours to get here. Had Emi been in this kind of pain the entire time? His hostility vanished to be replaced by fear.

He made his way down the hallway to where the sounds were coming from and stopped dead as he passed the open office door.

There was blood around the desk and what looked like journals scattered all over the place. They had been knocked from the desk, some lay open on the floor with splatters of blood across the pages and others were tent-like, fanned out, with their spines pointing upward. Had Emi discovered something — something stressful that had caused her to go into labour early? He turned away and headed to the bedroom where he heard voices — time to think about all that later, right now he needed to see Emi.

He quietly poked his head in at the bedroom door before becoming frozen to the spot as the scene unfolding in front of him suddenly seemed to come from a long way off, in slow motion. He could feel the blood drain from his face as he took in Emi, Matthew and Charlotte, the bed and the room.

Emi groaned and closed her eyes. Then opening her eyes, she started panting, loudly, in and out, through pursed lips. Her eyes were glazed, her hair matted with sweat. She thrashed her head from side to side, as if denying the pain would make it go away and leave her in peace.

Nobody had yet noticed him. Dez slipped into the room and took ahold of Emi's hand. She immediately gripped it and left fingernail moons in his palm. He wasn't sure if she knew it was him or not but he didn't let go.

'Emi, Dez is here,' said Matthew.

'Emi. Emi. It's Dez. He's here,' said Charlotte, running a cloth over her face and pushing her hair back before dripping a few drops of water into her mouth. 'Emi, see, it's Dez.'

'Emi, hold on to Dez, focus on his face, and I'm going to try to turn the baby. It's going to hurt, but you can do this, you're strong, and when this is over you'll have a beautiful little baby to hold.'

Matthew looked at Dez. Dez nodded in understanding.

'Emi. I'm here Emi. You can do this. It's going to be okay. Hold on to me. I'm here,' Dez said, stooping down to whisper in her ear, as he stroked her hair.

For a moment Emi's glazed eyes focused on Dez as she whispered his name, 'Dez,' before letting out an ear piercing scream.

Dez looked at Matthew questioningly.

'I managed to turn the baby a bit. Once more should do it…after the next contraction.'

Dez nodded, briefly bringing his lips to Emi's forehead as they waited for the next contraction to pass. The seconds stretched to eternity as Emi groaned and thrashed her head back and forth, gripping Dez's hand so hard he thought it might break.

Matthew sat back, expelling a pent up breath between pursed lips. 'That's done it. Hopefully now the birth can move forward and her body will know what to do,' said Matthew, looking at Dez. 'I can't tell you how happy I am that you showed up when you did. Her body has been too tense up until now for me to turn the baby. You're what she needed.'

Dez nodded, too choked up to utter a word.

The minutes turned to hours as Emi fought to bring a new life into the world. Charlotte, Matthew and Dez were confined to offering what comfort they could as time ticked by. Their focus shrank to the scene being played out before them…one of love and pain, death or life.

After Dez felt that he had lived his entire life over again within the four walls of that room, Matthew finally said, 'Okay. This is it. Emi, you need to push when I tell you. You can do this. You're almost there. Ready?'

Dez felt a squeeze to his hand and nodded at Matthew that Emi understood. A new phase to the ordeal began with them supporting

Emi as she strained to give birth to her baby, her body almost too exhausted to struggle through the last few minutes.

Dez's lips were on Emi's forehead and his eyes were closed when the cry of a newborn filled his senses. He looked up to catch the look of relief on Matthew's face. He closed his eyes momentarily and heaved a sigh, exhaling, thankful that the ordeal was over. He beamed at Matthew and planted a kiss on Emi's pale cheek.

Charlotte took the baby to clean and wrap up before placing the tiny bundle in Emi's arms. 'She's perfect,' she said, smiling down at Emi.

Emi kissed the top of her newborn's head. Now that the pain was over her eyes shone with happiness and love as she looked at Dez. A smile of contentment hovered at the corners of her mouth until her eyes closed and she lapsed into unconsciousness.

Dez glanced at Matthew questioningly.

'I won't lie to you. She's lost a lot of blood,' said Matthew in response to his unasked question. 'It might be best if you take the baby and let me take care of Emi.'

Dez nodded, the look of fear returning to his face, as he took his newborn daughter from Emi's arms and left the room.

———

A while later Charlotte joined Dez in the opulent living room. The room was the antithesis of all that she had witnessed in the previous hours. Pristine and elegant with masculine overtones and a lack of warmth or homeliness. Everything in the room screamed of impeccable taste, nothing was out of place and there wasn't a speck of dust to be found on a single object. It was not a place where Charlotte would want to raise a child.

'Hey, Dez, how you holding up?'

'Good question for which I don't have a good reply,' he said, as his lips tried to turn upwards in a half-hearted attempt at a smile. 'I don't know is probably my best response.'

Charlotte sat down next to Dez on the couch and pulled back the blanket to look into the baby's tiny face, her rosebud lips twitching as if she was already dreaming of being fed.

Dez looked up, his eyes glistening. 'She's so perfect. I never imagined…' he said, trailing off as he gazed down at his infant daughter.

'She's pretty cute,' said Charlotte, with a smile. 'And don't worry about Emi. Matthew is a miracle worker and I have no doubt she'll be fine.'

Dez nodded. 'I can't imagine life without her. Especially now,' he said, indicating his daughter with a nod of his head. 'I have to win her back, Charlotte. I can't have Edward raising my daughter, not here, in this,' he waved his free arm, indicating the apartment. 'Nor anywhere else, actually. I want the world to be a good place. A place where I can raise my children and not fear for their future.'

'I know,' said Charlotte, acknowledging the intensity inherent in Dez's emotions. 'One step at a time…that's all we can ever do.'

Dez looked up to meet Charlotte's gaze, nodding his agreement.

'Give her time Dez. Time to recover and time to sort through her own emotions. She never loved Edward. She only chose to be with him as she thought it the only way to maintain her role as leader, and protect her people and your baby when she thought you were dead. But I don't know if she'll be able to walk away from him while he's injured. You'll have to be patient.'

'I feel like I've been waiting years to have my life back.'

'Yeah. But we needed you, we still need you. And I have to say, I'm glad you've taken up your leadership role again. I don't think you realize how important you are to the salvation of the planet and the human race.'

'No. I don't suppose I do,' said Dez with a lopsided grin. 'Thanks, Charlotte. I'll try to be on my best behavior from here on out.'

Matthew came into the room, his shoulders slumped, a bead of perspiration across his forehead, and his clothes rumpled and blood spattered. They both looked up, not daring to say out loud the question that was forefront in both of their minds.

'She's resting. She's lost a lot of blood and had a tough time of it for a first birth,' he ran his hand over his face trying to dispel the fatigue. 'She should be okay. It's up to her now but I'm quite sure she wants to live. Her desire for life will help her pull through.'

Charlotte and Dez both let out their pent up breath at the same time.

'Thanks Doc,' said Dez, barely able to get the words out past the lump in his throat.

'Don't mention it,' said Matthew with a weary smile. 'I'm going to go. I'll check back in a few hours. And the next time you see me…I'll be a married man,' he added.

'What?' said Charlotte and Dez in unison.

'Zoe is waiting for me at my place. We had planned on marrying today. Thank goodness she understands the life of a doctor.'

'But…but I thought The Fringe couldn't marry outside of The Fringe,' exclaimed Dez.

'So did I. All this time I thought it was written into our laws. But I did some research and apparently it's not. It's just something that we have adhered to in order to prevent our DNA from becoming corrupted by genetically inherited toxins. But…well…since I discovered the vaccine, and since Edward chose Emi…I figure it's a good time to leave the custom behind us. I would have anyway.'

'Congratulations. Give my love to Zoe. I'm thrilled for you both,' said Dez, while at the same time wishing that it was he who was getting married to Emi and that his future looked that secure.

'I'll head out as well as long as you think you'll be okay,' said Charlotte.

Dez nodded.

After they left Dez returned to the bedroom and lay down next to Emi, with their daughter gently cradled between them. Like Emi, he was soon fast asleep.

# CHAPTER TWENTY-FOUR

Dez woke up feeling disoriented. His gaze took in the floor to ceiling windows, the luxurious carpet, the gleaming furniture, and the massive bed, before coming to rest on his tiny daughter and Emi next to him in the bed.

Her eyes were open and she was staring at him, a smile hovering around her mouth. 'Dez.'

'Emi, oh thank God. I've never been so scared,' he said, gently running his hand over her hair. 'How do you feel?'

'A bit tired…and sore…can I have…?

'…Her,' offered Dez with a huge grin, passing over the baby.

'What are we going to name her?' asked Emi, as the baby latched on to her breast and started to nurse.

'Are…are you offering me a say in the matter? I mean…what about Edward…and letting him think he's the father?' Dez asked, feeling thrown off guard.

Emi shook her head. 'I can't.'

Dez leaned down and kissed Emi gently on the mouth. 'That is the best news I've had since…since you told me about the baby,' grinned Dez. 'I thought I was going to have to patiently win you back but I was very determined to win and not take no for an answer.'

'I was planning to leave him anyway…once he's out of danger… even if you didn't want me back…but I…I read his journals…just before I went into labour. The journals aren't explicit but there was enough…enough for me to not want to be with him. Not that I really wanted to be with him…I…I just felt I had no choice. I'm so sorry I hurt you…didn't wait. It was the worst decision of my life.'

Dez shook his head and kissed Emi again, gently carressing her lips with his. 'It's okay. I understand why you chose what you did and, honestly, if you hadn't been in the position of being Edward's fiancee I don't know what would've happened. Things could have turned out so much differently…your influence restored Cloud III and started the seaweed farms projects. You might have just saved us all. I can't begrudge your decision because my emotions were hurt for a while.'

'So, what are we going to name her?'

'Well, the name Dez has been in my family for generations in one form or another but I think I would like a fresh start. How about Emma?'

'Emma…I like it. It sounds old fashioned,' agreed Emi, looking down at the tiny bundle wrapped in her arms. 'And maybe she'll get to grow up in something that resembles the old world that we've lost…the world where the planet provided for your needs instead of us providing for its.'

Dez ran his fingers over the top of the baby's head. 'Hello, Emma,' he said to the tiny scrap of humanity now fast asleep between them. He looked back up at Emi, 'I love you so much. But after all this time, I can hardly believe things are going to work out for us.'

Emi's face fell. 'I need to think. I can't just leave when he's so seriously injured. The Fringe trust us. We need to keep their trust. But you should look at his journals. Maybe they'll give you some insight.'

Dez's eyebrows drew down in a frown. 'Are you sure?'

'Yes. They're in the office. You should go and read them. I didn't get through all of them but it's better if you read it for yourself. And I need to rest,' she smiled at him as her eyelids began to droop.

Dez kissed Emi on the forehead before gently prising himself off the bed, trying to not wake the baby, and headed for the office. He was not looking forward to the task before him.

———

Dez ran his hand across his face. His eyes were weary from reading and his mind was heavy from what he'd learned. Was he reading too much into it? As Emi had said, the journals were not explicit but the implications were there. Reading between the lines it seemed as if Edward might have orchastrated everything. But were the journals really proof? It would be better for everyone if Edward died rather than re-gaining consciousness if he were behind everything that had happened to them recently. He had no idea how to share what he surmised with a population that worshipped Edward — the destruction of Sectors C and D, and of Cloud III — it seemed as if it were not quite what Edward had planned. It was the result of The Blues taking things too far and Edward had now wiped them off the face of the earth in retaliation. So all was good. Wasn't it? The fact that the raids had played into Edward's plans may yet be coincidence. The Fringe might even ignore the fact that Edward seemed to want him out of the picture — suggesting it was just boys flexing their muscles and wanting to win the girl. Dez ran his hand through his hair and tried to think about what to do.

His only thought was to bounce things off Abe. Abe had always had his back and he was level headed as well as kind…and forgiving. Though he was built like a house he never hurt anyone. The Blues had violently wiped out his entire family, leaving him with a lifetime of guilt, and yet he had adopted a Blue baby and refered to her as his little sister. Dez felt the need of someone's council who knew how to forgive and move forward.

Did Edward feel the need to kill him to get to Emi? That was something he still didn't understand. Why not try winning Emi by being the better guy? Maybe the answer would be in the other journals scattered around the floor, but his eyes were too tired and he didn't want to read anymore now.

He picked up the Sattcomm to get ahold of Abe.

'Hello.'

'Abe, it's Dez.'

'Dez. I've been hovering for hours waiting to hear from you. Is Emi okay?'

'Sorry. I should have called earlier. She's okay. She lost a lot of blood, she's weak, but I think she'll be okay and we have a baby daughter…Emma.'

'Congratulations. The girls will be thrilled,' said Abe, the relief evident in his voice. 'And how are you holding up?'

'Quite truthfully…I've never been so scared. I feel like I lived my whole life over again watching Emi in so much pain,' replied Dez. 'But we plan on being together, preferrably somewhere out of Edward's reach if he regains consciousness. Which is what I need to talk to you about. Do you think you could come out to New York? I have some things I want you to see…read actually. And I need your advice.'

'Sure. I think one of the Hovercrafts is heading back to New York fairly soon. It just delivered the last load of panels for Cloud III. I'll see if I can catch a lift,' said Abe. 'I'll call you back when I have everything arranged.'

'Great. Thanks. See you soon,' said Dez, hanging up the Sattcomm. He ran his hands through his hair, staring at the wall, deep in thought. He would have to have a member from The Fringe in on this as well or it could look as if The Network were taking over from The Fringe. Charlotte. She had served Edward faithfully for years and yet was a good friend to Emi. Her input would be invaluable. He reached out for the Sattcomm and hit the button for Charlotte's place.

# CHAPTER TWENTY-FIVE

Spike had managed to nurse Chi back to health. The wound in her arm was healing and didn't show any signs of becoming infected and though her ribs had been cracked it appeared that no bones had been broken. Over the weeks he had picked fruit from the trees, hunted squirrels and rabbits and caught fish in the stream. It was the most well nourished he had ever been and Chi's strength was now mostly recovered.

'We should head back to The Network soon,' said Chi, as she bit into the apple Spike had offered to her.

Spike's mouth pulled down in a frown. 'I don't think anyone from The Network is gonna want to see me,' he observed.

'You'll be with me. I'll explain. It'll be okay.'

He shook his head. 'Nah. It won't. Killed too many of your people.'

'But…but there's nobody else.'

'Yeah. It's my own stupid fault. Everyone always blamed me… guess they were right,' he shrugged with resignation. 'Don't care no more. I probably won't live much longer anyway but I'll help you get back even if it's the last thing I do.'

Chi stared at Spike in consternation, at a loss for words. He was right. The Network wouldn't be happy to see him and he probably didn't have long to live given his toxicity levels. Everyone he had ever known was dead and the rest of the world hated The Blues.

'I don't know what to say.'

'You were trying to help us. I need to help you. Make up for killing my own kid. It didn't even get to be born. Blown up because I smashed your Cloud…ruined all your plans. I need to help you.'

'Okay, but it'll be a long walk without the use of the Hoverboards.'

'Yeah. I've done it before,' Spike replied bitterly. 'We'll need to pack a lot of food. There won't be food drops along the way this time.'

'No, no there won't. And, rest assured, my mission when I get back will be to discover who the monster is who's had you execute the attacks. We can't have someone like that amongst us. They'll destroy everything we are working so hard to save.'

'If they haven't already.'

Chi had nothing to say. Hope was hard to find and harder to let go of.

———

Chi and Spike had spent days shelling nuts picked from the trees. Their fingers sore and cracked, sometimes bleeding, from the labour-intensive process. Yet they had little choice. They couldn't sacrifice any room in their packs to carrying the useless shells. They harvested whatever else they could find, whether it was ripe or not and filled their packs to bursting. Spike ripped his massive shirt in two and used it as extra sachels tied onto the ends of a short stick that he could carry over his shoulders. They would still have to carefully ration what they had but if they followed the stream it would at least guarantee them a supply of fish and fresh water.

It was time to start walking. Spike was not looking forward to it but, as Chi had pointed out, at least Sectors C and D were closer than Sector A and the Cloud that he had trekked to last time. Still he knew it would be too much for him. He wasn't feeling well and would have preferred to have a good long rest under the shade of the trees.

'Ready to go?' asked Chi.

'Sure, I guess.'

'You don't have to come with me. I'll be alright…follow the river, take it easy.'

'No, I need to come. Besides, I can carry four times as much as you can. And your arm is still not fully healed, you would have a hard time catching fish.'

Once again Chi knew he was right. Though he would consume some of the rations he would not eat as much as he could carry. And her arm was still weak, she would not be able to spear a fish. 'True,' she nodded.

'I've never bothered to look after anyone other than myself before. Maybe if I had, Shade would still be alive.'

'That was hardly your fault. You were bombed.'

'Yeah. But we were bombed because I smashed up your Cloud… I'm sure of it. The guy who gave me the tip-offs about who to strike and when was not the sort of person I should have thought of crossing. It was a mistake, a big mistake and I knew it.'

'Well, maybe we'll find the answers at the end of this treck.'

'Yeah. Maybe. Although the guy did say that if I ever came looking for him it would be the last thing I'd ever do.'

'Nice guy.'

'Gave me the creeps and I don't scare easy. Come on, let's go. I need to do this and we're running out of time.'

Chi followed Spike out into the blistering heat of the destroyed city streets, leaving behind the sanctuary of the orchard for the last time. It was going to be a long treck. One she hoped they would survive.

# CHAPTER TWENTY-SIX

Charlotte and Abe met with Dez and Emi at the apartment. Emi led them to the office and indicated the journals she wanted them to look through. Both looked uncomfortable. It was not something they wanted to do without good reason. Dez explained his thoughts and Emi divulged some of what she'd read that she found somewhat incriminating. Eventually, they were persuaded to pick up the journals and scan through them to see what they thought. Dez and Emi left them alone while Abe and Charlotte sat cross-legged on the floor and started reading through Edward's private thoughts.

'Well, what do you think?' asked Emi when they returned to the office a couple of hours later. She held her breath, waiting to see what their perception would be.

Abe shook his head. 'I don't know. It doesn't sound great, I must admit. Not the thoughts of a decent guy, but…I don't know that it's enough to definitely point the finger. The attacks still seem like they were coincidental and Edward just benefitted from them,' Abe shrugged his shoulders as he looked from one to the other. 'We all know the Blues are violent.'

'I've worked with Edward for a long time,' Charlotte piped up, 'he's obsessed with power…and Emi…but I never saw him do anything that ultimately endangered his plans for saving the planet. And he's never harmed anyone to the best of my knowledge.'

Dez nodded.

Emi's heart sank. Was she just imagining what wasn't there so she had an excuse? A way out of the mess she had created for herself? Were her gut instincts wrong because she was too emotionally involved?

'Sorry guys, but I think you need more concrete evidence. I mean for a while you thought it was Tom behind the attack on Sectors C and D. You can't guess again,' said Abe. 'Tom was forgiving about being asked if it was him. I doubt Edward would be quite so forgiving…if he wakes up.'

'Abe's right. You need to be certain,' Charlotte looked from one to the other. 'And it might end up being irrelevant if Edward doesn't come out of his coma.'

'That's true,' whispered Emi.

'Yeah. You guys are right. We can't go on gut instinct…especially with Edward in a coma. We have to be certain. How we'll ever find out though is hard to imagine,' said Dez.

'There are the other journals. Did you look at them?'

'I took a quick glance but they are from long ago and belonged to someone else…so I didn't see that they would be very relevant,' shrugged Dez.

'Well, we'll just have to wait and see I guess. Someone must know something about why the Blues smashed the Cloud. Unless it was just random violence,' said Emi, her forehead puckering in a frown.

'I wish I could find the missing link between the attack on Sectors C and D, Sam indicating it was a set-up and then the destruction of the Cloud. But I'm completely mystified.'

'Aren't we all,' said Abe.

# CHAPTER TWENTY-SEVEN

Spike and Chi followed the river. It was slow going. Even in the depths of the valley, with the shade of the trees, the temperature was stifling.

'Shall we stop for a rest?' suggested Chi. Spike looked a shade of grey beneath his blue. She was beginning to wonder if he was going to make it.

'Yeah. It's too hot to walk,' said Spike, looking up into the glaring brightness of the cloudless sky. By the sun's position it had to be midday. The trees offered little shade along the river at this time of day and it was too challenging to try and find a path through the forest.

'We'll wait 'til later when it's not so hot. My head is throbbing and I need a good long rest,' said Chi. It was not entirely true but she didn't want Spike to argue the point.

'Yeah, alright. I'm gonna soak in the stream. Cool off,' said Spike, dropping his packs to the ground under a tree. He lumbered over to the water's edge and lowered himself into the stream. The water splashed against the rocks and glinted in the sun as it washed the dirt and sweat from his body. Immersing his head, he held his breath, allowing the cool water to restore him before they were forced to continue their treck in the relentless heat.

Chi followed him in. She immediately felt her body temperature begin to lower and her headache receed. She cupped her hands and drank from the river. Though they were following the river there were many spots where access was too difficult to refill their water cannisters and it was challenging to stay hydrated in the glaring sun. Her headache receeded further as the fresh water alleviated her thirst.

She sat on the riverbed and braced herself against a rock, letting the cool water run over her, appreciating the peace of the moment. It was a beautiful spot with the sun shining on the water and the green canopy of the trees spread out on either side. If there had been more places untouched by human advancements such as this one, the world would have been a very different place.

After a while they retreived their packs and unrolled their thin, grass mats in the shade of the trees. They shared out a couple of apples and some nuts and feeling restored, settled down to rest for the hottest hours of the day.

They were soon fast asleep.

———

Although it was not all that far, the treck to Sector D was the hardest thing Chi had ever had to endure. With her injuries and Spike's increasing ill health their progress was slow-going. Food had always been scarce but the amount that she and Spike had to share was barely enough to sustain a small child. Though her injuries were largely healed, she was still weak from her ordeal and Spike could not carry their supplies and support her. By the time they reached the outskirts of Sector D they were both near to collapse.

Tom's place was the outermost shelter in the village and the first one they came to. Chi breathed a sigh of relief as they emerged from the forest and it came into view. It was late in the day, the sun was just starting to set behind the trees and cast shadows across the intervening space. Tom was obviously home as all the windows and doors were open to the cooler evening breeze. As they crossed the dusty road and came around the bend, Chi spotted Tom in his back yard getting water from the pump. He glanced up as she and Spike came into view. Chi raised her hand in greeting and grinned. Tom dropped his bucket of water before he froze to the spot and turned a deathly shade of white.

'Tom, you've no idea how happy I am to see you.'

'Chi?' gasped Tom, his mouth dropping open as his eyes darted a look at Spike and back. 'You…scared me to death. I thought I was seeing ghosts,' he rubbed his hand across his eyes. 'We thought you were…dead. How…how…?' he shook his head before enveloping her in a massive hug.

'I thought I was dead too,' she said after returning the hug and stepping back beside Spike. 'The rebar had gone through my arm but I thought it was my chest the pain was so intense. I passed out. Spike here managed to move the last couple slabs that you and Liz couldn't budge and then he…ahhh…nursed me back to health.'

Tom's gaze moved to Spike as he took a step backward. 'You. I've talked to you before.'

'Yeah. You gave me the game you'd caught so I wouldn't kill you,' Spike grinned causing the snake tattoos on his face to slither upwards.

Tom turned to stare at Chi. 'Why'd you bring him?'

'I didn't bring him, he brought me. I was still too weak…couldn't carry the supplies. And my arm was injured so I couldn't catch any food. Spike helped me get here. I promised him he would be safe… we wouldn't retaliate,' explained Chi, her voice hesitent and her eyes clouded with doubt.

'Don't worry, I won't hurt you,' said Spike.

Tom nodded. 'Right. Well, you better come in. It's probably best if Spike isn't seen just yet.' Tom shook his head as if trying to clear away the cobwebs from his mind. He retrieved his bucket and re-filled it at the pump. 'I'll get you something to eat. While you two eat, I'll go get Liz,' offered Tom as they headed indoors. 'I'll make sure she's sitting before I fill her in on your survival.'

---

Tom, Liz, Chi and Spike were gathered around Tom's table. Liz had mostly recovered from her shock. The remains of the meal Tom had provided had not yet been cleared away. Chi took a last piece of bread and happily munched her way through it. It was the most she'd had to eat in a long time and it was the best she had felt in weeks.

'So, Spike here is the one who planned the attacks on Sectors C and D and is the one who destroyed Cloud III?' Tom confirmed after listening to what Spike and Chi had to say.

'Yeah. But I wasn't told to destroy the Cloud. I was just supposed to kill the guards. Dunno why.'

Tom looked at Chi and Liz. 'Why would anyone want to have the guards killed?'

They both shook their heads.

'I think they bombed the city 'cause we smashed up the Cloud,' said Spike, looking from one to the other. 'Killed my kid. I wanna make sure that guy doesn't kill no more people.'

'But how are you going to figure out who it was if you don't know his name or where he came from?' asked Liz.

'Well, he wasn't one of you. Too, uhh, clean looking to be one of you. Hair cut, decent clothes, you know…you could just tell.'

'Okay, so it's not one of us. So someone from The Fringe. But there are a lot of people in New York and they are all 'clean' looking,' stated Tom.

'Yeah, well. It had to be someone who could give an order to wipe out a city by bombing it.'

Chi, Tom and Liz stared at eachother as realization dawned.

———†———

Abe took a step back from the massive guy who seemed to fill all the space in his small porch. He glanced at Liz and Tom, speechless, until Chi stepped out from behind. 'Chi!' he exclaimed in disbelief before stepping forward and enfolding her in his arms. 'You're alive. They told me you died. Buried when the city was bombed. How are you here?'

Chi rested in his arms, her head on his shoulder, not caring that the others were looking on, their faces beaming. 'It's a long story but Spike here saved me. We have a lot to tell you,' she said as they broke apart.

They sat on the stairs of the porch in the shade. The house would be too stuffy and confined for all of them. The breeze was warm but it was better than no breeze at all. Chi and Spike re-told their stories as Abe listed on in silence. He could hardly believe what he was hearing but as he listened, the pieces started to fall into place. The only thing that still illuded him was motive.

'So, what do you think?' asked Tom.

'I think the only thing we can do is to take Spike to New York. Peter will get us there in safety. I need to chat with Dez and Emi and then get Spike to identify the person who gave him his intructions. Beyond that…I don't know.'

As they sat making thier plans they were interrupted by the wail of a baby.

'That'll be Gigi waking from her nap. Back in a minute,' said Abe as he got up and disappeared into the house. He returned with Gigi in his arms, a small cannister fitted with a nursing tip held to her mouth and firmly gripped between her tiny lips.

'That's Gigi?' exclaimed Tom, who had not seen her since they had handed her over to Abe to care for.

'It is,' grinned Abe. 'Emi gave her the vaccine. Amazing isn't it.'

'I'll say. It's really quite startling,' said Tom, as he reached out to put his finger in Gigi's tiny fist. He turned to Spike. 'She used to be blue, like you,' he explained. 'Liz and I saved her, delivered her at the bombing site just before the mom died from the blast. We have a vaccine that gets rid of the toxins that make you blue.'

Spike stared from one to the other and then gazed at the baby. His jaw was working like he wanted to say something but no sound was emitted.

'You okay?' asked Tom. 'I guess you knew the mom, didn't you?'

Spike looked at Tom then back at Abe holding the baby and then managed to utter a reply. 'She's mine,' he stated in a strangled voice.

'What?'

'She's mine. Shade was due. Then we got bombed and she didn't move when I yelled at her. Got buried by the blast. When I came to she was surrounded by a pool of blood and the baby didn't move...I checked. Thought they were both dead.'

Tom and Liz had their eyes rivetted to Spike as he haltingly told his story. Then glancing at Abe and Gigi they turned back to Spike. 'Shade...she survived the blast. We pulled her out of the rubble and delivered the baby. Then she died. We brought the baby with us. Couldn't just leave her and didn't know what else to do. Abe here offered to care for her,' explained Liz.

'Can I have her?' asked Spike, holding out his arms to take the baby.

Abe swallowed and hesitently handed over Gigi.

Gigi waved her arms and pulled at Spike's hair as he held the bottle so she could continue to guzzle her milk. 'I thought she was dead,' he whispered.

They sat in silence as Gigi continued to wave her tiny limbs and pull at Spike's hair. When the bottle was done, Spike removed it and handed the baby back to Abe. 'It was good to hold her,' he nodded.

Abe looked questioningly at Spike as he took the baby from him. 'You don't want to keep her?' he asked.

Spike shook his head. 'No. I won't live long enough. She'll be better with you,' he stated bluntly.

Abe put Gigi over his shoulder and gently rubbed her back. Swallowing the lump in his throat, he inhaled loudly and nodded in understanding at Spike.

# CHAPTER TWENTY-EIGHT

'Abe, Charlotte, what on earth are you doing here at this hour?' asked Matthew.

Abe and Charlotte glanced at each other before Abe stated, 'I've come to turn off the machines keeping him alive.'

'Excuse me?' uttered Matthew, stepping in front of Edward, blocking Abe from access to the life support system. 'Did I hear you correctly?'

'Yeah, Doc, you heard me,' Abe replied calmly, nodding his head. 'He's a monster. Can't be allowed to live.'

'What are you talking about? You're not making any sense. I'm not moving,' replied Matthew, glancing at the button that would call security, but was just out of his reach.

'Don't do it Matthew,' said Charlotte, noting his glance at the security call button. 'I think you'd better listen to Abe first.'

Matthew turned questioning eyes upon Abe.

'It's him, he's the one behind the attacks,' said Abe, pointing his chin at Edward.

'Edward…behind the attacks. What attacks?' Matthew paused and looked questioningly at Charlotte and Abe. They remained silent, returning his gaze. Realization dawned. 'Do you mean the ones on Sectors C and D?' Matthew asked, incredulous.

'Yes, and the one on Cloud III that killed the guards and destroyed the Cloud…and almost our hope of survival.'

'That's not possible. He's the one who sent help after the attacks and is in charge of building The Cloud. You're not talking sense. Why would Edward undermine everything he has spent his life building?' Matthew shook his head. His eyes were haunted as he looked from one to the other and back again.

Abe leveled his gaze directly at Matthew before replying. 'It is him. We brought someone with us who can identify him…I think you'll find his story very interesting. And Emi has his journals…they weren't conclusive enough by themselves but they sure made us suspicious. Then someone found us who put all the pieces together and well…when you've heard, and read, all that we have…I think you'll agree with us. I have a journal here with me for you to see and, if you don't mind, I'll call in our guest,' he said, holding up the offending journal in his hand and gesturing with his head to the guest waiting outside in the hallway.

'Emi's been trying to find some kind of proof for ages. She's always had a gut instinct that something was off,' said Charlotte, 'and apparently Dez believed that some one set up the attacks on Sectors C and D but couldn't figure out who it was. He thought it might have been Tom at one point but then Dez confronted him and believed his defense. Then Dez heard the Blue who attacked him saying he looked like the guy who had tipped him off and put two and two together to figure out that it might be Edward…he does resemble Dez, even if he is a few years older. Anyway, Emi finally managed to find and open the safe in Edward's office and she found these,' she waved her hand to indicate the journal. 'There are quite a few. She's pretty upset about what's written as it makes for very unpleasant reading. But it's our star witness that really put it all together for us. And then we figured out the rest ourselves by reading between the lines, so to speak.'

Matthew didn't utter a word. He continued to look from Abe to Charlotte and back again, his face creased in doubt.

'He sent Elizabeth to recruit the help of Dez and The Network. While they were here in New York they seemed interested but reluctant to help. So we think Edward had a back up plan in place... just in case. He had Sectors C and D raided by The Blues so that he could then send supplies and his medical team to help The Network knowing that they would then feel obliged to help him in return.' Charlotte paused. 'It worked like a charm,' she stated.

'Good God!'

'But that's not all. He also met and fell for Emi...but she was not genetically pure so he resisted her...until your vaccine came into play. Then she was his for the taking...but someone let slip that Dez and Emi were planning to marry. So he arranged for Dez to be one of the guards of Cloud III on a particular day and for them all to be killed by The Blues. He left food drops for The Blues and made sure they could get there at the appointed time.'

'You can't be serious.'

'We have the witness waiting in the hallway and you're welcome to interview him if you like,' offered Abe matter-of-factly.

'But...why would Edward have The Cloud destroyed? I don't understand?' said Matthew, reluctantly taking the proffered book from Abe's outstretched hand. He looked at the journal as if it might bite him. He tried to focus on what was written on the page Abe had opened the book to but the words swam before his eyes, his brain unable to register what he was looking at.

'Edward had promised them food. There was no food to be found at the Cloud site, so they felt duped, and destroyed everything in their rage.'

'Good God!' Matthew turned to look down at Edward, a mirriad of emotions flitting across his features, shock and disbelief being paramount. His gaze shifted once more to the book. This time he read the page before him and then flipped through reading the subsequent pages. His eyebrows drew down in a frown, his mouth forming a grimace. When he was done reading he looked back up at Abe and Charlotte, patiently waiting for him to come to a decision — to help them or to stand in their way. His eyes reflected his troubled thoughts as slowly shaking his head he took a breath, as if to speak, but he found he could find nothing to say.

Charlotte stood quietly, her gaze shifting from one to the other and occasionally to the man in the bed who she had served for most of her adult life.

'I think you'd better bring in your guest,' said Matthew. 'The book is not proof enough...as you said...and your reasons for his actions are...hypothetical at this point.'

Abe exited the room and soon returned with the most enormous person Matthew had ever seen. He filled the room with his height and width...and he was completely blue and covered in sinister looking imprints of spikes, snakes and gore.

Matthew took a step back. 'Good God!'

'This is Spike. He's the father of Gigi and the member from the Blue tribe that Edward made contact with.'

'Good God!'

Spike nodded his head at Matthew in greeting. 'I'm sorry,' he said.

'Sorry...to me...for what?'

'I'm the one who planned the attack on Sectors C and D and also the attack that killed your guards and smashed up your Cloud.'

'Good God!'

Spike looked at Abe. 'He doesn't talk much does he? Is that all he can say?'

Abe snorted with laughter. 'I think he's just a bit startled at the moment. Give him time, he'll come round.'

Spike returned his gaze to Matthew and waited. Then his eyes shifted and he took in the form lying in the bed hooked up to all sorts of tubes. 'That's him.'

'What's him?' asked Matthew

'Him. In the bed. He doesn't look as good as when I last saw him but...that's the guy who asked me to do the raids. He promised us food. We didn't get...enough...not like what he said we'd get.'

'But why?'

'I dunno why he wanted the first raid done...he said he had his reasons,' Spike shrugged. 'The second one he wanted us to kill the guards. Had to be on a certain day and he wanted the guard dead who looks kinda like him...at least he fooled me.'

Matthew looked back at Abe. 'Good God. This is...unbelievable.'

'Yeah, we know,' acknowledge Charlotte.

'He killed all my people. Bombed them. Guess he was mad. We destroyed your Cloud,' stated Spike. 'But we'd also served our purpose. He didn't need us no more.'

'Yeah. The Network won't work for Edward now. How do we know he won't destroy *us* when we've served *our* purpose and provided him with a new world to rule?' asked Abe.

Matthew stared at Abe and then turned to Charlotte. 'And Emi... she knows all this?'

'Yes, she knows,' answered Charlotte. 'But she didn't want to be here.'

'And Dez?'

'Yes, he knows as well but he didn't want to be here because he thought it might make it look like revenge on his part and...' Abe trailed off.

Matthew massaged his forehead with his fingers and then pinched the bridge of his nose as he stared at the floor. He looked up, shaking his head, at a loss for words.

'Turning off his life support…it's a political statement for all of us…and justice for those he's killed,' stated Charlotte.

Matthew looked from one to the other, nodded his head and stepped aside. They all turned to stare at the man in the bed.

His eyes were open.

———————

Dez and Emi were at the apartment. Dez was sitting on the couch, his head clutched in his hands, his eyes fixed on the floor. Emi was standing at the floor-to-ceiling windows staring unseeingly out at the city scape, her back to Dez. Every once in a while she paced back and forth but neither of them spoke.

Finally, Emi spun to face Dez. 'I should go. I should be there,' she stated loudly in the quiet room, as if trying to convince herself of what her actions should be.

Dez looked up in time to witness the look of torment on Emi's face. 'Go if you feel you should but it won't be…easy…for you.'

'Nothing in this life is easy,' she countered. 'And as horrible as all this is, he still cared for me, gave me all he could in this forsaken world. I should be there. Not being there is…is…cowardly.'

Dez was at a loss for words. He had never much cared for Edward, had never been able to warm to the guy but it was different for Emi. Edward had obviously loved her and she had agreed to share her life with him. There were ties there that were not easily broken regardless of what they now knew.

He puffed out his cheeks and exhaled as he ran his hand through his hair. There was no perfect way forward. 'Come on then. I'll ask Zoe to come and watch Emma and I'll walk you to the hospital,' he offered, knowing that deep down she felt the need to be there and would gain strength from his support.

———·———

'Oh God. He's finally woken up,' stated Matthew.

'Impeccable timing,' said Abe, taking a step forward.

'Edward?' questioned Charlotte, wondering how aware he was.

'I've been awake for a while,' he rasped '…listening.' He gave Charlotte a look of pure loathing. 'I trusted you,' he stated accusingly. He reached out for the glass of water that was on the table by his bed. His hand shook — was it from emotion or his physical state? He drank thirstily, spilling the water down his front. He stopped, choked, and then sipped more cautiously. He returned the glass to the table with a clatter, drew a deep breath and fixed his gaze on those filling the doorway of his sterile hospital room.

Charlotte glanced at Matthew, unsure of what any of them should do now.

'You won't kill me. I'm the leader of the new world we're creating. I've lived my life dedicated to saving the planet and the human race,' Edward stated with certainty. 'You can't *possibly* take his word over mine,' Edward demanded, his face turning an angry shade of red as he surveyed the group. 'Nobody will believe you,' he said, his eyes fixed on Spike.

'They believe me,' said Spike, indicating the others in the room. 'And I….' he trailed off as the door swung open and Emi walked in.

Emi froze to the spot as she looked into Edward's eyes. 'You're… you're awake,' she gasped, her eyes darting to those gathered in the room as all the colour drained from her face.

'Emi. *Thank God!*' Edward gasped. 'They've all lost their minds. Want to kill me. They think I planned the attacks on Sectors C and D and on The Cloud. Please, talk some sense into them.'

She stood, shaking her head. Finally her eyes came to rest on Charlotte who was looking at her questioningly.

'I have this,' said Spike, pulling a Sattcomm from his pocket. He handed it to Emi. 'It's what you need. My word against Edward's.' His eyes darted to Edward. He nodded his head to indicate the Sattcomm. 'It's from Edward. Gave it to me so we could talk. I pushed some buttons and I guess Sattcomms record messages. If you play it back you'll hear what you need to.'

'Emi. Please…no,' Edward whispered.

Emi pushed the play button and they all listened as Spike and Edward's voices filled the room. The first conversation was Edward telling Spike to go ahead with the plan as instructed and the second conversation was Spike telling Edward that the raid was done while in the background was the hum of conversation as if a party was in full swing.

Emi stared at the Sattcomm in her hand as if it had come to life and bitten her.

'This is enough to link him to the raids on C and D but it still doesn't explain the destruction of The Cloud and I'm afraid it is that which most people will be upset about,' stated Matthew.

At that moment Dez walked in.

Everyone turned to stare at Dez. The room was now crowded and hot as tensions ran high. Edward's heartrate monitor was beeping loudly, his heart rate elevated. As Dez walked in, it went up another another notch.

'Dez, what are you doing here?' asked Emi.

Dez stared at Emi. 'I was waiting outside and…it just seemed like what I was meant to do. That somehow the pieces would fall into place.'

Spike was turning his head back and forth, staring at Edward and then at Dez. 'See, they do look alike.'

'Of course we do. He's my brother,' stated Edward.

All eyes turned in Edward's direction with expressions varying between doubt that Edward was in his right mind and shock.

'Brother?' stammered Dez.

'Yes. Your father is Caleb Black — my father. Such a fool. Procreated with someone not genetically pure. You were supposed to die,' Edward turned an accusing stare upon Spike. 'Knew you were too stupid to get the job done. Destroyed The Cloud instead. My lifetime's work. So you all have nothing on me. It was Spike here who took things into his own hands and went too far. Put us all at risk. Had to be stopped so I bombed them.'

The room was quiet other than the beeping of the machines. Edward's audience stood transfixed until Spike took a step forward and with a sudden movement that was surprising given his bulk, snapped Edward's neck.

Edward's head lolled sideways, his glassy stare unseeing.

'That was for Shade.' Spike turned and exited the deadly silent room.

Not even the monitors were beeping.

Emi stared from one to the other then to Edward's lifeless form and back to the Sattcomm in her hand. 'So there was always the plan for The Network to be the slaves necessary to build The Cloud. Edward wasn't convinced we would agree to help. He had his own backup plan in place. If we didn't agree then he'd have the Blues raid the villages, he'd save the survivors thus obliging us to help him in return. When we met on the street in New York we indicated we were reluctant. When he realized this he put through the call to Spike. Spike raided Sectors C and D and then called Edward to say it was done. Spike's call happened to come through during the first dinner party we ever attended here...when Edward fell in love with me.' Emi's words came out in a rush, as if she was rehearsing a monologue or talking to herself.

The truth of Emi's words reverberated in the room.

The pieces had fallen into place.

The countenance of each person in the room reflected their understanding and their horror. Slowly, one by one they exited the room, too shaken up by the turn of events to know what to do or what more to say.

Matthew was once again alone with Edward — his body lifeless; the machines quiet. Matthew stepped forward and pulled the sheet over Edward's face. He no longer wished to look upon the man he had served so faithfully for his entire working life.

Matthew turned and left the room.

# CHAPTER TWENTY-NINE

'Dez. Come on in,' said Emi, opening the door wide to let him into the apartment.

'How are you holding up?' asked Dez, taking her in his arms before planting a kiss firmly on her mouth.

She kissed him back, then shrugged her shoulders in response to his question before turning and leading the way into the living room.

After the birth of Emma and then Edward's death, they had thought it best for Dez to return to The Network until things settled down. Decisions had to be made about what to tell The Fringe and The Network. Should they let them think that Edward had died from his injuries or should the truth of his duplicity be revealed? It was a difficult decision and one they could not leave unanswered for long. Peter and Elizabeth were brought in to the conversation that otherwise only included Dez, Emi, Abe, Charlotte and Matthew. They had finally come to the conclusion that those on the board should know the truth but the rest of the people did not need to know all the details. There was a certain amount of fear that if The Network knew what the leader of The Fringe had done there could be further bloodshed. They had a right to be angry, but hatred and bitterness would not help their cause. And so Dez had agreed to return to The Network to continue in his leadership role there and Emi had agreed to stay in New York to sit on the board of The Fringe.

Emi had now fully recovered from the ordeal of the birth. Emma was a cute four-month old. Life had settled down. People had come to terms with Edward's death and the board was managing to lead as a committee. The restoration of Cloud III was complete and the seaweed farms were being planted all over the world. It was now a waiting game — waiting to see if all their efforts would restore balance to the planet in time for them to survive. They would probably not have any definite results for years, but Emi was determined to live her life, and give Emma the best chance of survival that she could. Dez and Emi found that they finally had some of the freedom they'd craved for so many years.

'Can I get you anything?'

'A beer wouldn't go amiss if you have one.'

'Sure, have a seat,' she said, gesturing to the couch and then heading for the kitchen to fetch the beer. She returned, passing the cold beer to Dez and placing her glass of water on the coffee table, taking a seat across from Dez.

'What's up?' asked Dez, trying to read her emotions and failing. She seemed a bit more reserved and on edge that normal.

'I…I asked you to come over because of these,' she said, indicating a stack of books on the coffee table.

'More journals?'

'Yes, but these ones aren't Edwards.'

Dez looked at Emi, his forehead scrunched, wondering what was coming. Nothing good ever seemed to be written in journals so far. 'Whose are they then?'

'They were in with Edward's journals. When I went to clean up the office I noticed the handwriting was different. They belonged to…Caleb Black.'

'Oh.'

'So you know how Edward set up the attack where Cloud III was destroyed but that was just The Blues taking things into their own hands and going too far…. Edward's purpose was that he wanted you killed.'

'Yeah, I know.'

'And we thought he wanted you killed so he could have me.'

'Yeah.'

'And to think he almost succeeded,' said Emi, quietly under her breath, tears welling briefly in her eyes. She looked away, to the cityscape shining beyond the floor-to-ceiling windows. Although Edward had not killed Dez, he had still managed to separate them, had made their relationship strained and on edge from all that he had put them through. And things were still not as they once were — the trust had to be rebuilt. Gathering her courage, she forced the air from her lungs between pursed lips and took another deep breath in. 'They explain some of his irrational jealousy. The fact that I loved you and not him was…the final straw. As far as he was concerned you had taken everything from him.'

'But…I'd never met him before we came to New York. I didn't even know he existed. How can I have taken anything from him?'

'I think it's better if you read the journals…it's too much for me to explain and I'd probably do a poor job of it. But I think, in the end, what is written there…will help,' said Emi, offering him a hint of a smile in encouragement. 'I'll be in the bedroom feeding Emma if you need me,' she said as she exited the room.

Dez stared at the stack of journals as if they were going to attack him, then taking another deep breath, he reached out and took the first one from the top of the pile and began to read at the page that Emi had left open.

*Journal entry: Year 2175*

*I have decided to leave New York. There are fatal flaws in my son, the same ones which I also see in my wife. I was fooled by my wife's charm into believing that she loved me. I have lived to learn that she only married me for the position of power it would bring to her, and to her offspring. Though my son has the same charming and intelligent personality, I can already see that these characteristics are a mask for his underlying nature of control and manipulation. He has too great a need for power and I fear if he one day becomes leader it will be cataclysmic for the rest of humanity. If I leave now the governing board will be forced to rule until my son is of age and by then, I hope, they will have seen his true colours and be able to deal with the fall-out. If I stay until he is older he will simply follow in my foot-steps — there is no voting here unless it is offered by the leader to the people, if I offer it they will just vote for him, and he will not step down, not offer someone else the role of leader — and I dread to think of what the outcome may be.*

*My plan is to take a Hovercraft and to go and live at Sector A. I have a younger son, one nobody knows of, as it is illegal to procreate with anyone outside of The Fringe, but he is bright and compassionate and will be a great leader when he grows up. I will train him up to be the leader the world needs. His mother is already teaching him the old ways — the pleasures of playing, dancing, singing, and drawing, and the necessities of hunting, planting, harvesting, gathering, cooking, and even swimming, as well as the vital abilities of reading and writing and to think for oneself. Simple things, I know, but life is so harsh that most have lost these abilities. Even now, at the age of four, he is being taught some of our terrible history and how we managed to destroy our world and to leave most of the human race with no hope of survival. We are so close to a solution, to solving the world's problems. It will be his generation that will lead us into a new future — a future where we can lower the earth's temperature and regenerate the toxic soil. A future where we can re-introduce the extinct species, and crops, that are so vital to our existence. I must leave The Fringe to ensure that, when the time is right, it is my younger son who becomes leader. His name is Dez.*

*Caleb*


Dez sat back on the couch, lost in thought, barely taking in the words written on the page — by his father. His mind reeled as thoughts flitted through his brain. Edward had been his brother. And Edward had known they were brothers and he had hated him. Their father had abandoned Edward and his position of leadership in favour of a subsistance living amongst The Network and raising him to be leader in Edward's place. That Emi had chosen him over Edward as well must have been an enethma to his soul. It was amazing that Edward had managed to hide so much hatred behind the charm for all the time he had. Dez shook his head. Had Edward always planned to have him under his thumb? He would have surmised that Dez would become leader of The Network and that one day The Fringe would need their help. To rule over him would have been sweet revenge, he was sure. But his own popularity as a leader must have rankled with Edward. And then for him to have the love of the woman that Edward loved — Edward had been willing to run the risk of sacrificing the world to exact his revenge. Dez shook his head again. He couldn't hate Edward, he wished things could have been different, but mostly, he realized, he felt sorry for him — a feeling Edward would have loathed above all else.

His mind turned to memories of when he was four years old. He vaguely remembered a man who came to stay. He remembered his mother's laugh, dancing in their tiny kitchen, learning to swim in the rockpools, being read to in bed at night and then the birth of his sister, Isi. But he couldn't remember the man, Caleb — his father, being there anymore after the age of eight. His mother had ceased to laugh; she would smile at him but the smile rarely reached her eyes. He recalled that he was hungry more of the time and that his mother would have to leave him alone to look after Isi while she went out to find food for them. Life had become much harder and he'd suddenly had to grow up. What had happened to his father? Where had he gone? Why had he left them?

He reached out for the journals and flipped backwards through the pages to an earlier year. He scanned what was written, trying to glean the answers to his questions. The thought of ever abandoning Emma was unimaginable, unless it was somehow to her benefit. He needed to understand his past.

*August, 2160*

*My wife gave birth to our first child. We have named him Edward. He is a handsome little fellow. It is a strange thought when looking at a newborn to think of him being ruler of what is left of the world one day…but so it is. My wife is so happy, so proud of her tiny newborn son. And I, I will work hard to make sure there is something left for him to govern. We are so close to solving the world's problems…problems that we the human race have inflicted on our planet. It is only right that we should be the ones to try to solve the problems and restore the planet to health. If we don't do it soon we will lose everything. We are running out of time. I must give my son a future. I am filled with so much love that I am determined to bring about the changes we need.*

*December, 2160*

*I have just returned from my quarterly visit to Zach. Their lives are so hard. I wish I could do more but it would be impossible for those of us in New York to feed all of those in the villages scattered throughout the barrenlands. Until we lower the earth's temperature and detoxify the soil we are simply not able to feed everyone. I have followed in my mother's footsteps and continue to take food to Zach and his daughter Dezzie. I do not know if they would survive without my help, although Dezzie is tougher than she looks. She is kind and compassionate, but has an inner resilience that one cannot ignore.*

*June, 2165*

*I have to admit to being disappointed that my wife refuses to have any more children. It would be good for Edward to have a playmate. His mother demands too much of him at such a young age. Her vision is only for her son to be leader of the world and she leaves no time for him to just be a child. I try to do what I can to ensure he has fun — we go to the park to play ball and I make sure he has other children to play with, but generally he seems to just boss the other kids and they do not like it.*

*September, 2167*

*Edward is beyond his years in intelligence. He has already learned that if he bosses other kids around they do not like it and will not play with him so he has learned instead to be charming…and they do exactly what he wants. He is a lot like his mother.*

*I have again just returned from visiting Zach and Dezzie. Their life seems increasingly hard. The latest trouble is that as the south becomes more barren, The Blues are moving further north to the abandoned cities that are close to where they live. I have started referring to those outside The Fringe as The Network; although in reality they are just individual families scattered about, living hand to mouth, and helping one another when the need arises. I have tried to encourage Zach and Dezzie to form more of a cohesive group as I think they would be better off working together. But food is so scarce it is hard for them to imagine people being willing to help each other on a permanent basis. I must admit, though their life is so hard, that I enjoy my visits, the conversation is always stimulating and their experience of life is so different from my own.*

*This visit was not quite the same as visits in the past. One, it seems to me that Zach is not as well as he used to be. I do not know what Dezzie will do without him as she will be left to fend for herself. She has grown into a very beautiful and intelligent young woman…but still, to be on ones own in such circumstances will not be easy. I'm going to start to visit more regularly to make sure they are okay. My mother rescued Zach as a baby, and when she died she made me promise to look after him and his family. I cannot let her down no matter how hard life gets. Although, I have wondered if Dezzie has a crush on me and maybe I should send someone else with the food they so desperately need, but I find I can never bring myself to not go…I look forward to her company.*

*November, 2168*

*The weather should be cooling off by now as winter approaches, but it gets later every year and this year it still feels stifling out. There is no coolness to the breeze. We must perfect The Cloud soon or all our efforts will have been in vain. I can feel that we are rapidly running out of time.*

*Edward continues to grow and flourish. He is intelligent, quick witted and charming although I sense a selfish streak in him that he keeps well hidden. I pray he will grow up to be a good leader and that his selfishness will drop away as he matures and realizes that the world as a whole is in peril and needs a selfless leader to survive.*

*I have been going once a month to see Zach. I take what I can. Today my wife confronted me when I returned, accusing me of taking food from our mouths to feed those less worthy and demanding that I cease bothering with those not worth saving. She was okay when I only went once every three months, figuring it was a duty I owed to my mother, but she does not like my more frequent visits…considers them unnecessary. I refused to cooperate with her wishes and she is now barely speaking to me.*

*January, 2169*

*That was the hottest 'winter' on record. The predictions we have for the amount of time we have left in which to change things are dire but I feel we are very close to reaching our goals. I spend many hours pouring over calculations and maps, trying to pick the best locations around the world for The Cloud sites. There are so many variables to consider — weather, size of each site, location, safety, distribution, transportation, and the workforce needed. It is so all-consuming it is hard to think of anything else.*

*It has been four months since the argument with my wife and she continues to barely acknowledge my existence or utter a word to me. Unfortunately her attitude is also being picked up by Edward. I tried to talk to him about how hard existence is for those trying to live off our infertile land and he agreed that it was good that I help them…but then he left me speechless as it was his opinion that for our plans for The Cloud to work we would need the people as a workforce. He didn't think we had enough manpower to make it happen on our own. But there was something about the way he said it that made me think he meant to have The Network as slaves and we, The Fringe, would be in control. He may be right about us needing help in the form of a bigger workforce, but I was astounded that an eight-year-old would think of such a thing in such a way. It left me quite unsettled.*

*February, 2169*

*I have decided to no longer visit Zach and Dezzie in order to appease my wife, and I mentioned to them that my visits might once again be less frequent. They took it with good grace, realizing that my commitments to The Fringe and all that we are trying to accomplish are my priority. It has been seven weeks since I last visited them and I wonder how they are doing without the food I bring. Last time I was there Zach seemed in much poorer health and I have to admit I miss Dezzie more than I can say. I have fallen in love with her but I don't see any future for us so I keep it to myself.*

*My wife continues to ignore me. I truly begin to worry for the type of man Edward may turn out to be.*

*May, 2169*

*Today was the first day that I have visited Zach and Dezzie since January. It was not good. I could hardly believe how much worse off Zach was. There are no nutrients left in our soil, it is almost impossible for people to feed themselves anymore. The tall grasses are the only things that can grow, they have taken over, but have no value other than to be woven into mats or used as a broom head.*

*Dezzie was holding up okay but in my compassion I gave her a hug and one thing led to another. We made love. I told her I loved her but I couldn't leave The Fringe. She loves me too, but knows how important my work overseeing The Cloud is. She is content to see me when she can. I feel torn.*

*June, 2171*

*We have a son. I cannot admit that anywhere but here as it is frowned upon to produce children with anyone from outside The Fringe as they are not genetically pure. But he is a delight and Dezzie is the happiest I have ever seen her. Her only regret is that Zach did not live to see the birth of his grandson.*

*The plans for The Cloud and the detoxification of the soil continue to move forward...although at times it feels as if it is at a snail's pace. Still, the forecasts are very promising.*

*Edward will be eleven soon. I can never tell him that he has a baby brother. To care for another human being would do him good. His charm and his selfishness have combined to make him manipulative...he is very good at it. I try to be a good father to him, and show him how to be a good leader, but his mother holds more influence over him that I do. I watch and worry.*

Dez came to the page that Emi had left open for him. He read it through a second time and then continued with the journal. He wondered as he flipped the pages what Edward would have felt as he read these same words. To have a father who went from loving you to wanting to abandon you because he thought your character was flawed. Dez shook his head, and running his hand through his hair, picked up another journal.

*December, 2178*

*Dez is turning out to be everything I hoped he would be. He has the resilience and compassion of his mother and the natural instincts of a great leader. I can see it even in the way he cares for his little sister, Isi. The last few years have been the happiest of my life, even though the living conditions are so much harder. I have managed to keep tabs on what is happening in New York through one person whom I trust there. The Cloud and the soil detoxification plans are close to complete. The board has managed to rule in my place, but as Edward nears his eighteenth birthday he becomes more and more involved in their decisions and though they see he is headstrong, they cannot prevent his intervention. I have considered returning, at least for a time, so that Edward cannot take control ( though most presume I am dead so it would come as a bit of a surprise to many ), but I do not know that I can bring myself to leave Dezzie and the children.*

*Today I must go out hunting as we are in desperate need of meat. I'm hoping I don't meet up with any Blues as I'm pretty sure they have been in this area lately but I must get some food as I can't stand to see Isi looking so thin.*

That was the last entry. How had the journals ended up here in the office? Had Caleb returned and hidden them or had he died at the hands of The Blues and his mother passed the journals to Caleb's contact in New York. He would never know. But at least he had more answers to the questions that had plagued him for much of his life. Dez put down the journals, closed his eyes and rested his head on the back of the couch. He had always wondered who his father was. Somehow he had never put two and two together and thought of the man who had lived with them for a few years when he was little. Here was his whole history laid out before him. It almost sounded like his own story with Emi, but upsidedown or backwards.

If Edward had read these pages he could see that it would have filled him with jealousy. Poor Edward.

He got up and headed to the bedroom. Poking his head in at the open door he found Emi awake and the baby sleeping soundly next to her.

'Hi,' whispered Emi. 'You okay?'

He nodded and gently lowered himself on to the bed on the other side of Emma. 'Yeah. It was a lot to take in but it has answered a lot of questions.'

'And did it help?'

'I think so. At least I knew my father loved me and wanted me to be leader…thought I would be good as a leader. I now realize, I do have some memories of him.'

Emi nodded and gave him a hint of a smile. She had found the whole story bittersweet. It was all very complicated, but then people were.

'It made me feel sorry for Edward though.'

'Yes, that was my reaction too and I can't imagine how he felt as he read those journals. But…and this may sound terrible…but I'm glad he isn't alive. If he had lived…he would have hated that in the end I chose you over him, that Emma was not his, and that he could no longer be the leader. Once it was known what he did, he would not have been trusted and his charm would no longer have worked its magic on anyone. I can't see him living like that.'

'No. I didn't like the way his life was ended...but at least we can keep the rest of this story to ourselves.'

'That seems fair,' said Emi, her gaze one of contentment as she stared at the two people she loved most in the world.

# EPILOGUE

Emi sat on a rocky outcrop watching her children paddle in the brook, a smile hovering at the corners of her mouth as she rested her hand contentedly on her swollen belly. She glanced up to see Dez making his way toward her, his head down as he followed the footpath through the pinky-purple sea of heather.

Arriving at her side, he plonked down beside her on the ledge before giving her a kiss on the cheek.

'I can never get over the beauty of this place,' she smiled at him.

'I know,' he smiled back. 'It's really incredible, isn't it?' he said, turning his head to survey the scene before them.

The heather was in full bloom, the purple hills rolling away from them in every direction. With the bracken, still bright green against the purple backdrop, and the rocky outcrops, stacked like pancakes, scattered throughout the hills, the view was breathtaking. The brook added to the idyllic scene, as it meandered slowly down the gorge, splashing off the large boulders that created small paddling pools for their children to play in.

'I could hardly believe this place existed when I first came here. Although, it's even nicer now that when I first saw it. The cooler temps are already making a difference,' he said, wrapping his arm around her.

'I'm so glad we were able to move. Coming here made me realize how much I needed to leave the past behind,' she said, leaning her head on his shoulder.

Dez tightened his hold and kissed the top of her head. 'I have news.'

'Good news?' she asked, glancing up at him.

'In our world, yes,' he replied, grinning down at her upturned face. 'Abe said the river is back up and Cloud III is providing enough cloud and rain that the area is beginning to flourish. They even burned off some of the grasslands, regenerated the soil and planted corn, wheat, and a variety of fruit trees and vegetables in its place. This fall will be the first time they are able to harvest crops from outside of the valley.'

'You know, I think I could quite like living in a world where the news is good,' said Emi. 'Although, it might take a bit of getting used to.'

'Well, you're going to like this then. Abe also said that Jon and Amy are doing a fantastic job of overseeing the seaweed farms. They're now using the seaweed as a natural fertilizer for the crops and as a food source. And to top off the good news, Tom and Liz had a baby girl and Abe and Chi a little boy,' said Dez, with a grin that lit up his face.

'I can't think of anything more perfect,' Emi smiled up at him. 'And the girls?'

'Peter is teaching Lea to fly a Hovercraft and Fie is acting as her co-pilot until she is comfortable enough to learn to fly herself. And Gigi apparently spends all her time reading. Abe says she wants to open a school when she grows up.'

'Abe. I miss Abe, but I'm glad he has a family to care for again.'

'Like us,' said Dez, looking down at his children happily splashing about in the brook.

'Will they have a future?' whispered Emi, her voice catching as the baby kicked at her hand.

'I got a report from Charlotte as well. She said that Matthew and Zoe are doing an in depth report on how the chemicals and toxins destroyed the planet and our health over time. They hope that the mistakes of the past won't be repeated if the evidence is researched and documented. And she said that the earth's temperature has dropped by almost one and a half degrees. It's not enough…not yet…but it gives us time. And with Charlotte in charge what could go wrong?'

Emi nodded. 'I'm so thankful she took up the task of being leader. She has to be one of the best people on the planet and, of course, working with Edward she knew everything and everyone. I was happy to relinquish my role, I must admit. Looking after our own small brood is much less demanding. It'll be up to them to finish what we've started,' she said, as she and Dez watched over the next generation.

Their lives now were not so much about being leaders to all the people but simply about being parents; raising up their children to be people who would care for the planet rather than destroy it. Each family had to do its part, make their own choices. She had learned that you couldn't control all the people, as Edward had tried to do. You could only hope the choices they made would be the right ones — and try to lead by example.

Dez kissed the top of Emi's head. They had done all they could to ensure that their children would have a future — the type of future they would have would be in their own hands.

—·—

# ABOUT THE
# AUTHOR

G.J. Page lives in the Peak District in England with her family. She is passionate about conservation and the environment.

She is also the author of the popular children's series *The Travel Adventures of PJ Mouse* and *The Animal Pack* series. Her other books can be found online at www.gwynethjanepage.com and www.pjmouse.com.

Ingram Content Group UK Ltd.
Milton Keynes UK
UKHW041832310523
422675UK00004B/173

9 781989 302132